The Broke Brothers' Revolution

#brokepower

The Broke Brothers' Revolution

J. Shawn Durham

Dedication

For my parents Julia Durham and the late Joseph Durham, Jr., who knew that every revolution starts at home.

Contents

BOOK ONE: Broke

Chapter 1: The Broke Brothers' Manifesto

(Brother Carlos)

"Y'all on some bullshit," I said as I snatched the cash out my wallet. I didn't mean to be a jerk. But damn that. Lola and I had just seen a movie, and afterwards she suckered me into meeting her friends for somebody's birthday celebration. I smelled a trap.

"Birthday? Whose birthday?" I quizzed as we walked into the restaurant.

"Adrienne's," she said. "And what do you have against my friends?"

"Baby, it's not that I have something against your friends. But you know they got something against me. She can stop having birthdays, far as I'm concerned."

"That would mean her death, Carlos."

"I'm just kidding, Lola," I said with half a smile. I got the feeling that I was being set up. We walked into Strip, the steak and sushi joint where it cost money just to blink. And it's hard not to get caught up in a place like that. The smell of grilled meat and seafood is a carnal aphrodisiac. And Strip was always full of pretty (and wannabe pretty) folks who willingly paid the cool tax just to be there. But it *was* a chill spot. Huge ceiling. Big, rectangle-shaped bar in the middle of the joint that could seat an army. And a deejay constantly spinning some generic, dance music tripe. And the house was always packed. It's like a Walmart of fine dining, and honestly, I get ADD in the place.

When we reached Adrienne's table, Lola and her friends got their *fake on.*

"Hey, girrrrrrlllllll!" Adrienne said to Lola.

Then more fakeness.

"Ooooooh, hey baby! It's so good to see youuuuuu!" Lola said back.

That's a lie. It was never good to see Adrienne. Not for me, anyway.

"Girrrrlll, I love that top!" Lola then said to Julia. But that was a lie. No way in hell she could love that top. It looked like the Crayola mascot took a shit on her chest.

Anyway, Adrienne was with her Insane Clown Posse aka, Lola's gang: Julia, 40, was a hot chick, but hung out with girls 10 to 15 years younger. Yep, she tried to compete with the young girls. And there was Tomeka, 31, who worked with Julia and followed up on everything she did. And then there was Adrienne.

My favorite fantasy involved Adrienne walking in her five-inch heels and breaking her ass in the most embarrassing and public way possible. I know it's bad to hate someone, but when I say I hated Adrienne, I *really* hated Adrienne. Lola and I had been together for years and Adrienne was the girlfriend who always accentuated the negative about me: "He ain't got this and he ain't got that," and all that noise.

What I did have was a size-11 foot to wedge dead in her fat butt. Even more irksome was that Adrienne—knowing good and damn well she didn't like me either—smiled and acted like we were the best of friends. And since it was her birthday, I figured out why. She wanted me to pay for her and everyone there! Damn that.

I did buy a round. Just *one round*, mind you. Then the bill came. And like an ass, the waiter placed it in front of *me*. So that's when I defiantly said: "Y'all on some bullshit."

When I said that, Lola coiled her neck like a viper and Adrienne tried to shame me.

"I'm sorry?" Adrienne asked as if she didn't hear me. Bitch, you heard me.

"You mean, your girls aren't treating you, Adrienne," I asked and then looked at Tomeka and Julia. "Y'all don't really expect me to foot this, do you?"

They looked at me like I was crazy, but I was serious. Lola and I joined them late, ordered one drink each and I bought a round. How the hell did that make me responsible for the other $200 they ran up for a woman I didn't even like? Oh, hell no.

"It's like that?" Tomeka asked. "I'm surprised, Carlos. I thought you appreciated the company of four lovely ladies."

"Trick, I already paid for the company of *my* lady and I hardly like her ass," I said.

Okay, I *wish* I said that. Instead I laughed and said: "And I do love your company. But my responsibility is to Lola. Besides, this is y'all's celebration and we've only been here 15 minutes. And I even bought everyone a round of drinks, so happy birthday."

Lola cut her eyes at me. And the way Adrienne mouthed her lips, I think she said "cheap ass," but I couldn't make out the words over the crowd noise. But I didn't care. I wasn't going to drop two bills on women who talk shit about me behind my back. I thought the episode was amusing until I felt the side of my face burning from Lola's devil-red stare.

"I may have overdone it this time."

✳ ✳ ✳

"You *always* overdo it, Los," Vanessa said as she lifted her eyes from her computer screen and shook her head at me. "Why couldn't you just pay the bill? That would've spared you Lola's wrath."

"I wouldn't have been spared shit," I said, playing with her stapler. "I would have been out $200! Why would I pay for other people's good time when they were responsible for most of the bill?"

"Because—gimmie that stapler before you hurt yourself—because you're a man. A gentleman, Carlos. And for ladies, most gentlemen would—"

"My Visa bill was due, so later for that. It had nothing to do with being a gentleman. Besides, they ain't ladies. They're demon women. A pack of pairaka."

"A pack of *what*?"

"*Pairaka*. It's Persian for a group of female evils who are most active through the night and have witch-like personalities."

"I gotta use that, 'cause these pairakas be hating on me all the time."

"You're not using that right. Anyway, Lola's girls don't like me, but they got gall. Don't women have to have manners and be likeable before they start demanding shit?"

"But they don't like you because you don't treat them like ladies," butted in Williams, an editor. We all still wonder why *The Atlanta Journal-Constitution* hired him as a "people editor." Not any of the writers, not me, or V, knew what the hell a "people editor" was. And to be an editor, he didn't edit anybody. None of the *AJC* writers turned in copy to him. Williams' total existence was complete and utter bullshit.

"Was either one of us talking to you?" I asked. I think he liked being disliked.

"Why not split the bill five ways and pay for the birthday girl?"

"Because that would've had me on the hook for eighty of that $200, with me and Lola's cut at $40 each. That ain't fair!"

"But it was her birthday," V said. "Why are you so tight?"

"Because my money isn't for random women. It's for stuff that matters. Not on chicks playing nice 'cause I'm the only man around."

"If you weren't already attached, you'd get no play," Williams said. "Face it man, you're cheap! Pop quiz: if Lola was out with her girlfriends and you didn't know her, what should you do? Should you a) offer to buy just Lola a drink; b) offer to buy all of her girls a drink and talk to Lola; or c) offer to buy no one a drink?"

"Are my boys there with me?"

"Uh-uh," he said.

"What do you think, V?" I asked.

"Oh no," she said. "I want to hear your answer."

"Well, I would choose, 'D'."

"Los you can't do that!" V chided. "There is no, 'D'!"

"Yeah!" Williams said. "What is 'D'?"

"D is me walking over—with my swag on, you know—acknowledge her girls, lay some of my mature, grown man rap on her, ask for her number and keep my money in my pocket." They looked at me, shook their heads, and laughed.

"So you don't even buy Lola a drink?" V asked.

"Not until we do some talking," I said. "When her throat is dry from all the stimulating conversation we just had, *then* I offer the lady a reasonably priced beverage."

"And she will offer you a reasonably cold shoulder," V said.

"Better hold on to Lola 'cause you'd never get a woman," Williams said.

"Really?" I asked. "So what's the answer then, Playboy?"

"It's, 'B.' Buy her girls a drink and talk to Lola. If you don't, they will clown you when you walk away. Then they'll call you cheap and that'll be the end."

"But Williams, I'm not cheap. It's just that my money is valuable. By going with 'B' I'm out 50 bucks before I say 'hi.' We can't all be cake daddies like you, Duncan Hines."

"Okay, Carlos," Williams said as he put on his sports coat. "Call me what you want. But this cake daddy gets mad frosting!" He walked off smiling. Damn pretty boy. I hate that dude. A twenty-something clown like Williams could spread his money around all he liked, but he'll end up in more debt than Cuba before it was over with.

"'Gets mad frosting, yo?'" I mocked. "I bet he has mad bad credit too."

"He's got a point," Vanessa said, giving me the side eye before she resumed typing.

"Maybe he does. But I can't operate like him. I got mouths to feed."

"Yes, you do. But face it: Lola's crew tried to pull a fast one on you. Some women try to make dudes feel bad by calling guys cheap. But why is Lola so upset with you?"

"Because she's *canine*. And she really dug in my ass when we left the restaurant."

"Well, you were being an ass. But she should have checked her girls and stuck up for you. Don't sweat it. She just wanted to show them she was running thangs, that's all."

"You really think she was showing out?"

"Yes," V said as she stopped typing to look at me. "And you *know* that, Los."

"Yeah," I said. "Lola's crazy."

❋ ❋ ❋

I picked up my blazer and headed out the office when Daniel, the guard at the security desk in the lobby, stopped me as I walked by.

"I liked what you wrote the other day," he said. I didn't know the nigga could read.

"Wait. You've read my stuff?"

"Man, I read all of your stuff. I got a lot of downtime here, and it's not like I'm really securing shit. Who the hell wants to bust up some writers?" When he said that, he pulled his dreadlocks away from his face. The dreads covered most of his front, so when he pulled them back, it revealed his massive chest. Dude was huge.

"True," I said while noticing his burliness. "You used to play ball or somethin'?"

"Yeah. I was a tight end at Douglass and played in college at Chattanooga. Didn't play long though. Couldn't do the books 'cause I was doing hoes, know what I mean?"

"Yeah," I laughed. "I know *exactly* what ya' mean." I had no fucking clue what he meant. I was 29 years old and I've *looked* 29 since I was 19. See, I'm short and pudgy with a receding hairline. By comparison, Daniel was a freakin' Adonis. As much as it pains me to admit this—as a straight man, mind you—Daniel is simply a handsome dude. He's 6'4, 240 pounds, dark-skinned, with dreads. Daniel played the "Office Adonis" thing to the hilt, too. I've seen him work the sistas at the security desk from afar. Compared to him, I had no command over women. So no, I couldn't really relate at all. I couldn't relate because I didn't know what it was like to be a man-whore. But it did feel cool just talking about that stuff with him. And I felt like I needed more guy friends to kick it with to buffer against the *paraika*. We continued to talk. Before I knew it I knew it, I was talking to the cool *AJC* security guy for nearly an hour.

"I like that you expose hoes for being hoes," he said. "Some of the baddest chicks in Atlanta are all about one thing." He rubbed his fingertips on his right hand together. That brought a smile to my face.

"You know, you should hang with me and my boys sometime."

"Y'all ain't gay or on the down low or any shit like that, are you?"

"No!" I said immediately. "We like girls, man." And that brought a smile to *his* face.

"Cool," he grinned. "Nigga, this Atlanta. A brother gotta be sure."

✳ ✳ ✳

I didn't often come home to the smell of hot food because Lola was a horrible homemaker. If you ain't gonna work, you can at least make yourself useful around the house, right? Cook a meal. Clean up. Do *something*. But Lola couldn't cook and didn't think she had to cook. She didn't clean and didn't think she had to clean. And instead of sticking a chicken in the oven, she stuck her hands in my pockets and spent my money.

But I walked in the kitchen and I saw my favorite girl, my little brown-faced Jordan, seated at the table trying to eat some sort of fried rice dish. When she saw me, she shimmied out of her chair, and ran to me for a hug.

"Daddy!" she yelled. I picked her up and gave her a kiss.

"Hey, Baby! What you tryin' to eat?"

"Fwyied Wice! Mommy bwyought Chi-nese food!"

"Sure did," said the Princess of Darkness as she entered the kitchen. Sometimes you don't need A/C when Lola walks in the room. She can be a damn Ice Queen.

"You get enough for me?" I asked as I placed Jordan back in her seat and moved over to kiss Lola hello. But Lola flinched...and dissed me!

"What's wrong?" I whispered to her.

"You act like last night didn't happen," she said.

"Oh. Well, about last night...I was wondering...why you set me up like that?"

"Set you up? Would it have hurt you to pay for a friend on her birthday, Carlos?"

"Yes, Lola, it would have. And Adrienne isn't my friend. I'd rather spend that money on you or Jordan, or on something we need around the house."

"It doesn't matter, Carlos. You embarrassed me in front of all my girls."

"What?" Then I stopped myself. "You know, we shouldn't argue in front of Jordan." I leaned in again for a kiss. Still quiet, Lola tilted her cheek toward my lips.

"And you're cheap," she said, dryly. "Your food's in the microwave." She then left for the living room. I grabbed the food, sat with Jordan and sighed.

"What you think, Baby?" I asked her. Jordan cutely shrugged her shoulders.

"I don't know, Daddy," she said and kept eating. The girl can eat.

"I don't either," I said as I wiped her mouth while she laughed.

For some reason, the moment triggered a brainstorm. I pulled out my laptop and punched away at the keys to explore a subject, stopping only for a quick, crunchy bite of a flaky eggroll. I was writing in fits and starts and didn't want to lose momentum, so Jordan left her Old Man to work.

"Bye, Daddy," she said, waving as she slid out of the kitchen chair.

"Hey! Where you going, Little Girl?"

"SpongeBob!" Ah, Nickelodeon. Every parent's favorite babysitter.

I got back on my brainstorm. And what I completed 548 words later was syndicated by Cox Newspapers, published Feb. 22, 2008 in 125 newspapers across the country:

Good Riddance to Ladies Night
By Carlos M. Tyrone

This is for my fellow bachelors caught up in the struggle.

Women are cheap as hell. Gents, you ever wonder how some women can afford vacations out the yang, home décor that would make the "Queer Eye" guys jealous and have random shopping sprees for ridiculously narrow stiletto-heeled shoes on a salary as restrictive as yours?

It's simple, man. Some women don't have to pay for jack when they go out. Instead, all the money they would spend on cosmos and cover charges is tucked away into some hoity, toity financial account, bankrolling their playgirl lifestyle. Do you realize that dames can actually plan a night out while crying poverty and still have a good time? How is *that* possible? Simple: because they know we guys (aka, suckers) bring spending money for us AND for the women we meet. By night's end, we're left with, like, six dollars for McDonald's.

That's why David Gillespie is my hero. Gillespie brought a discrimination suit against a New Jersey nightclub and got "Ladies Night" promotions barred in taverns across the state.

Last week, New Jersey's top civil rights official (who is male) said "Ladies' Night" promotions of discounted drinks and other financial incentives for women discriminated against men.

That's one small step for man, one giant step for mankind.

I suppose it's the double standard that women should own. As James Brown would say, 'It is a man's world.' Chivalry is incumbent upon pleasing the woman—as it should be. (Besides, you'll get prosecuted if you try that "caveman's club to the head" jazz.)

What's interesting, however, is that we live in a time when feminism has put some forward-thinking women in a predicament. You would think that with women making more money than ever before, going Dutch would be a regular thing. In some instances (not just in the Whitney Houston/Bobby Brown household) women—take black women for example—are making more money than their male contemporaries.

But my friends, here is the dirty little secret that many feministas won't admit to you. Most women don't want to be an alpha woman. I repeat, most women don't want to be the alpha woman.

Some women yearn for the chivalry of their mother's and grandmother's generation, where a dashing, white tuxedo-clad, Cary Grant type walks in, lights her cigarette, orders Gibson martinis and glides her across the dance floor. Even intimidating professional skirts want the man to make most of the moves. When was the last time a woman bought you a drink? For me, the only time that occurred was during the Clinton Administration.

Fellas, there is nothing wrong with women wanting Cary Grant. But y'all, some of these chicks are getting over on us. Meanwhile, we go broke. Some dames even want us to finance drinks for their freeloading girlfriends. I once dated a girl who thought I should buy drinks for her AND her girls. I think I said something to the degree of "Hell No," but I can't recall.

We should take up the cause of David Gillespie! We should be outraged! It's revolution time, damn it!

Just one thing, guys: Can the revolution wait until after this weekend? I put in overtime at the office to pay for the Valentine's Day date I had last week.

When I started editing it, Lola entered the kitchen.

"Baby, you still mad?" I asked as I tapped the keys.

"I'm not still mad," she said.

"Well, you're still *something*. What's wrong?"

She poured a glass of chardonnay, pulled herself a chair at the kitchen table, took a couple of sips, and then—seemingly disgusted—looked at me.

"What are you writing?" she asked sourly. When she asked that, I stopped typing and looked at her. Why, all of a sudden, did she take an interest in my work?

One time I told Lola I was writing a story about The Modern Man and I wanted her to read a draft I put together and write some adjectives to describe me. (It was a first-person article). But she didn't even do that. And it pissed me off that she never read *anything* I wrote. She didn't even read the piece I wrote for *Essence* that won me the Silver Pen Award. Unbelievable!

After that, I began adding up all of my grievances with Lola. By time I was done, it was clear that it she didn't care about me. So I didn't have the energy to talk. I just wanted to write.

"Carlos, dear...what are you writing?" she asked again. I looked at her like a cop trying to evaluate if what a witness was saying was credible.

"Are you sure that you care?" I asked as I leaned back in my chair. She clearly didn't like that, so she got up from the table.

"Oh nevermind," she said, irritably, with wine in hand.

"Lola, are you alright? If this is about Adrienne's party, then—"

"I don't want to talk about that, Carlos."

"Okay," I said as I turned my gaze back to my laptop screen.

"It's just that none of this is how I thought we would—"

I lifted my eyes from the laptop again. "This isn't *what*?"

"Don't worry about it."

Silence.

"Is Jordan asleep?" I asked, looking behind me.

"She's been in bed for about a half an hour."

"Damn. But she usually gives me my kiss goodnight."

"I told her you were working. Are you mad I sent her to bed, Carlos?"

"No, of course not. I just like to make it a habit to kiss her goodnight, that's all."

"You know you can go check on her. The girl acts like she can't sleep without saying goodnight to you anyway."

More silence.

"Well, I'm going to bed." Lola said. "But no, I'm serious. What are you writing?"

"My next column. Wanna see it?" I asked as I swiveled the laptop toward her.

"Nah," Lola said. "Honestly? I'm tired." Typical. Lola did sound tired. But so was I.

"You about done here?" she asked. "Because I can turn off the living room T.V."

"Yeah," I said lowly. "I think we're done."

Chapter 2: Monty, Chili and the Curious Case of Brokeitis

(Brother Oscar)

"Kiss my ass, Monty," I muttered as I waited for the car salesman to finish up with another customer.

Would I get any money for my raggedy truck in trade? *Hell no,* I thought. But I didn't care. I just wanted to wash my hands of that no good son-of-a-bitch. When I think of what my old truck put me through, my blood boils. Monty—that was my truck's name—was my 1991 Mitsubishi Montero. And Monty deteriorated to the point that I had to carry around a homemade, makeshift Piece-of-Shit-Car Care Kit.

If you've ever had a piece-of-shit car, then you know what's in a Piece-of-Shit-Car Care Kit, which could include any or all of the following: quarts of oil and/or transmission fluid; a jug of antifreeze or water; a rag to check fluid levels; duct tape; a can of soda to break up the corrosion of the battery cables; some Fix-A-Flat for when the tire goes flat for no good reason; a flashlight to see how messed up the car is when it breaks down at, say, 11 p.m. along the South Carolina border on I-85 when you're two hours away from your Atlanta destination; a list of curse words to call the piece-of-shit-car when it breaks down; a gas can because the gas gauge is broken and there's no way to know how much is in the tank; two quarters for when the piece-of-shit-car breaks down and you have to walk down State Route Scary-Ass Highway to make a call to whomever because your cell doesn't work in the dead zone where your ride broke down; and— this is key—a baseball bat for protection.

"Punk-ass car," I mumbled again as I flipped through the pages of a magazine in the showroom lobby.

"You okay?" a wonderfully smoky voice dipped in honey said. I looked up and wow. She was only about 5'4", but she seemed taller and had the complexion of a graham cracker. Now take that and dip in honey. Delicious.

"I'm sorry. I was just swearing my car. It broke down on Sugarloaf."

"Maybe your car knew what you were up to."

"I think so, too," I laughed. "Are you looking for a new ride?"

"Nah. I'm getting it serviced. My problem is that my 'check engine' light will not go off and it's driving me nuts."

"Like a steering wheel on a pirate's crotch?"

"Ha! Exactly."

"Wait," I asked. "You actually *got* that joke?"

"Yeah, it was cute," she said.

Cool.

"Why don't we curse our cars together?" I asked as I removed my coat and newspaper from a chair. "Please. You're welcome to join me."

"That sounds fun, but I think my car is ready. I just wanted to say hi."

"Oh, okay," I said as I stood up to shake her hand. "Well, it was nice meeting you. I hope they fix that light. I know that can be annoying."

"Yeah," she said. "I guess I just needed a good fix."

Pause.

"I'm kind of an idiot with innuendo," I said as I tried to size up the moment. "But was that a double entendre?"

"I plead the fifth," she said, smiling like the cat that swallowed the canary. "Well—I hope you find what you need here. Take care."

Then she walked away. I wasn't joking about being dense about stuff like flirting. She did come on to me, right? At least I thought she did. I shifted my focus from Ms. Check Engine Light back to replacing Monty. Monty was good when he ran well. But most of the time, he whooped my ass. And like all fools in an abusive relationship, I over-hyped his love. If Monty made a seven-mile trip to the mall, then I was like, "Hey, Monty didn't overheat today!" But damn it, it's a car. It did what it was supposed to do.

I replayed my encounter with Miss Check Engine Light, trying to see where I went wrong when my phone rang. It was Carlos.

"What's goin' on, Los?" I asked.

"Nothing much. What you up to? Carlos asked.

"I'm at the car lot. I'm finally getting rid of Monty."

"Do you need a therapist or some shit?"

"Shut up. Anything turn up at the *AJC*? It's been three weeks."

"Nothing you'd want. Maybe in a few weeks, though. Listen: I'm rounding up some guys at Archie's tonight around eight. We're gonna have a meeting."

"A meeting? About what? Shooting pool?"

"No. Not about shooting pool," he said cryptically. "It's more serious than that."

"Then what's this about? If it's a pyramid scheme or something you can forget it."

"No, man," he said. "Nothing like that."

"Then what is?" I asked as a salesman walked toward me. "I gotta go." I hung up.

"Mr. Ruark?" he asked shaking my hand. "Tom Ryan. You wanna see the Durango?"

"I sure do," I said. "And please, call me Oscar."

"Well alright then, Oscar. Let's go see that truck! Now, were you looking to trade-in your current vehicle?" Uh-oh.

"Um...yeah."

"Great. Is it here?" he asked.

I sighed. Kiss my *entire* ass, Monty.

I first got Monty about two weeks before I moved to North Carolina for better pay, an exciting atmosphere and a lot more possibilities. There, I took a job at the local newspaper and became a stud. I worked hard. But I played hard, too. It had only been a few months since the move but Monty and I had it going on. I upgraded my wardrobe and bought some serious threads. And when I got soup, Monty got soup: a fresh coat of paint, new stereo, fresh tires and rims (not gaudy) and a timing belt for under the hood.

Professionally and socially, I took off. I hung out in posh bars, worked radio shows, wrote trendy columns and—get this—even made the local indie paper's Most Eligible Bachelor list. You couldn't tell me *nothin.'*

And then I met Ol' Girl. Ugh.

One day I got a call from one of the editors at the Boston Globe who wanted to talk to me about writing a column targeting the Gen X/25-34 year-old crowd. Music to my ears! I thought it'd be music to my girl's ears, too. Boy was I wrong.

"Where?" she asked as she pulled turkey legs out the oven. She loved to cook for me. That's how she housed me. "Oscar, you've only been at the paper for a year. You think you're ready for big move like that?"

"Who cares? Interviewing for the job is good experience even if I don't get it."

"But Boston called you, so I don't see how you wouldn't get it."

"Why do you make that sound like a bad thing?"

"No, it's not bad—for you," she groaned. "But what about *us?*"

"Baby, this could be great for me *and* you," I said. "This could be a chance to see if we are each other's finish line—if we are the pot at the end of each other's rainbow."

"The end of each other's rainbow? What black man says stuff like that?"

"I do," I said as I slipped the oven mitts from her hands and kissed her fingertips. I then wrapped my arms around her and kissed her forehead.

"Baby, we can make this work," I continued. "You know how I am."

"Yeah, I *know* you alright. You and Monty will be on those streets slumming for some big-booty Boston bitch."

"They have booties in Boston?"

"Can you be serious, Oscar?" She hit me playfully. "Long distance sucks."

"But it's more money and exposure. If we did get married and—"

"If?" she asked pulling away from me. I didn't realize all the Samsonite Ol' Girl had. It was perfectly reasonable for a 24 year-old to say "if" about a relationship that was ten months old. But she had more issues than a New York City newsstand.

"If you don't think about us together, then what's the point, Oscar?"

"Baby, that not what I meant—"

"I know what I heard, Oscar."

"So baby, what do you want me to do?"

"It's your life. You've made that clear. Do what's best for you."

So what did I do? I blinked. And the weeks after I turned down Boston, Ol' Girl used our conversations *about* Boston to second-guess our relationship. She was determined to be negative. And when she got sour, coincidentally, so did that bastard Monty. Out of nowhere, he needed a computer. What car needs a freaking computer? *Knight Rider*? Then he needed more shit: Brakes. Tires. Rotors. *Rotors*? Really, Monty?

Then I hit a wall at work. Like a lot of young reporters on the verge of burnout, I struggled with some deadlines. It *was* a problem, but I had always righted my ship before. Besides, the paper had a history of sweeping reporters' problems under the rug. The cops reporter had a DUI and never got disciplined. Another guy took his shoe off during a staff meeting, stuck his toe in the pit of a woman staffer's crotch under the conference table and got as little as a reprimand. And another reporter was warned twice about making up quotes and stories—the ultimate no-no—before they showed him the door. So surely the bosses would understand when it came to me, their young, hard-working, but burned-out star, right?

But um, no. No, as in, hell no. No, as in a "Don't let the door-knob hit you where the Good Lord split you, Nigger," kind of no. After three years of dedication, those crackers showed my ass the door. Even worse, two weeks after I got fired, Ol' Girl dumped me.

"I can't be your girl anymore," she said, crying one day in my kitchen. It made me stop stirring the chili I had on the stove. "I can't do this anymore."

"Where is all this coming from?"

She teared up and stayed quiet.

"Well, tell me what's wrong? I mean, I'll get back on my feet. Tell me you want me to go to church with you or something. Tell me you're celibate. Tell me anything, Baby. Just don't tell me I lost my job and now I'm losing my girl, too."

She just pouted and stood there in silence.

"Don't just stand there. Damn it, talk to me! Say *something*!"

"I have my own issues and so do you. And I just think—"

"You just think what?" I asked as I took the wooden spoon out the chili and waved it wildly. She had a scared look on her face.

"Are you going to hit me?"

"No, I'd never do that."

"Then quit waving that spoon at me."

I put down the spoon and she relaxed a little. "We're going in opposite directions, Oscar. This isn't a good time for you."

"Is it not a good time for me or is it not a good time for *you*?"

"It's not like that at all, Oscar."

"You're right. The knife in my back actually feels quite nice."

"I can't talk to you when you're like this."

"When I'm like what? Down and out of work?"

"Look, I can't talk to you right now. I just can't. I should go."

Without hesitation, I opened the door and just looked at her. She lowered her head and walked out. We never saw each other again.

"Damn!" I shouted as I slammed my palm flat on the hot stovetop. I raced to the faucet to let the cool water soothe my burns. With a force that I cannot explain to this day, that's when I cried out to God, cursed her and sobbed most of that night. And I never ate the chili. In fact, it took four years before I had another bowl of chili.

Then hell broke loose. Monty's radiator and head gasket busted at the same freaking time. Repairs? About $3,000. I didn't have it. Bills piled up and I didn't have any money to pay for it. I fell behind on rent and got evicted. Before I knew it, I was homeless. I crashed on a friend's sofa most nights but was essentially a vagabond. I lost my furniture, my clothes, some of my early writings. And my health failed. I was never a big guy, but 30 pounds were gone from my 6'2 frame. I was down to a gaunt 165.

Because Monty sucked, I rode the bus. And one night, I was the only passenger and the bus got into an accident. No lie! The damned thing ran up against the concrete dividers and turned over. I wasn't even hurt enough to make any money in a lawsuit. I walked away with minor freakin' injuries.

So fuck you, Monty, for triggering my brokeitis. Brokeitis is a crippling, debilitating condition that ravages everything: relationships, future hopes, dreams, faith in God—everything. I went from top shit at the paper to a part-time coffee jerk making $7 an hour. It was an awful bout of failure for a young man to go through. In between shifts serving up coffee at a café, I caught the bus to have a needle stuck in me at a plasma center for a few measly bucks, two or three times a week, every week for almost a year. Eventually, I had to swallow my pride, move back to Georgia and stay with my folks. I soon landed a job selling insurance, which I hated. It was a far cry from my old days at the paper, but at least it was something. Selling insurance put some money in my pocket and I was soon back on my feet and able to afford my own place again. But truth be told, insurance sucked and I desperately wanted back into the business. But I couldn't find anything.

"Kiss my ass, Monty," I mumbled again.

"I'm sorry?" Ryan asked as we stepped into his office.

"Oh, nothing," I said.

"It felt good when you drove it, huh?"

"Yeah, it did."

"I can see you in it."

"Me too. I like it, but I don't want to pay too much down on it. What do you think you can do to keep the down payment low?"

"Well, that depends," Ryan said. "We would have to check out the truck and see how much you can get on it in trade. How many miles does it have?"

Shit. I gave Ryan the stats—more like lied to him knowing that car wasn't even on the lot and knew the jig would be up as far as trade-ins. I was about to fess up when—wow—The Check Engine Light hottie from earlier appeared.

"Hey, Babe!" she said as she walked up to me and gave me a hug and a kiss on the cheek. "Can I borrow him for a second, Tom?"

"Yes ma'am," Ryan said. We stepped outside his office.

"I'm sorry, Miss," I began. "But—"

"It's Angie," she said with a smile. "I drove by where your car broke down. Do you know you left the door unlocked with an extra key in the glove compartment?"

"Oh, yeah, I do that a lot."

"You just don't care about that car anymore, do you?

"Yeah, I can't even get anyone to steal the damn thing."

"It just overheated, so I was able to drive it here. Besides, it's easier to get value when it's on the lot." Angie pointed out the glass doors and there was Monty. I swear he was *smiling*. I gave Angie a great big hug.

"Lady, you have—"

"It's Angie," she said giving me that wonderful smile again.

"Oscar," I said, shaking her hand. "I owe you a dinner."

"How about tonight? It's as good as any other, plus it'll be your first evening with your new truck." She gave me a wicked grin.

"You're a bad girl, Angie."

"You have no idea, sir," she said arching an eyebrow. Then she shrugged it off with a girlish laugh. "I just like to have fun, that's all."

"I can be down with that. I like to have fun, too."

"Cool, well give me a call and let me know how it goes and I look forward to that dinner tonight." She reached in her purse and pulled out a business card. When she gave it to me, we held hands a little longer than usual.

"Absolutely," I said. "Hey, can I give you a ride back to your car?"

"This is *my* dealership, Oscar. One of my service techs will give me a ride. By the way, I suggest you run after you sign the deal because your truck is a piece of shit!"

"Yes ma'am," I said. And then she left. I took a look at her business card: ANGELA RIDENOUR, ESQ. Then I watched her walk off.

Chapter 3: The Broke Brothers' Revolution: Inquiry Meeting

(Brother Daniel)

"Bitch, come!"

"Oh *shit*!" she cried as her nails dug in my back.

"Ow, Sabrina!" That shit hurt.

"Ooh, ooh! Sorry baby!" she said. Just for that, I was gonna make her walk *extra* bowlegged for that shit. I slid my forearm under her waist and clutched her back. That's when her legs flew open and she got so wet that I needed a lifeguard. I moved my hands from her titties to her neck and gave it a little squeeze. She liked that shit.

"Oh, Daddy! Oh! Oh! Dontstopdontstopdontstopdontstop... Oh! Oh, *shit*!"

I made a long thrust and left it deep inside her. She took a deep breath to take in all my inches. I know it hurt, but she liked it 'cause I was all up on that button. Then, like a tidal wave, the bitch came. And she came *hard*.

"*AHHHHHHHHHHHHHHHHHHHHHHHHHHHHHHHH!!!!!!!!!*"

She was done but I wasn't. "Girl, you got some more," I said. I sat her up, flung her legs over my shoulders, pressed her back against the headboard and grooved in it with big, long strokes. "Oh *shit*!" she said as she got wetter. Her big, sweaty titties slid against my chest. And when the strokes got good to me, I reached down to make sure the condom was still on. When I felt that it was, that's when I got off inside her.

"Grrr...Grrr...Ugnnh! Ugnnh! *MMMMmmm!*" It was so good. But then she had the nerve to try and cuddle. Sorry, but after I come the hoes gotta to go.

"Yo, I gotta be going soon," I said getting up before she got too comfortable.

"Oh," Sabrina said, realizing that I was kicking her ass out. She got up and went to the bathroom but left the door open. I hate that shit. Girl, I don't want no conversation. Just leave, ho!

"The boys still ask about you." She had two boys, and them little niggas were so bad, you'd think they were raised by wolves. I gave her a look when she mentioned them.

"Relax, D. I know what this is. You made that clear."

"And you still cool with that?"

"I guess I got to be. We're just two grownups hooking up, right?"

Damn, right. Chicks say they can play around like men but they can't. The more you give it to her, the more she hangs around. And when she hangs around, she gets used to you and wants you to be her man. Every booty call wanna belong to someone. I felt bad about Sabrina 'cause she's a mom and they don't get out too much. Sometimes sexing single moms is like stealing booty. But what can I say? It was some good booty.

We kicked it for about a year, and I wanted to bounce before that, but then my birthday came up. Since I spent mad cash on her birthday and Valentine's Day—I always meet bitches when they birthday or V-Day is 'round the corner and we all-a-sudden break up after that shit—I made sure I got my payoff with Brina. And the shit did pay off. Brina got me a PlayStation 3, an iPhone, a trip to Vegas for a poker tournament and even a suit to wear on the casino floor. I didn't feel bad 'cause, hell, Brina came from money. Her folks were loaded, so those few G's she spent on me didn't hurt her any. But two months after that, I broke it off. This how I did it:

"Brina, we two different folks. I'm black, and you, like, *alternative*. I mean, yo' folk don't even like black people."

"You know my background, D." I only knew she had two boys and two big-ass titties. I gave her a blank-ass look. "I'm Indian!"

"Don't y'all Indians hate black people?"

"What? Indians don't hate black people."

"Yeah the hell they do. I saw *Mississippi Masala*. And we ain't got the same God. That means a lot to me."

"Religion didn't mean much when you had me bent over doggy style earlier."

"Well, whatever. I'm a Christian, Brina, and you're Muslim."

"Most Indians are Hindus, not Muslims. Besides, I'm Methodist!"

"Methodist? See! That's some David Koresh/Jim Jones shit, yo!"

"You're an idiot!"

"I'm not an idiot. I'm a Christian...terrorist."

"Terrorist! What? Fuck you, Daniel!"

I pissed her off on purpose 'cause I ain't want no serious shit with her. We ain't had shit in common since she was Sri Lankan or whatever the fuck she was. But I wanted to keep her 'round 'cuz the booty was great. And Brina wasn't goin' nowhere 'cuz she was dickmatized. So the moral, fellas, is to lay it down and split her right. She'll call you names. She'll cuss you out. But one good dicking and she'll orbit yo' ass like the moon. Money and good dick are the two things that keep chicks in your stable. I ain't got much of one...

"Talk to you later?" Brina said when I walked her to the door.

"Sure," I said as I smacked her on the ass.

"Why are you so bad, Big D?"

"Whatever, Brina. You know you like it." She walked to her car, smiling.

...But I got plenty of the other.

✳ ✳ ✳

"There's nothing but brothers here!" Josh said when we walked into Archie's.

There were 'bout 40 niggas and Josh was the only snowflake there.

"A lot of niggas here, huh Josh?" I fought back a smirk.

"There sure are!"

"Ha! I caught you! You didn't say it but you agreed that we niggas!"

"C'mon, Danny. I didn't mean that—"

"Chill. I set you up for that one. Just try not to get yourself lynched."

Josh normally don't trip like that because he thinks he black. Josh is my whother—as in my *white brother*. Not my *real* brother, but he's cool. He's also my hook up on some weed. And that night, he was my ride.

Anyway, the night at Archie's had a Million Man March feel to it, and in my mind, whatever Carlos had planned was probably better than *that* damn waste of a Tuesday. That was my senior year in high school and my Ma allowed me to go with my boy Ronnie and Atlanta's 100 Black Men. Ronnie and I even fasted until sundown like Farrakhan told us. Well, we fasted 'til I got hungry. When my stomach growled, I told Ronnie, "Dawg, fuck this. That nigga Farrakhan will talk all day. That nigga made his point so fuck that. Let's eat." So we found a dude around The Mall selling fried fish. It wasn't sundown, and the other 999,998 niggas out there were mad we broke our fast, but fuck them niggas. We were happy while everyone else had the white mouth. Not having kids eat? Hell, naw, Farrakhan. That's child abuse.

Anyway, the meeting actually started on time, so Josh and I tiptoed to the back. Carlos saw us, gave a head nod and turned to answer a question.

"Y'all wanna do *what?*" asked a dude up against a pool table.

"Picket the bookstore," Carlos said. "The Borders on Peachtree."

"That's the biggest bookstore in town!" Pool Table Dude said.

"Yeah, but the point is to protest Brenda Jacobs," Carlos said. "Jacobs is having a book signing for her newest book to piss-off all men, *"To Hell With Him, Girl!"*

"I'm so tired of Jacobs' man-hating," said this tall, Mario Van Peebles-looking dude as he stood up behind Carlos. He had these small, narrow eyes, stern cheekbones and the squarest muthafuckin' jaw I ever seen. His hair was cut low and he wore some old, civil rights era/Malcolm X glasses. He wasn't as tall as me—about 6'0— but the nigga was intimidating. He looked like a militant Clark Kent. "Stuff like Jacobs' books and all of these stupid movies and songs and other bullshit screwing up people's thinking."

"Gent's right," Carlos said looking back at the Van Peebles/ Clark Kent-looking dude whose name was apparently Gent. That's how they ran the meeting. Carlos preached, Gent amen-ed him, and the brothers ate it up:

"Women want us to pay for everything!"

"*Yeah!*" the brothers in the room yelled.

"They got funky attitudes and are emasculating us!"

"*Yeah!*"

"Ain't you fed up? I am because these women are out of hand!"

"*Yeah!*"

"Let's march on the bookstores!"

"*Yeah!*"

"Let's say 'stop' to poisoning women's minds against men!"

"*Yeah!*"

"To hell with Ladies Night! Where's the Guys Night? Buy *us* a drink!"

"*Yeah!*"

Even Josh got caught up in the hysterics. "Let's go to small claims court and file suits to get our hard-earned money back that we spent on these ungrateful hoes!" he yelled out. The room got quiet fast. I was prepared to abandon Whother Josh, but the mob approved.

"*Hell, yeah!*"

Feeling it, Carlos stood on a stool and kept getting niggas worked up. He raised his fist and everyone else did the same.

"It's time for us to get our balls back and not take this crap anymore. It's time to get our shit together and be men. Pump your fist in the air. It's time for the Broke Brothers'...REVOLUUUTION! Say 'Broke Power!'"

"Broke Power!"

"Say 'Broke Power!'"

"Broke Power!"

The energy in that motherfucka was off the charts! But when the chants died, some nervous nigga raised his hand.

"I got a question—two questions, really."

"Go ahead, Jamal," Carlos said, raising an eyebrow.

"What's 'emasculate' mean?"

"Aw, shit," Gent said.

"Ha. I'm just playing. It's when you have sex and you come, *right*?"

"What?" Gent asked. "Anyone have a real question to ask?" We all laughed at him, but Jamal looked at Gent like he wanted to whoop his ass.

"But for real, guys," Jamal continued. "T.V.? Radio? On Saturday?"

"Is there a question in there somewhere?" Gent cracked. "You're not making sense."

"T.V. and radio, yes," Carlos said. "We want to draw attention. Why? What's up, Jamal? You got something to do Saturday? March Madness doesn't start 'til next week."

"Well I—" then Jamal paused.

"Well you, *what*?" Gent sniffed.

"Well, I told my girl I'd take her to McDonough."

"MCDONOUGH!" yelled all 40 of the brothers in the room.

"As in 'The Outlet Malls are in McDonough?' McDonough?" Gent asked.

"Um...yeah," Jamal said lowly.

"A shopping spree, Jamal?" Carlos asked piggybacking Gent. "Seriously?"

"Not really a spree, but we just going to look at some—"

"Are you bullshitting?" Gent asked cutting him off. The crowd could not hold back its full-bellied laughter anymore. We were rolling at dumbass Jamal's expense.

"We are The *Broke* Brothers'!" Carlos said with his hand on Jamal's shoulder.

"BBR, brotha!" Pool Table Guy called out.

"That right," Carlos said nodding his head. "You can't take chicks on shopping sprees and be in The *Broke* Brothers Revolution! We're trying to send a message here!"

"Y-y-yeah, yeah, you right, Los," Jamal said, backtracking. "I feel what you saying."

"So you still down, Jamal?"

"H-h-h-hell yeah, I-I-I-I'm d-d-definitely down," Jamal said as he looked at Gent, who gave him one of the best "Nigga, please," looks I've ever seen.

"So what you gonna tell your girl?" Carlos asked Jamal.

"I-I-I-It'll be straight. I got it covered." Jamal said.

"You sure?" Carlos said.

"Yeah. We'll just go to McDonough on Sunday."

"No, fool!" Carlos said shaking his head while the whole room groaned. "Shopping the day after a Broke Brothers' rally? Look: I got over 3,000 emails from that column I wrote in February. There is serious interest in this. But we should have fun, too."

"Fun? So this shit ain't serious then!" Pool Table Guy yelled.

That nigga. I hated niggas who had a comeback for everything. Ol' counterproductive dick. But Carlos paid them no attention. He then reached into a box, pulled out a T-shirt and raised it over his head. "Gentlemen, let's just see how far we can take it." The black shirt had a "black power"-style fist clenching cash in the middle. And the international symbol for "no"—that red circle with that slash in the center—was stamped over the fist.

"What is that? *Cashbusters?*" joked a brother who entered the room. It was this tall, bald, dark-skinned dude with this hot chick on his arm. Carlos stopped the meeting and he and Gent walked over to greet the couple. But were they a couple? This was Atlanta. Gay niggas rock bad bitches all the time. I had to see if this shit passed the smell test.

"Semmi, I'm going to talk to her," I told Josh in my best Eddie Murphy from *Coming to America* accent. I walked over to see what was up because homegirl was fine as hell. But what was she doing at the meeting?

"Glad you could make it, Oscar," Carlos said. Oscar? Fuck. That was Carlos' homeboy. "Angie, I didn't know you knew Oscar?"

"Carlos?" Angie said, looking shocked. "Well, Oscar and I met earlier today."

"Yeah, she helped me get the Durango, today," Oscar said. "Angie, me, Los and Gent went to college together," Oscar then looked at me like, "Who the fuck is this nigga?"

"Oh!" Carlos said, finally realizing I was there. "This is Daniel. He works in my office. Daniel, these are my boys, Gent and Oscar. And this lady is Angie—"

"Just call me, D," I said, cutting him off and getting right in there to dap everyone. "Good meeting y'all boys. Los told me a lot about y'all. And how are you, Ms. Angie?"

"*Ms.* Angie?" Carlos asked. "You mean *Mrs.* Ridenour, right?"

They got quiet. But it took a second for my slow ass to catch up and get it.

"What's your last name, Oscar?" I asked.

"Ruark," he said, looking at me like I was crazy.

Wait. *Mrs.* Ridenour? But they didn't have the same name so— Oh.

"Carlos," Angie asked him, smiling. "What is all this?"

"I can't say because it's really for brothers only," he said. "How's the Congressman?"

"Jack's in Washington doing Congressman stuff, I guess," she said.

"Wait," Gent said with an irritated look. "How do you two know each other?"

"I used to write a politics column at the *AJC* and Angie was a good source when she worked on Ridenour's campaign," Carlos explained before turning back to Angie. Well, that shit made sense. "So does the GOP want to face Hillary or Obama?"

"What are you, trying to get a scoop?" Gent butted in. "The brothers are waiting!"

"Y'all stick around," Carlos said. I'll buy us a quick round afterwards."

"Cool," I said.

✳ ✳ ✳

"So that Angie chick—she's married?"

"That's what Carlos said," I told Josh as we cruised on the highway.

"So why was that bald dude with her if she's married?"

"I guess they're trying to get down on the down low."

"But dude looked like that was the first time he knew she was married."

"Well if Oscar didn't know then, he sure as hell knows now."

Whother Josh was annoying me. But I was thinking about stuff after the meeting because Carlos inspired me. He was doing thangs. But me? I didn't even hang with niggas with prospects. I began to think it was time for me to trade in my old friends for some new ones. I was 27 and not hitting on shit. All I had to show for myself was booty from simple hoes and a lame job.

Brina texted me to see if the meeting was done. But I ignored it because I wasn't in the mood to see her. Then, a few minutes later, I got a text from April, this 20 year-old who worked at Chess King at South DeKalb Mall. April wanted to come over, but I knew why: she wanted my weed. I always told April that if she was gonna get my weed, she had to get the dick, too. This was fair to her and so we developed an understanding. After the meeting, I was a little depressed. So I told April to come over because a little smoke and sex usually was my quicker picker upper.

"Nigga, you holding?" I asked as Josh turned on Memorial Drive.

"Holding some smoke?" he said. "Naw, but I can get some."

"Cool."

As Josh wheeled his 300M onto Flat Shoals, I got sad. Old bullshit popped in my head: the handshake with my college coach when I signed to play ball in Chattanooga; the tears when I got kicked out of college for dicking around; the job I had at the Ford plant in Hapeville and getting laid off when it closed. I mean, my life seemed harder than it *needed* to be. Shit.

Josh pulled into his man's place and there were these white boys on the PlayStation, drinking and smoking shit. We were supposed to get the weed and then split. But then they passed a controller to play Madden. And then they passed a beer. And a joint. So instead of it being just a few minutes, it was some hours later when Josh took me home. I straight forgot about April. But when we got to my place, she was waiting outside my apartment door. So then Josh drove off, leaving me with the youngin'.

"Come here, boy!" she yelled in her squeaky voice. I guess she had just gotten off work and came over soon after she clocked off. She still had her nametag on and shit.

"Don't give me shit, April. I know I'm late, but Josh and I—"

She shut me up by giving me a big, wet, sloppy kiss with lots of tongue. She was jonesing to smoke and fuck and her mouth tasted like Newports.

"Been smoking them menthols again, huh?"

"Shut up and come here, boy," she said pulling me closer to the door. My big body covered her tiny body, so if you saw us from afar, you wouldn't see her. She unzipped my pants.

"Oh word?" I said, smiling. "Well, it has been a long, hard day."

As her lips and hands got good to me, I tilted my head up in the air. But then I noticed a folded yellow note stuck to my door.

"Hey, hey—stop," I said. "Chill out for a second."

I looked at the letter. It was a fuckin' eviction notice. Damn landlord was buggin' again. I didn't have the money, so I could only hope that dude would accept a payment plan or something. But I couldn't do shit about it at 11:15 p.m. on a Monday.

"What's wrong, Boo Boo," the young girl asked. I hated when she called me that.

"Nothing, April. Let's go inside and get fucked up."

That eviction note set off a lame week. On both Tuesday and Wednesday I went back and forth on the phone with that bastard landlord to work a deal on the rent, but he was being a dick. He said he "had to think on it." Then that Thursday, both Brina and April kept blowing up my phone, making up all sorts of stupid shit as an excuse to see me. Both were chasing the dick. Both got straight ignored. Pimpin' can be exhausting.

So when Saturday came around, I ain't wanna do shit. But I wasn't gonna let Los down, so I set the clock to make sure I made the BBR rally. Los told us to show up at Borders at 10:30 a.m. I didn't know why he wanted us there so early because Jacobs' book signing wasn't until noon. But when me and Josh got to the bookstore around 11:30, I saw why: the other niggas hadn't showed up. It was just Carlos and Gent, who had the back door of his SUV open as the two sat on the bumper. They wore their Broke Brothers' Revolution T-shirts and looked sad as hell.

"Who you gonna call? *Cashbusters!*" Josh said as he greeted them with his hand out for dap. You shoulda seen the scowls on their faces. Josh can be corny sometimes.

"I struggle to find the humor in this," Carlos said.

"Um, I think I'm still fucked up from last night," Josh said. "I'm going in for coffee. Y'all want any?" We shook our heads and he walked into the bookstore.

"He's actually a cool dude," I said after Josh walked off.

"I guess," Carlos said. "At least he showed up."

"Yeah, where is everybody?" I asked.

"Maybe them boys got scared," Gent said. "Or maybe they think this is silly."

"Well, it *is* silly, ain't it?" I asked. We looked at each other and then Oscar stormed onto the lot and pulled up next to the truck in his Durango.

"Hey, Los!" he said. "You got another *Cashbusters* T-shirt? I left mine at the crib."

"Yeah, I got you," Carlos sighed. I looked at him and Gent.

"We've known Oscar since college, so it's cool if he's a smart-ass," Gent said. "Your wannabe black white friend? Not so cool." That made sense to me.

Thirty minutes before rally time, and our numbers were short. It was me, Josh, Gent, Oscar and Carlos. Carlos didn't seem fazed, but I was pissed. Where were them niggas?

"I just spoke with the manager," Carlos said. "He's okay with us wearing our T-shirts and carrying our signs in and out of the building. We can even chant a little bit."

"That's fair," Gent said. "As long as we don't cut the fool. If we do, pissed sisters will make the Selma marches look like nothing."

"Wait—we could get beat up?" Josh asked as he came back with his coffee in hand. Man, I had no idea how much bitch he had in him until right then. He was punking out.

"Man, calm down," Oscar said. "No one's getting beat up."

"Exactly," Carlos said. "Where is my T.V. crew? They said they'd be here at 11:30."

"At least I'm here, Los!" chirped this sexy light-skinned chick with frizzy red hair that sat on her head like a fern. She was a tall mama too—5'9—with a pretty round face and light freckles.

"Vanessa?" Carlos asked. "What are you doing here? Are you on assignment?"

I thought I seen her before. Vanessa worked at the *AJC*.

"Nope," she said. "Just curious to see how many sistas will toss their books at you."

"They're gonna get down like that?" fretted Josh.

"For the last time, *no!*" Gent said to Josh. "Vanessa, you're scaring the white boy."

"Ok, Mr. Serious," she said to Gent. "I'm just teasing. You guys have my support."

"Thank you," Gent said.

"And I'm here if you guys need a ride to the hospital."

"Very funny," Oscar said over her shoulder. She turned to him and did a double take.

"Damn, he's cute," I overheard her whisper to Carlos about Oscar before speaking up again. "Why y'all choose a Brenda Jacobs book-signing? She's the angriest woman on earth! You may as well walk on the set of *Oprah* and flip all the women the bird." Vanessa was funny. And I wanted to palm that big, luscious watermelon booty of hers.

"Are you drunk, V?" Carlos asked.

"Tipsy," she said. "I had an early brunch date at Aria. Bottomless mimosas."

"How was the date?" Carlos asked.

"I'm here now with you instead of with him, so there's your answer."

I peeped the bookstore entrance and a saw a few of the brothers from the inquiry meeting showing up...with their women! Even that jackass Pool Table Nigga walked up to the Borders entrance and held the door for some chick with him.

"Hey!" I yelled to him from our parking lot spot. "We're set up *here!*" He shrugged and walked into the store. Then another dude walked in with his woman.

"Something's not right," Gent said as he slid his glasses below eye level.

"Johnny!" Carlos yelled and ran toward them, stopping the second man before he got in the store. But the whole thing was out of earshot. I couldn't hear anything, so I turned my attention to the beauty with the booty.

"You write a lot of money columns, right?"

"Yep, that's me. Front desk in the lobby, right?"

"Yep, that's me."

"Yeah, I heard things about you. Stacy Mack said you're a man-whore. Do you remember Stacy?" Hell naw, I didn't remember that ho. But I couldn't say it like that.

"Stacy...Stacy...*Stacy*? I don't recall her," I said after pretend-thinking.

"Stacy said you're a Fido. Rover. Bow wow. Arf, arf. A *dogimus maximus.*"

"You can't believe everything you hear."

"Well, Robin Atwell in accounting said the same thing." Fuck. Did the bitch have a fuckin' FBI file on my ass? Thankfully, Carlos came back to our huddle.

"Johnny said a lot of the fellas' women won't let them stand with us."

"Why doesn't that surprise me?" Vanessa asked.

"Well it surprises me," Gent said. "It doesn't make sense."

"What up with dat, man? Dem fools is trippin', fellas," Josh said in his whother voice. He was getting on everybody's nerves by then.

"Who the hell brought the Beastie Boy?" Oscar cracked.

"Anyway," Carlos said, rolling his eyes. "Johnny thinks some-one contacted Soror Books and they got in touch with Jacobs. She posted something on the web and—"

"Oh no," Gent nodded.

"Exactly," Carlos said. I didn't get any of that nuanced shit.

"Oh, shit," Oscar said as he looked to the store. About 30 mad-looking bitches oozed out the Borders and made a slow march toward our camp in the corner of the parking lot.

"They know our plans," Carlos said. "This is a big set up."

"A set up?" Oscar said. "Who'd drop the dime on us? And who has the stroke to get in touch with Jacobs? Don't we have to be established before we can have snitches?"

"I know, right?" I said. "Hey, where Josh go?"

"He left when he heard one of y'all say 'Oh shit,'" Vanessa cracked. "Those women are slowly walking here like this is *Thriller*. Good luck, Los." She waved and took off. She was right. Things got bad fast. We were shorthanded, Los' plans had gone to shit and a bunch of pissed-off women were *Thriller*-walking toward us.

"I'll go talk to them." Carlos said to us. "Y'all stay back here. We don't want too much of a scene." Carlos walked out to meet them.

"I heard you came here to disrupt my book signing," Jacobs said to Carlos. She was a tall, healthy broad with a low-cut, blonde natural. And the bitch looked like she could fight. "What is this 'Broke Brothers' Revolution' mess, sir?"

"Ladies, my friends and I don't want to start any trouble, we just—"

WHOOMP! A rubber band-bound newspaper flew over Carlos' head about 60 yards behind him and landed at our feet. It was catapulted like some shit you'd see in *Braveheart* or something. Who threw that? Mike Vick? I unfolded the paper and Gent and Oscar looked at it over my shoulder. Carlos's first BBR column was circled in red.

"Uh oh," Oscar said. "These women are pissed."

Then a T.V. crew pulled into the parking lot. Gent checked his watch. "Our T.V. crew was supposed to be here at 11:30. But they show at noon."

"And the book signing is at noon!" Oscar said, looking at Gent. They turned to me.

"I don't get it," I said."

"Listen, D," Gent said. "The TV crew isn't late."

"They're here, but not to cover *our* protest," Oscar said.

I looked at the newspaper with the circled column.

"So," I said, taking a crack at it. "Jacobs wanted the T.V. crew..."

"Yeah," Oscar said.

"T.V. is here...but at noon, but not for us..."

"You're getting warmer, man," Oscar said.

"So the T.V. folks are here to really show us get punked! Did I get it?"

"Yeah, you did!" Oscar said. "You win a new car!"

"Y'all two clowns straighten up!" Gent said to us, still about business. "Los is out there in no man's land!" Then he yelled to him, "Los! It's a big-ass trap! Run!"

When the women heard Gent, they surrounded Carlos and a big-ass assault of newspapers, magazines, and books were fired at us. Them bitches were super pissed!

"We need to get out of here!" I called out to Oscar.

"I know!" he said. "Because at this rate, someone is going to seriously get hur—"

FOOP!

"Ow! I'm hit! I'm hit! My God, that hurts! That shit really *hurt!*"

I turned and saw that Oscar got cold-cocked upside his head by a copy of *Beloved* and that thick-ass book drew blood. The direct hit freaked me out.

"What the fuck, man!" I yelled. "Man down, Gent! Man down! Oscar's been hit!"

"Shit!" Gent said, ducking flying books. "Both of you! Get in the truck! Now! We gotta get out of here! Los! Bring your ass! Now!"

Carlos dropped his BBR sign and hauled ass toward Gent's truck. The four of us—me, Oscar, Carlos and Gent tossed our shit in the back, piled in the ride like bank robbers on a getaway, and sped off with the tires screeching. When we left, the women cheered.

The whole thing sucked. Even worse, the shit was on T.V. and it even got 200,000 hits on YouTube. The Broke Brothers' Revolution was a damn punchline out the gate.

"Fellas? The revolution will not be televised," Carlos said. "We can't afford it."

Chapter 4: Lola the Terrible

(Brother Carlos)

"Gent, I can't sign off on that."

"Why not, Los?" Gent asked from the other end of the line. "Don't you think it'd be great if we got rid of all the junk on the radio?"

"Lobbing Molotov cocktails into the windows of record labels would land us in jail. And my pretty, yellow ass wouldn't last a prison shower. I'm about to hang up because tossing Molotov cocktails is one of the worst ideas *ever*. Oh, before I let you go: Did you see my interview in *Sista Girl*? The reporter made me look like a real asshole."

"You made yourself look like an ass," Gent said with a chuckle. "Why'd you do it?"

"I thought the BBR needed a different tactic. Ya know, regular press stuff. Columns, interviews—stuff like that. We can't picket shit until we build ourselves a strong base."

"We should do something about these dumbass songs on the radio. I just heard a song from some fool named Young Mann. It's about a girl baking a pie while giving a guy head! The hook was to the tune of 'Mary Had A Little Lamb,' except the words were 'Gary Got A Little Head.' Is that some shit or what?"

The song Gent referred to was disgusting, terrible...and *catchy as hell*. But I couldn't tell my militant friend that. One time, we went to The Atlanta Hip Hop Film Festival and during a forum on black vernacular, Gent stood to ask the producers of *N*gga Come Lately* a question.

"Why do you guys constantly use the n-word?" he asked, sincerely.

Their response? "Nigga, sit your black ass down and shut up!"

Gent got so pissed that he formed petitions to end the festival. That's my best friend.

"Gent, quit bullshitting. Lola will be here soon and—"

"Los, songs about girls baking pies giving strange men head are a problem."

"Would you rather the girls give familiar men head while baking pies?"

"Not funny, Los! This sorry-ass rap music has to be stopped."

"Well, I can't stop it today. Lola will be here soon and I got to get my mind right."

"Why? You finally gonna break up with her?"

"I don't know what else to do, Gent. I swear I'm so damn tired of her."

"I hear you. But whatever you do, don't kill her."

"Right."

"Just put a little foot up her ass."

"What?"

"It's a metaphor, Los," he said. "Just give some of the hell she gives you back to her. At least give her two or three toes. A few toes would do Ms. Crazy some good."

"Bye, fool," I said as I hung up the phone.

✳ ✳ ✳

I met Lola in Chicago. I worked for a wire service there and she did PR for a theater on the Southside. And then the condom broke and she got knocked her up.

In retrospect, Lola and I were like oil and water. But I wanted us to work. I guess I had been so bad with women—so emotionally unavailable and so distrusting of them—that I wanted to give us a real shot. After all the years of being with people who didn't understand me or my line of work, I thought Lola got me. I guess I was wrong. Fool.

Do you how tough it is to be a brother and *not* get tagged with bullshit labels that sisters lob at you? Some sisters cling to their phobias about black men like their purses when they walk down dark alleyways. Brothers can get any and all of the following labels: homosexual, bisexual, on the down low, too pretty for her, white woman lover, man-whore or player, deadbeat, bitch-ass nigga or punk, mama's boy, stupid, abusive. And of course, broke.

Yet chicks wouldn't know a real man if he was the Son of Man, dig? I could imagine how some hens would cluck about Jesus:

"Girl, Jesus ain't hittin' on shit! He's a carpenter, so he ain't got no money. And he's always hanging out with them busters."

"I know, right? 'The Disciples.' They sound like some gay dudes living on the down low if you ask me, okay?"

"Now Judas is cool. I heard he just came up on some silver and got paid. Let's see if he'll take us to the Waffle House."

"Yeah! I may be a sophisticated diva with special wants and needs that many men can't fulfill, but I'll do anything for waffles."

"Judas is cool?" "Anything for waffles?" Wow.

Brothers who extend an olive branch to these finicky, yet, simple women don't stand a chance. Some sisters get their noses opened wide by Mr. Gimmick, with his bling and bullshit. Meanwhile, honest, hard-working, quality brothers get berated, emasculated and ignored. Dismissed like some second-class citizens because we aren't a gimmick. That, in a nutshell, is as good a reason as any for The Broke Brothers' Revolution to exist.

Looking back on my time with Lola, she really had nothing to offer except a pretty face. I got caught up in her looks—she's 5'6 and looks like Tyra Banks. I'm 5'9, 200 pounds, and look like Martin Luther King's long-lost, moon-headed brother. I'm a yellow man with hairline issues and a little Buddha-belly, so when I met Lola, I thought I hit the jackpot. Especially since short, light-skinned men are out of style. But being light-skinned has its advantages. Here's a joke: What do you call a black man with good credit? LIGHT-SKINNED. *Ba da BUMP!*

Anyway, blinded by beauty (and since I knocked her up), I changed my world for Lola. We moved to Atlanta so that she could go to art school. And we lived together. Big mistake. Lola wasn't nearly as together as advertised. She had $62,000 in student loans and $11,000 in credit card debt. She couldn't even borrow from her 401(k) because she had an outstanding loan from a trip she took to Italy with her girls. She took out the loan without my knowledge a little after we moved in together. I busted my ass to get *us* out of *her* debt while she was being careless with money.

And the last straw came when I overheard Lola on the phone with a girlfriend:

"Yeah, I know girl....It ain't the best, but as long as I'm getting mine....Yeah! Girl, he paid the car note AND moved me to Atlanta.... Well, as long as I give him some every now and then, I don't worry about a thing....Oh girl! Last night at the club, there was this fine-ass man and...."

My heart sank. Scheming, heffa.

Gent warned me from the beginning that Lola was just a pretty face with hella issues.

"Los," he once said. "It's the Eve Syndrome. As in Adam and Eve. God makes the pretty women the most ridiculous to see how we men will act around them."

Gent was right. That's what I got for being cheap. I thought it was good for Lola and me to live together to save money. But Gent warned me about "living in sin" with her and I should've listened. Of course, Gent's the same man who wanted to toss Molotov cocktails at buildings, so go figure. And the way I saw it, I already did a bunch of sinning while living by myself. So that wasn't ending any time soon. So why not do what I do in a two-income household? I just assumed we would get married someday. Fool.

Then Lola pulled up in the driveway. I wanted to talk but I worried that things could get ugly in front of Jordan and Lola had picked her up from the daycare.

"Hey," Lola said waltzing in the house with shopping bags. Guess whose money she shopped with? "I got some stuff for that room upstairs. What you doing home?"

Jordan ran to me and gave me hug. "Hi, Daddy!"

"Hi, Baby!" I said. "Go upstairs and see what Daddy got you."

Jordan happily ran upstairs to her room, while Lola looked at me with suspicion. And she was right to do so. See, I bought Jordan a Spongebob luggage set, and had packed most of her things. Jordan and me were gonna stay with Uncle Gent until I got a new place. I was leaving Lola but would be damned if I left Jordan with that lazy wench.

"What you get Jordan?" Lola asked. "I'm curious since you say we spend too much."

"I'm glad you took that to heart," I said looking at the shopping bags. Why are you home so soon? Weren't you starting a class today?"

"I decided against taking the class," she said. "I didn't feel like the time was right for me to take on a full load this year."

"Oh, *you've* decided? I must've missed that conversation. Lola, we've been through all of this. You can't sit up here all day or just go shopping. It's stretching us thin."

"I help out around here, Carlos." How the hell did she figure that?

"Well you're not 'helping' enough, Lola. We moved here because you wanted to live in Atlanta and go to an art school that you don't even attend now."

When I said that, our postures changed. Suddenly we faced each other, bowlegged, like gunslingers in the Old West. This was it. No more complaining to friends and coworkers. No more pent up anger. It was time for all of our drama to come to a head.

"Did I tell you to move down here for me?" she charged.

"Yes. You said art was your dream and you wanted to live in Atlanta."

"Well...so?"

"*So?*" When someone gives you a stupid one-word come back like that, it means they know you're right and they're wrong as hell. And I sensed that Lola was about to get ghetto. I always forgot about how ghetto she was until we argued.

"Let's cut the shit, Carlos," she said. "So what's the deal, huh? You ain't feeling appreciated? Huh? Is that what this is about? You want me on my knees to praise you?"

"Lola, lower your voice. Jordan is upstairs." Lola dropped to her knees.

"Maybe you want me to pray to God and thank him for such a good man in my life!!"

"Don't be so dramatic, Lola! Get off your *knees*!"

"No. I need to be here on my knees and pray to God! Or maybe I should pray to you? Yeah! That's it. Maybe I should just kiss that underappreciated dick, hmm?"

"Kiss it? But the baby is upstairs!" I said through my gritted teeth. I didn't want Jordan to walk in on her parents cutting the fool. But Lola unfastened my belt and actually pulled my dick out. Her touch turned my angry cries of "Lola! Lola!" into a softer, sexier "Lola...Oh, baby...*Lola.*" I wanted to tell that heffa where to go, but she was good at using sex to change my mind. She'd been stingy with it since the Strip fiasco, so when she touched it, I got my hopes up. But again, God had a sense of humor and the scenario didn't play out as I'd planned. Because then—

"Lola...Lola...Ow! What are you doing! Lola! *That hurts!*"

The bitch wrapped her hands around my junk and pulled down on it *as hard as possible.* I fell to the floor and we were both on our knees—me with my pants down, writhing in pain, and Lola squeezing my rocks like a near-empty tube of toothpaste.

"You are not the boss of me, Carlos," she hissed. "You hear me?"

"Lola!" I shrieked in an octave I didn't know I had. "Please! Let go!"

But she didn't let go. So I took my hands, wrapped them around her neck and squeezed. I had been warned about this woman, and now she wouldn't stop bringing the pain to my privates. How pathetic was this? My daughter was a stairway away and her two college-educated parents were about to be the Two Dumb Niggas on *Cops*. I don't do violence. But Lola's Tonkin Death Grip was killing me. So I hissed back:

"Lola, if you don't let go of my shit right now, I will pop your neck like a zit. Now our daughter is upstairs and if she sees us—"

"Daddy?"

We looked up the stairwell and saw Jordan with a puzzled look on her face through the railing. That made us quickly let go of each other. I pulled up my pants and ran to Jordan. It was the most painful 10-yard run ever because my junk felt like it was on fire. But the adrenaline made it possible to tend to my crying daughter. Lord, have mercy.

❋ ❋ ❋

"It could have been worse," Gent said as we pulled out the driveway of my condo in his truck. "She coulda cut you."

"She slashed my tires, man!" I said from the passenger seat. "She did the shit when I went upstairs to get my bags. You're an accountant, Gent. Do the math: she cost me $50 on a wrecker to the tire shop and about $600 in tires!"

"While you packed, it gave Lola a chance to stew. How you gonna have Jordan packed, but not have yourself packed? You've been planning this for a while, right?"

"Yeah, you're right. I guess worrying about Jordan made me forget about me."

"Real classy to leave her a couple of months mortgage, though," he said.

"I shouldn't have left her shit. It's my damn condo." I turned to the backseat to spy on Jordan, who looked so precious sleeping. I was surprised that Lola let me take her without a fight. But I think deep down she knew she couldn't take care of her. Her immaturity showed that she wasn't ready for parenthood. But she took my leaving better than I thought. I felt good. So good, in fact, that Gent and I even entertained the idea of going to Daniel's strategy session/party for BBR the next night.

"Well I ain't messin' with Daniel's dumb ass," Gent said. "I know you've gotten to know him pretty well and all that, but I don't know. We'll probably talk BBR business for about 30 minutes, and after that, the shucking, jiving and cooning begins. No sir. I can't fool with them clowns. I gotta get up in the morning and drive to Natchez anyway."

"Oh yeah, that's right. How's Mattie holding up?" I asked.

"She's taking it better," he said with his voice lowering a bit from his normal, chest-thumping baritone. "You know it'll be 13 years since tomorrow...on my birthday. I don't think she got used to seeing me knowing she lost a son that looks just like me."

"Freaks her out?" I asked as I felt the mood get a little heavy.

"More like breaks her heart." It got quiet for a second. But I had to ask:

"You think she still blames you for losing Nate?"

"I don't know, Los," Gent said. "I always thought Nate was the one to blame. I don't know. I just know that something is telling me I should go see her. I don't what it is, but it's nagging the hell out of me. You know me. I don't do Mississippi for my birthday."

"Hell naw," I said. "Shoot, you and me would drive past it to do New Orleans."

"Yeah," he said with his voice trailing off. "Well, that was the old me." By the "Old Me" Gent meant, The Old Asshole Hellraiser Who Always Got Into Shit. But he changed a lot after college. I've known the man for years and I still don't know everything about him. But I know that while he was in college, he hardly went home. So for him to go on his 30th birthday, something must've bothered him.

"Well, for what it's worth, happy birthday, and tell Mattie I said 'hey.'"

"You know I will."

We got quiet. Then halfway to Gent's place I got a text message. It was Lola:

"The truth is, I tried 2 get n 2 u, but the feelin just was not there. I did not like kissin u—I absolutely hated lying beside u in bed but I did."

Damn. That hurt. Where was she going with this?

"What's wrong?" Gent asked.

"It's Lola. She just sent me some bullshit!"

"Keep it down," Gent said. "You'll wake up Jordan."

Another Lola text came in:

"So I tried 2 get n 2 u. Just couldnt. Its why I couldnt answer the questions...And..."

And what? Another Lola message:

"...And sex, I never met a man whose dick curved down. It was uncomfortable and a gay friend said that curved dicks were common in that group so I wondered if you were bisexual!!! U just were not MAN enough. Its why we stopped sleepin 2 gether."

"What?!" I yelled. I was so damn mad I wanted Gent to turn the car around so that I could get my hands right back around Lola's neck.

"Keep it down, Man! Your daughter is trying to sleep!"

"But this heffa Lola—!"

"Keep your voice *down*," Gent said in a loud whisper.

"Lola wrote she thought I was gay because my dick curves down. She talked to some gay dudes and they said that meant I was gay. The bitch thinks I'm gay! Hell naw!"

"Wait a minute, is it, like, boomerang-shaped or something?" Gent asked.

"No," I said. "Just kinda like a banana."

"What's wrong with that?" Gent said. "My shit is like that too. Brothers with big ones often curve down," he said with a chuckle. We gave each other a fist bump.

"It's genetic, man," Gent continued. "There's even an operation you can have to take away the curve. I already looked into it. But shit, I know some women who love my curve. Waitaminute? What the hell is she doing listening to some gay men anyway?"

"Because she's stupid. That's why. But I got something for that."

As I started to text Lola back, Gent groaned.

"Oh, Lord," he said. "You're starting a text war. I hope you got some fast fingers. That shit is going to go on for a while."

He was right. The Lola Text War was *on*. And it got pretty nasty.

> Me: "U so stupid. U listen 2 some gay men—your rival in dating—and let them nose around in our shit? there is nuthin wrong with my dick. but its clear that u r dumb as DICK."
>
> Lola: "i have had longer and thicker and loved them all and they pointed in the right direction. they didn't feel like they were fuckin me n the ass from the inside."
>
> Me: "whatever minnie mouse. u r the small one. in fact, fucking u was like fucking a KEYHOLE."
>
> Lola: "i don't have the defective DICK.
>
> Me: "but you have the defective KEYHOLE...Ow! My PENIS!"
>
> Lola: "u r gay. admit it."
>
> Me: "go lick carpet, dike-zilla"
>
> Lola: "you turned me gay cause u ain't a real man."
>
> Me: "what the hell do you know about real men? Daddy left u and your fam years ago dumbass."
>
> Lola: "all u can do is call me names b/c u no its true that i made a fool of u and u cant deal w/it. Now whos the ass?"
>
> Me: "and u r proud of shitting on me. amazing. real lady like. I will devote my life 2 make sure our daughter don't turn out like your bitter, evil ass."

She got quiet after that. But just to be certain, I fired off this final shot in the text war:

Me: "By the way, u r talking on MY PHONE and MY BILL. THIS SHIT WILL BE DISCONNECTED IN AN HOUR."

"Sincerely texting you my middle finger, Carlos."

Chapter 5: Gent's Dead Brother

(Brother Gent)

I wanted that drink. But I'd chilled on the drinking some time ago. And by chilled, I mean, I stopped drinking to get drunk. I still had a beer—or two or three—every now and then. But I just didn't want to drink before hitting the road. Some things you need to feel sober for. The point of driving eight hours to see Ma in Mississippi was to take her to see my brother on his birthday, and it wasn't what you'd call a toasting occasion.

Of course, there are times when you want to numb yourself against your pain with whatever alcohol is strongest and nearby. That's what I was thinking as I drove down the road—that I regretted passing on that drink with Oscar, who I saw right before I left Atlanta to grab some CDs he burned for me for my drive.

Hell, I needed to drink with Carlos to talk about the jive Lola pulled when she showed her ass and slit his tires. Still, Carlos had his act together, and he was determined to not take shit from Lola again.

I wondered if the BBR could get our shit together and get these young boys off the streets. Maybe encourage them to do something with themselves. Sometimes I think we raise brothers to fail while young sisters are told they can be the next Oprah. It almost seems that people think it's masculine to suck. You studying to be a doctor? Soft. You want to speak good English, wear suits and practice some grooming? Sellout. You think today's hip-hop is some janky, jivey bullshit? You ain't real. You ain't down. Bullshit. It was only April during the thick of the primary season and I was on hands and knees praying for Obama to get in the White House. His victory would mean a lot to young brothers: they could see the most powerful man in the world look like them. Congratulations to all the professional black women doing their thing. I'm not hating on your success. I'm just saying that brothers need the boost.

I got loopy on the highway. Something about the drive home always did that to me. Random thoughts filled my head: *Tupac didn't live long enough to cash in his 401(k). Do rappers have 401(k)s?...Did Los drop the dime on us at Borders? He'd do it for publicity...I hope Mama hasn't started smoking again. I hate visiting Nate and Mama's never up to seeing him...*

I struggled to keep my eyes open during the drive, so I popped in one of Oscar's CDs—some vintage '80s and '90s R&B. The first track was "Criticize" from Alexander O'Neal. Did you know that Alex was really from Natchez? Word is, we're related some kind of way. Through my pops, I think. That kinda makes sense because Pop was a musician who'd pack his guitar and hit the road for gigs. He was on the road when Nate went away which made me wonder if he were home would Nate still be with us.

The CD helped me make it all the way to Jackson and I always perked up once I got there because it meant I was only about an hour from home. Driving from Atlanta to Natchez meant navigating a funky jumble of back roads and poor highways. And every 20 miles or so, the warm, fresh and putrid stench of hogshit, roadkill and polecat rose from the Dixie asphalt and flowed dead into my nostrils. It's one of the reasons I hated that damned drive. The only reason I made the drive was to see my mom.

Mattie Hawkins is a sweet and sour little black Catholic woman who should leave the Pope and his funny hats alone and just pray to The Big Man himself. Instead, she spills her guts to a shadow in a confession box who prescribes her some Hail Marys and she thinks that's it. Bullshit! How can some dude who's probably fantasized about going wild on some altar boys do shit for Mama's conscience? Her *soul*? I was done with the Catholic Church years ago. About round the time Nate was gone, actually.

Maybe God lets us go through stuff and figure it out as we go along. At least that's how I feel. I'm kinda Baptist right now.

Those guys are some fools, too. But I like the way they approach God. I don't have to talk to Him via dudes with corny headgear on. Baptists say I can talk to Him personally. And who's to say that if you go through a mediator, your message to God won't get screwed up? Before you know it, you're in Hell with a pitchfork in your ass, wondering if it's a misunderstanding.

When I finally crossed into Natchez city limits, bad memories came back to me. God, I hate that town. I used to want to move back home and try to save the city. Be the town's first black mayor or something. Maybe build, like, a restaurant or a movie theater or something. Do some of that Magic Johnson, entrepre-negro stuff. But folks there were too busy being or getting girls pregnant by age 16, or doing and/or selling drugs.

Selling drugs. Damn you, Nate. Goddamn you.

It was the dead of night when I got to Mama's and all of the lights were on. The house looked as I remembered it: small and quiet. I rang the doorbell. Mama cracked the door open and slid Betsy's nose through the opening. Betsy is Mama's pistol.

"That you, Genthaniel?" a gravelly voice asked from the other side of the door. At 58, she was too young to have a gravelly voice. Something was up.

"Yeah, Mama, it's me. Could you put Betsy away?"

"I'm sorry, baby," she said. She opened the door to reveal her lean, cherry brown face. But she was wearing a wig, which was kinda weird.

"My nerves bad," Mama went on. "These niggas here act like they lost their damn minds." I cringe every time she uses that word.

"I know, Mama," I said walking in. "Sorry I'm late. I had to help Carlos out with something and I didn't leave till about nine or so."

"Yeah? How Carlos doin'?"

"He's okay. He and his little girl are staying with me till he finds a place. Looks like he and Lola are finally done for good."

"Mmt," she grunted as she grabbed a pack of Newports and plopped a cig in her mouth. Ugh. She was smoking again. Damn it. "He ain't kill her, did he?"

"Naw!" I laughed. "He just put a little foot up her ass though!"

"Good! A little foot in the ass never hurt nobody. At least give her a couple of toes."

"That's exactly what I told him. Carlos finally got tired of her mess. So how're things at the bus line?" She got quiet.

"Oh, it's okay," she said as the words crawled out. Mama was lying. I could tell. "You got a plate in the microwave. And yes, I'll let you eat in the living room."

"Cool!" I cheered as I gave her a kiss on the cheek in passing and I made for the microwave. She grabbed a broom and started sweeping the kitchen floor.

"Anyway, ya know I'm on leave from the bus right now?" she said in between broom strokes. She tried to sneak that one in there. How was I supposed to *know* that?

"No'am," I said, removing foil off the plate of smothered chicken, creamed potatoes and English peas. I grabbed some hot sauce, a grape soda and camped in the living room.

"Nigga, get yo' feet off the coffee table!" she said whisking the broom at my ankles.

"Aw, my bad, Mattie," I said.

"And I done told you about that 'Mattie' shit," she growled with the lit cigarette dangling from her lips. "Kids 'sposed to call their mamas 'Ma' or 'Mom' or shit like that." Oh, to hear the sweet little Catholic lady cuss like a sailor.

"Well, if you can call me nigga, why can't I call you Mattie? At least I'm calling you your name. Nigga is a negative representation of—"

"Nigga I don't care!" Mama said, snickering at her own silly joke. Her nerves must've been bad, though. She was sweeping the living room floor at 2 a.m., seemed skinnier than usual and was smoking again. I was too hungry to probe anymore. Instead, I studied my plate of food. But I couldn't stop wondering what was really up.

"What time we gonna see Nate tomorrow?" she asked.

"Can you be ready at seven?"

"Seven? Nigga why? Tomorrow is Saturday. Don't we have all day?"

"No'am. We've been over this. It takes two hours to get there and we can only see Nate at certain times. After that, we can't expect to see him much past—"

"Genthaniel Elmore Hawkins, they givin' us bullshit and you know it! I can't go and see my dead son on his birthday anytime I want to?"

"Mama, please don't call Nate your dead son."

"Well he *is* dead. He all locked up and may not live to get out. And if he do get out, he ain't gonna be no good to nobody so what's the point? It's his birthday!"

I furrowed my brow. "Mattie, you *do* realize it's my birthday too, right?"

She stopped sweeping, put out the cigarette and looked up at me. It was like she *just* realized that my face was Nate's face and that we were identical twins. She looked at me like she wondered what her other son would look like if he hadn't messed with drugs.

Mama turned away, and spoke in a low voice, "Yeah, I remember it's your birthday, too." She paused. "I'll be ready by seven and I'll make breakfast. Good night, son."

She left for bed. This all pissed me off. I drive down to Natchez on my birthday and seems like her only concern was for Nate. It was my birthday too, damn it. I was tired and irritated. So after I cleaned my plate, I went to the bedroom Nate and I had shared. All his stuff was still in there: Spider-Man comics. An old box of condoms. And a family picture: Me, Mama, Nate and Pop.

I put the picture back in the box and noticed a bottle of brown. It was a Crown Royal bottle. The seal was broken and it was half full. I opened it up and took a sniff. It smelled fresh. Had Mattie been drinking? That would explain the oddness I couldn't put my finger on and why she was on leave from driving the commuter bus to Jackson. Pop used to drink, but I never saw Ma drink. But no one else had been there. No one else would put a bottle of brown in their kids' old comic books box unless they were in that room themselves. Mourning. Maybe she was just missing Nate. And missing Pop. Hell, maybe she even missed me a little. I didn't know. What's worse is that I wanted a taste of it.

I unscrewed the cap and thought about Pop. Pop had a stroke and died months after Nate's trial. God, I miss him. He was so cool. So strong. And I wanted to be just like him. Funny thing is that he and Mama were so different, but they worked well together. Sir Lee Hawkins—that was his actual name—was all left brain. Sir was a handsome, charming brother that drank, smoked, played four instruments, told the best jokes and stories and had friends in every town from Natchez to Nashville. Sir was a country Mississippi boy with big-city mentality. Mama, on the other hand, was sweet but stoic. She wasn't a dreamer like Sir. Instead, she was practical and pragmatic. And she took shit at face value. Mama never taught me and Nate to think in "what ifs." She taught us in "what was." Mama was Sir's anchor and she was good for grabbing him by the ankle whenever his head got in the clouds.

But she loved him and didn't mind—well, I won't say she didn't mind as much as I should say tolerated—Sir's road trips as long as he promised to have income from a job more stable than music. So Pop's crazy ass found steady work as a dealer at a casino. Problem was that shit was an hour and a half away in *Vicksburg*.

I guess a man like him needed to work where there was some action. So he'd work in Vicksburg a few days a week, and on his off days, he'd be domestic at home and tend to me and Nate while Mama pulled shifts at the bus line. But on some off days, he'd hit the road to play a few gigs.

I always wanted to go with Sir when he played. When I was real little—I'm talking about six or seven years old—I'd sneak down to the basement on those Wednesday nights to see Sir practice with his "Few Times" band (named that because Sir would say, "Shit, I can only play with them sorry niggas a few times"). Mama would roll her eyes when Sir talked to us about his music. But the more I think about it, the more I think Sir's free spirit really turned her on to him. And her deep-rooted pragmatism is what drew him to her. Mama and Sir worked well together. As a kid, I like the folks' act. But Nate seemed interested in other shit when the parents tried to tell us stuff. Like he always had bigger fish to fry.

Although we are twins, Pop would remind me that I came out of Mama first. So he put a lot of responsibility on me to do shit. But I think about it now and I kinda figure that he did that with me because I was his favorite son. Or did I become his favorite son because I doted on him and Nate didn't? It's not like Nate and Pop didn't get along or me and Mattie didn't get along. It's just funny how two boys living in the same house—twins, at that—turned out so damn different.

But Pop loved me *and* Nate. And it really did hurt him when Nate went away. But it was me who failed you, Sir. I was supposed to look after Nate while you were gone. But I failed. God, I missed the Old Man. I raised the bottle to my lips and took a swig for Pop.

I'm sorry, Pop.

I looked at the photographs, comic books and the old baseball glove.

"Fucking drugs," I snarled. "Goddamn you, Nate."

At 3:09 a.m., I took a big swig for Mama. Why was she on leave? I didn't know. The folks said that all Hawkins have the gift of clairvoyance—or something.—And my sixth sense was nagging me: *Mattie's been drinking. Maybe she showed up on the job drunk.*

Maybe that's my fault, too. Leaving her alone in a house full of ghosts. Another swig.

I'm sorry, Mama.

At 3:14 a.m., I took a third swig and the Crown started to kick in. So what? I had to toast my baby brother. I'm the oldest by only six minutes, but I always felt like the oldest.

I looked around the room and envisioned Nate at 17 years old. That was the last time I saw him as a free man. Nate was the jock. I was the ladies' man. At least I thought I was the ladies' man. We shared a beat up Toyota Cressida and since I had the car, I was supposed to pick him up from basketball practice at 5:30. But I was running late. Why? Because I was getting the goods from this chick with a tiny waist and an onion booty. God, it still haunts me. You know I've been celibate ever since? Well, *not quite* celibate. But I haven't enjoyed it, since Nate's um...well. I don't know how else to put this—I don't come when I do it. Messed up, huh?

So I was late picking him up, but when I got there, I learned that Nate's friend, Anthony had given him a ride. I never liked Ant. Never trusted him. But Nate needed a ride and Ant offered to give him one. Nate never came home. He got involved in Ant's scheme to move bricks of weed. They both got busted. Nate was charged as an adult and got 15 years. Even worse, they sent him to Central State Prison. Central State is one of the roughest places on earth. And then wouldn't you know it, an inmate tried him there and Nate *killed* him. He didn't mean to kill the man—at least they say it was self-defense—but it didn't matter. More years were tacked on to his sentence. But that kinda stupid shit happens when you're caged up like an animal. And for what? Wanting to sell people shit to get high? The same shit states are legalizing so rich people can be relieved of their pain and suffering for "medicinal purposes?"

There I was taking shots of whiskey to the head—and alcohol had been as big a killer as anything else in this country—and my twin brother was locked away for weed? I know Nate was in the wrong, but he was just a kid when it happened. Now he's hardened and may never get out. And like Mama said, what good is he gonna be to anyone whenever he does get released?

But I didn't care. I loved my brother. It was his birthday. *Our* birthday. Nate was 17 when he got in prison and wasn't due for parole for another 12 years when we're 42. And that's only if he can keep his nose clean.

I'm sorry, brother.

I looked at the clock as it turned 3:16 a.m. *Something important about 3:16, ain't it?*

The whiskey was winning. I wasn't doing well. But I picked up Nate's Bible and looked up the verse. John, right? I read it aloud: "For God so loved the world that he gave his only begotten son." Amen. I took a really big swig.

I'm sorry, God.

After that, I mentally said "Fuck it," and turned up it all up. I must've cleaned out half the bottle. Of course, once I did that, I promptly blacked out. Shit. My glum stroll through memory lane had turned into a patented Hawkins meltdown. It'd been a minute since I curled up into a bottle like that. And of course, God woke me up about two hours later with a monster headache. When I sat up, it felt like I bench pressed heaven and earth with my forehead. God I was hurt. I fell out of the bed. *THOOM!* I tried to be quiet, but I stumped the hell out of my toes against the hard-ass bedpost.

"SHIT!" I yelled loud enough to wake the dead. My God it hurt. I stumbled in the bathroom and slammed the door behind me. That woke up Mama.

"Genthaniel! You alright?" Mama must've been in a good mood 'cause she didn't cuss or call me "Nigga."

"I'm fine, Mama." I said as I slid my fingers over the shelves of the medicine cabinet and clumsily knocked her insulin and pill bottles to the bathroom floor.

"Well, I'm 'bout to make breakfast. You want anything special?"

"Coffee," I said on my knees, squinting to read the pill bottle labels. "Lots of coffee."

"I can drive since you got in so late last night. You tired, ain't cha?"

"Yep."

"And drunk as hell."

"Yep."

"You one drunk ass, ain't 'cha?"

"Yep."

"I can smell it. See ya when you get out. And you owe me another bottle of Crown, nigga." I heard her walk away toward the kitchen, humming a hymn. Funny lady.

After what seemed like endless fumbling around that medicine cabinet, I finally found a bottle of aspirin and popped two of them. But then I noticed the bottle next to it: EMEND. I read the inscription: TAKE FOR NAUSEA.

Huh? I grabbed my cell phone and Googled it:

EMEND (aprepitant) Helps Prevent Nausea/Vomiting for Breast Cancer Patients.

I slouched in the bathroom corner. Even terribly hung over, I was able to put it all together: the wig. The weight loss. The time off. I hadn't seen Mama since Christmas. It was now April. So she may have known then and didn't tell me. Shit.

God, I can't lose her!

I got teary-eyed and didn't know what to do. In that moment, the toilet became an altar that I knelt and prayed to. I cried like I hadn't cried since Pop died. Mama heard me from the other side of the door.

"Gent! Genthaniel! Is you crying in there?"

"No, ma'am," I lied, sniffing.

"Well, whatever you *ain't* doing, stop it! Get your ass up, son and get out here! You ain't gonna make me miss Nate today."

"Yes'm," I said, slowly getting off my knees and wiping my eyes. I put the Emend bottle in my pocket. It was going to be a long day.

✳ ✳ ✳

"You okay, bruh?" Nate asked me from the other side of that small-ass table the visitors and inmates sit at during visiting hours.

"I should be asking you that," I said. "I'm fine. How you doing in here?"

"Oh he's good, ain't 'cha, baby?" Mama said.

"Yeah," he said reluctantly. "I'm fine. Just another 12 years."

"Jesus, Nate," I said shaking my head.

"Jesus ain't got nothin' to do with it," Nate mumbled.

"Nathaniel, don't cuss the Lord like that. Watch your mouth, son."

"I'm sorry, Mama."

She then sneezed and both Nate and I flinched.

"Mama, you shouldn't be here in your condition," he said.

Did Nate know? I looked at him and then at Mama and then back to him. A stale silence came over us. Nate knew! I couldn't believe Mama told Nate and didn't tell me.

"Boy, I ain't got no condition," she snapped at Nate, getting back on message after trying to sneak him a look. She didn't think I caught it but I did. "Don't mind me. It's your birthdays. And I wish your Daddy was here to see how big y'all have gotten."

"Ma, my being here killed Daddy," Nate said. "You know that."

"Now don't you say that, Nathaniel," she said.

"Yeah, man," I said. "Don't blame yourself for that."

"Shut up, fool! It's your fault that I'm here in the first place!"

"Say what? Nate you can't be serious."

"Boys!" Mama said, trying to stop the unstoppable drama.

"If you'd picked me up like you said, then I wouldn't be in here."

"Nate, you're kidding, right? We were 17!"

"No, I ain't kiddin'. And you didn't come for me. You was with some chick instead of picking me up like you 'sposed to."

"I know where I was, Nate," I said, staring him down. "Do you remember where you were? It wasn't my plan to get up with my friend and to sell drugs. I ain't do that, Nate."

"It wasn't Nathaniel's fault though," Mama jumped in. "Anthony set up the whole thing. It was the wrong place at the wrong time, Genthaniel."

"That's not true, Mama. And Nate know it. He and Ant had cooked that crap up for a while. We been through this. I'm not rubbing it in, it's just—"

"Hush, Gent!" Mama said as she teared up. "You know your brother didn't set the whole thing up and I can't believe you in here talking to him like you had no part in this."

"Now Mama, *you* can't be serious."

"Yeah she is," Nate said with a small grin.

"Mama?" I asked.

She was quiet. And she gave Nate another look to be quiet.

"She hadn't even told you, huh?"

"Told me what?" I asked. I knew where he was going. But I needed to hear it.

"Hush, Nate!" she said. But Nate didn't care anymore. He had to get me.

"You don't even know that Mama has—"

"Nathaniel! No, son!"

"Breast cancer! She been sick and on chemo for like, four or five months. Even cut one off. You can't tell she wearing one of them special bras?"

"Lord have mercy, Nathaniel," Mama said, sobbing.

I just looked at Nate.

"How it feel, Gent? You out working your good job, sending Ma money and shit, and she tell me her shit but don't tell you? I bet she wasn't gonna tell you nothing neither."

"Boy, whatcha doing?" Mama sniffled quietly, shaking her head.

It was then that I knew Central State had gotten the last bit of my brother's humanity. It was bound to happen sooner or later. I just didn't think it'd happen like this. Mama always said that Nate was as good as dead in that place. But this time I really saw it. The brother

I knew was completely gone. The guards saw Mama crying but they didn't do anything. I guess every mother probably cries when they visit their sons in prison.

"I think I'm ready to go, Gent," she said, wiping her eyes.

I looked at Nate. He was my twin but I didn't see any of me in him. His skin seemed hardened, his cheekbones more profound, a jawline more rigid than ever. He sported a scar above his eye. His hair was in cornrows.

"You didn't answer me, bruh," he said. "I asked you, how did it feel to have Ma keep that kind of shit from you?"

We got up from the table and stopped walking out when he said that.

"Makes me feel like I lost a brother, Nate. I'll see ya around."

Then we left Nate there with the rest of the assholes.

✳ ✳ ✳

Mama and I didn't talk the entire drive back to Natchez. We stopped to get her that bottle of Crown because she was serious about me replacing it. But we didn't speak. Instead, I stewed the whole time. Stewed, I tell ya. I was so pissed! It was so frustrating. Just 24 hours earlier, I thought I was going to see my brother and my mother, and that was it. Instead, I learned my mother was drinking and smoking as a cancer patient, and both still blamed me for bringing down the House of Hawkins. Wonderful.

We finally made it back home. I sat down at the kitchen table while Mama put down her bags and sifted through the refrigerator.

"You wanna eat?" she asked. "I got pork chops and cabbages already done. And I can make some creamed potatoes."

"Why didn't you tell me, Mama?"

"I didn't think it was important, baby."

"How the hell did you figure—?"

"Don't use that tone with me, boy!"

"Yes ma'am," I said, correcting myself. "But Mama?"

"What?"

"*Why?*"

"Boy, I said it wasn't important!"

"But you told Nate!"

"It's only me and Nate down here. So I just never got around to telling you."

"But you've known for months. Were you sick at Christmas?"

"Listen, Gent: I got the damn cancer. I got the cut off breast and I got the damn chemo. So I don't need your shit. Understand?"

I held my head down for a moment, but then I remembered a smiling Nate who seemed so satisfied with my shock and disgust. I almost did what I always did with Mama. I almost backed down. But then I reached in my pocket and pulled out the Emend pill bottle I discovered that morning, and put it on the table.

"How sick are you, Mama?" I demanded.

She slammed the pot of cabbages on the stove top.

"What the hell you want, Gent?"

"I want you to be straight with me. Tell me if you're dying or not! You smoking again. That ain't good for a cancer. You drinking whiskey when I ain't ever see you take a drop in my life. And you're keeping secrets from me, Mama. So excuse my language, but I'm giving you shit 'cause you giving me shit. Right now, you acting like you got a death sentence when I need to know what's going on. I'm your son and you're stonewalling me. So answer the question, Ma Are. You. *Dying?*"

Mama turned off the cabbage and sat down at the table. I know I shouldn't have done this, but I broke the seal on that new bottle of Crown, grabbed two small glasses, and poured some into each one. Straight. No chaser. I pushed one glass towards her and picked up the other one. And I asked softer this time. "Mama? Are you dying?"

She struggled before the words came. "I don't know, son. They keep telling me that I should be okay. But I don't know. This is just some intense shit, son."

"Why didn't you tell me?"

"You back on that again?"

"Yes."

"I don't *know*, Gent," she said, trailing off. She sipped her drink and I sipped mine. We got quiet again. I didn't know what to say. So I told her what I should always tell her.

"Mama?"

"Yes, son?"

"I love you."

"I love you too, son. Happy birthday, Genthaniel."

"And happy birthday, Nathaniel."

We clinked our glasses and sipped again. Then Mama got up to make us both plates.

After dinner, she pulled out a cigarette and lit it up. She nearly put it out when she saw the face I made.

"No, don't do that, Mama," I said. "It's okay. Have your smoke."

That's my mother. If she dies, I want her to die doing whatever makes her happy. Even smoking. I didn't know her exact condition. But she wasn't telling, and we'd bumped heads enough for one trip. I looked at my watch.

"You leaving tonight?" she asked. Mama sounded like she didn't want me to go.

"No, I'm leaving tomorrow."

"Okay."

"Mama?"

"Yes, son?"

"Come back to Atlanta with me. I'll look after you until your treatments are done. I know you may not want to leave the house and Nate, but—"

"Okay."

I was stunned. No resistance. No nostalgia. No cuss words.

"Don't get drunk like you did last night. I'll be damned if I'm driving us to Atlanta."

"Yes, ma'am," I said, laughing my first good laugh of the whole visit.

Chapter 6: The Last Night with Angie

(Brother Oscar)

Daniel called me to—and this was a direct quote—"Do what revolutionaries do."

What do revolutionaries do? Apparently, they meet in backrooms of seedy pool halls to drink, smoke, and talk about women they'd like to bone. Not exactly highbrow stuff. I really wasn't enthused to see any of the bozos who punked out while books were thrown at our heads. (That copy of *Beloved* left a bruise for weeks!)

I'd only known Daniel for a short time and I had a read on him. My take? He's an idiot—a pothead I can't take seriously.

Here's what brothers like Daniel don't get: It doesn't matter how handsome or buff you are. Your charisma doesn't even matter either. At the end of the day, it's about ambition and your willingness to get your butt out of neutral and in gear. But Daniel and his boys were like a lot of brothers these days: dudes who don't go the extra mile to become professionals. They don't own a suit and don't mind living with Mom at age 30.

Still, I had a real need to get out of myself and break loose. Daniel's BBR-themed "meeting" would be a good time to relax. The mundane nature of my insurance gig frustrated me, my search for a writing job was going nowhere, and I had a crush on a married woman, which I knew wasn't cool. In fact, I worried God would send a million locusts to bum-rush my ass.

So I took Daniel up on his offer to hang with his homeboys at Archie's Pool Hall. It didn't take long for the haze of seriousness to leave the room, and the haze of weed and alcohol to enter. And all the brothers there seemed to be DANs: Dumb Ass Niggas.

Weed never did it for me. All those different lips touching one vessel—being passed around like a $5 hooker at a frat party—just ain't sanitary. Especially when said mouths belonged to scroungy ne- groes who looked like Grady on *Sanford and Son*.

I'd *usually* demure and say "No thanks" to this kind of scene. But Daniel got me liquored up first. Then when Whother Josh turned to me with the joint in his hand and said, "Daniel told me to give you this," I didn't say no right away.

"What happened at the book store last month was kinda fucked up, huh?" Josh asked glassy-eyed. "Did Los ever find out who snitched us out?"

"Say, didn't you haul ass out of there?" I shot back, looking at the joint, then Josh, then the joint again. "I should kick your ass for cowardice just on principle."

"Oscar—you gonna smoke this shit or what?" he asked, ignor- ing my objection to him. "I mean, I know what you sayin,' but it seems like you got a lot of shit on ya mind and it's like McDonald's, man. You deserve a break today."

"Why thank you, White Boy," I said, giving him a cold look.

I was too pissed to smoke by then and Josh left me alone after that. And that's when my cell rang. It was Carlos, which was cool because I'd been meaning to talk to him since he and Lola spilt.

"What's up, Los?" I answered. "You hate living with Gent yet?"

"Naw, man, Gent's cool," Carlos said. "He left for Mississippi tonight, so Jordan and I got the place to ourselves."

"Yeah, he dropped by my place before he left," I said.

"Oh, okay. So—is it Niggapalooza there yet?"

When Los asked that, I stared at the joint in Josh's hand and surveyed the room. Jokers were off to the side gambling on video games, shooting dice, playing pool and cards. If I told Carlos the truth, he'd clown me to no end. He's kind of a buster like that.

"No, it's not Niggapalooza," I lied. "It's okay."

"Whatever, sucker. Gent's birthday is tomorrow. He might still be in Natchez, but when he gets back, we all should take him out to celebrate."

"How old is he turning anyway?"

"He'll be 30. We're all about the same age. He just seems older."

"Being crazy will do that, I guess. Anyway, I'll holler at you later."

"Cool, man. Oh, and I got some ideas for The BBR I wanna share. So on Friday, all this can go down. I'll call you to let you know what Gent wants to do. Peace."

The BBR *is* a joke, I thought. Just like everything else had been in my life: a joke. I was in a funky mood and I needed to chill. So I walked back over to Josh, plucked the joint from his fingers and hit it. Hard. It'd been seven years since I last smoked and that was only because of some peer pressure from my ex in North Carolina. Any man would've given in. Ol' Girl was 5'10, half-black, half-Puerto Rican, and all *fine*. So I smoked with her.

I thought I was completely done with weed. But thanks to my mild depression, I found myself standing there next to Josh, puffing. I may not have dug it much, but after what Josh handed me, I felt calm for the first time since I lost my job in Carolina.

I was so tightly wound I could've snapped. After brokeitis set in, a sad job hunt and getting whacked by a book to the head, I had to chill. But you know what *really* chills me out? Women. And I needed one that night to get me calm. Get me high. Get me *laid*.

I was good and buzzed as I watched the boys play Madden on the PlayStation. Daniel asked if I wanted to play. I took another hit of the joint, sat in front of the TV and took the controller. Then my cell went off. It was Angie sending me a text message. She wanted to see me. Angie and I were getting close and over coffee a few days ago, she blew my mind with some shit.

"He raped me," Angie told me, raising a mug to her lips. We were talking about old lovers and sexual experiences.

"Who?" I asked. How's a man supposed to respond to this?

"This guy back in college. One day I visited him at the school he went to and I was a virgin at the time and I just loved him so much. I—" Angie stopped to take a breath before she continued. "When he did it, he seemed just done with *me*."

She was so still. My God, she was so damn still.

"I'm sorry, Angie."

"It was so many years ago. I'm 35 now and I still can't get over it, but I worked hard to get past it. You know, try to not let it affect me in other ways."

"Men can be pigs," I said, looking at her. She relaxed after I said that.

"I took some time to figure myself out. I went to law school. I dated some but didn't take anyone seriously. And I didn't trust black men anymore. So that's how I came to marry Jack. He's a nice guy and I never thought I'd marry a white man, but here I am."

"It doesn't hurt that he owns all of those car dealerships, huh?"

"I have my own money, Oscar. Before we met, I wasn't super paid like Jack, but I have my own. I didn't need to be with him. I just think he was good to me."

"Do you love him?" I asked.

"Jack's never been what I ideally wanted. But he's a good man."

"Did you want the furthest thing from the type of man that your ex was?"

She thought a while before speaking again. "I don't know, Oscar. Jack gave me attention I never had before. He was different from all the others. And he was older and he was genuine. That made a difference. I thought he'd give me what I needed. I thought he'd be enough." She sipped her coffee. "Jack gave me security."

"What do you mean, 'He gave you security?' You just said you made great money."

"It's not about the money, Oscar."

"Don't let the President of Women hear that."

"Hush," she said laughing. "Seriously, I'm not talking about financial security. Jack treated me like I was the only woman in the world."

"So what's wrong with him?"

"Well he isn't who I thought he was," she said shaking her head. "I'm his trophy wife. And I'm good at it. Maybe I was running from that rape. Maybe he is what I needed at the time. But I don't think I need that now."

"Being different than your ex doesn't make Jack perfect for you. Men are still men."

She smiled. It's tough to have a friendship with someone you're attracted to. But maybe I needed just this kind of relationship after my time with Ol' Girl. Besides, I wanted to be that one good man Angie could count on. So when I saw her message asking me to come over, I relinquished the controller and left Daniel's party more lit than a Christmas tree.

✳ ✳ ✳

"Where's your husband?" I asked.

"Long answer? He's touring Iraq with his flunkies," Angie said. "Short answer? I don't know and I don't care."

"He needs to tour New Orleans and see all the shit that hasn't been done to clean up after Katrina. Anyway, I just had to be sure where he was."

Yeah. I really got to be sure before I'm caught banging another man's wife in his house. In fact, my flight impulses were in overdrive. Oh Lord: *Thou shalt not covet thy neighbor's wife. Thou shalt not commit adultery.* Did I want to go to hell over a cute, 5'4, 130-pound caramel-colored woman with nice chest, butt and lips?

I tried to justify spending time with Angie. Since she was married, sex on her part was adultery. But since I wasn't married, I was only *fornicating,* right? The Commandments didn't say anything about fornication. I beat God on a technicality! Ha! Take that, God!

(I once shared this logic with my mom and she slapped me harder than Prince slapped Apollonia into that shelf of preserves in *Purple Rain*. Fornication was a no-no, she reminded me, and I would be hell-bound on a nuclear-powered, gasoline truck. So Goddamn Angie. Literally).

Nevertheless, there I was, on the doorstep of Angie's sprawling Atlanta Country Club home. On one side of the threshold was me, looking my normal handsome self. At 6'2", I was as dark as the cups of coffee Angie and I shared weeks earlier. I looked good, too. I wore a brown, pinstriped blazer with a burnt orange oxford shirt and some dark jeans. And I had just shaved my head, so I really felt confident. I may have been broke, but I never looked it. Angie stood on the other side of the threshold where her beautiful brown body was draped in a silver teddy that showed through a silver satin robe. Damnit, *that* wasn't proper, platonic-friend attire. A month had passed since I met her at the car lot. We'd gotten chummy, but funny business never went down. It was tense though. When she greeted me with a hug, she pressed her perfect breasts against my chest. Oh my.

"When I first met you, Oscar, I had my doubts," she said. "For some reason I thought about Snagglepuss. We are in Atlanta, you know."

"Snagglepuss?"

"Yeah. You know Snagglepuss was, like, the gayest cartoon character of all time. And, you are so beautiful—and so *proper*—that I kinda thought you were a little sweet."

"Well, you got me wrong. Do I actually come off as sweet?"

"Not at all," she said giving me the once over. "In fact, you're a real gent."

"No. I'm Oscar. Gent is my friend. And Snagglepuss ain't gay."

"Yeah the hell he was. Snagglepuss was gay, Popeye and Bluto were down low lovers, and Wimpy was Sweet Pea's baby daddy."

"Snagglepuss, was *not* gay," I said. "He was just metrosexual. Remember, he dated that yellow lion Daisy? At any rate, Snagglepuss was the coolest, straightest cat out."

"Oh really?" Angie asked gliding across the floor toward me.

"Yes, really," I replied. "And I'm certain that cat loved pussy."

Now why did I say that? It woke Black Magic up.

"Clever," she winked. "But I didn't call you over here to talk about old cartoons."

"You called me over to make love to my mind, right?" I laughed again.

"Oh, I love your mind," she said as she turned around and walked towards the living room. "So much that I want to fuck your brains out."

Aw hell. She poured some drinks and smiled slyly. Then, she took my hand, raised it to her mouth and sucked and nibbled each finger. Suddenly, my fingers tingled and got numb. She leaned in closer and wrapped my arms around her satin-laced back. I pulled her into my chest. My tingling hands—what was up with them?— held her face and tilted her lips up toward mine. We kissed. And I heard—in my head at least—a crowd cheering as if I was about to score. I felt so guilty. She was married, for God's sake! But guilt and all, we kissed at an escalated pace. Sweat trickled down from the top of my head to the sides of my face. But Angie framed my face with her hands, wiped away the sweat, and—wow—*licked* the leftovers from my face and whispered, "I want this, Oscar. I want this tonight. Give it to me. *Please.*"

"Angie, I can't come between you and your husband. This is hard."

"I know it's hard, Baby," she said, as she reached down and wrapped her hands around Black Magic. "I can feel how hard it is. *Mmm.* I like that."

"Angie, wait," I said to no avail. Black Magic, meanwhile, was so excited he hurt. She ignored me, pulled off my blazer, slid her hands into my shirt and rubbed my shoulders. She lowered her head to my chest and worked it: *Kiss. Lick. Nibble, Nipple.*

I surrendered. "Don't stop...doing...*that,*" I exhaled.

Angie reached into my back pocket, got a condom out my wallet and showed it to me like she pulled a magic trick. Yeah, she was ready to work Black Magic. She unbuckled my belt and dropped my pants. Then, more slight-of-hand. She showed me the condom, which she had somehow gotten out the wrapper. Then she placed it in her mouth and—this was so awesome—used her mouth to roll the condom over Black Magic. *Bravo.*

It was so on. It was 12:30 a.m. and the crowd in my head was still cheering me on: *"Os-car, Ru-ark! Clap-clap, clap-clap-clap! Os-car, Ru-ark! Clap-clap, clap-clap-clap!"*

I picked up Angie, wrapped her legs around my waist and pressed her up against a wall. The crowd got louder. And that annoying tingling returned to my hands.

Lord, please don't let me have a heart attack. I have two fears about my death: one, dying while doing something embarrassing to my family. And two, dying while doing something totally sinful before I can ask God to forgive me. Screwing another man's wife fit both bills and would likely get me a first-class ticket to hell. I pondered this while standing butt-naked grinding Angie against her kitchen wall. I worried about God. I worried about my hands tingling (Was it the weed?). I worried that with my pants at my ankles I couldn't make a getaway if some shit went down.

Another concern? Angie's husband was U.S. Congressman Jack Ridenour, an ultra-conservative son-of-bitch. Arguably the whitest man on earth and likely related to Paul Bunyan. Angie literally married THE MAN.

"Isn't Jack in the NRA?" I asked mid-grind. (Translation: "Don't that cracker own a gun?")

"Fuck Jack," Angie said as she planted on me the slowest, deepest kiss in the history of kissing. She then gave me bedroom eyes and said: "Fuck me."

"Fuck me is right," I said, giving in.

We got our bodies off the kitchen wall. Now with both of us totally naked, she took my hand and led me to the bedroom. Her brown body blended with my black body as we rolled around on that immaculate bed of hers for hours. The moon peeked on us through the window and caught us in a serious groove. I kissed her until my lips were numb and my throat was dry. She couldn't sing, but before, during and after fucking me, she moaned some of the sexiest notes I never heard before.

I knew I couldn't make this a regular thing. But it all felt so damn good! I pressed my chest against hers, and we made our final movements into each other. Then one last, long, hard thrust—*Oh!*— and my tense arms eased. Her thighs trembled. And she finally made that sound that all men want to hear from his woman: *"Ooooooh!"*

I gave her a look. She gave me one back. Then a kiss. And then another. And another. It was so good it was fattening. I couldn't stop tasting her. I wanted some more. So we did it again—harder—with hands on throats and legs everywhere. When we finally stopped, we fell asleep in each other's arms. And when I woke up, I was staring up the barrel of a rather shiny black pistol.

"How long ya' been doing her?" Jack asked with the gun in my face.

"Jack! Let me explain!" Angie pleaded as she scrambled to put on a robe.

"L-L-L-let *me* explain, sir," I stammered. My hands were completely numb now. But I still heard crowd noise. Why was I still buzzed?

With the gun still aimed at me, I slowly pushed myself upright in the bed. I don't know why, but Black Magic was hard as hell! Morning wood, Black Magic? Seriously? Jack saw my massive erection and turned crimson. His square jaw clinched tighter than butt cheeks in a prison shower. He turned to Angie.

"So this nigger's dick what you been wanting, huh?" He cocked the gun. Oh shit.

"Is that what you like, bitch? Let's see how you like his dick now!" He aimed the gun at me. *Oh my God.* The numbness in my hands extended to my entire body. My chest tightened. I couldn't breathe. It happened so fast and then—

BLAM! One shot.

Oh, Jesus. Is he aiming the gun at Angie?

BLAM! BLAM! Two more shots.

Am I dead? Did he shoot Angie? Did he shoot himself?

All I saw was black.

When I came to, I was back at Archie's backroom at Daniel's party with a massive headache. What the hell? First thing I did was check to see if my dick was okay. Yep, Black Magic was still there. Second thing I noticed was that I had a PlayStation controller in my hands. And my fingers were numb from all of the pushing. It was the game creating the stupid crowd noises. Then Daniel walked up to me.

"Man, you are fucked up," he smiled. "Will you please give the controller to someone else? You been pushin' buttons for 30 minutes. Nigga, your fingers don't hurt?"

Apparently, I was really baked. But did Angie really call? I checked my phone. It was only 11:47 p.m., but I saw that she *did* text me to invite me over. I had even texted her back saying I would after a game of Madden. Damn. What a trip!

"What the hell was in that joint?" I asked Daniel.

"Just a little bit of angel dust, that's all."

"What! You jackass! You gave me a joint laced with PCP? You can't hand out joints with PCP! Grow the hell up, fool! I'm out of here!"

Daniel needed to quit hanging around Josh. Josh's family owned six liquor stores and a Popeye's Chicken off Candler Road. Meanwhile, Daniel's mom was a housekeeper and waited tables at Waffle House. While leaving, I overheard Josh to Daniel:

"So he didn't know the joints were dipped in formaldehyde?"

When I heard that, I turned around and started swinging to beat the holy hell out of both Josh and Daniel. To be blunt, I went apeshit. I walloped Daniel in the jaw and straight backhanded Josh.

I threw everyone there by surprise and the guys had to separate me from Josh and Daniel. I hadn't been violent since grade school. And I don't pride myself on this moment. But I had been drugged and I couldn't tolerate that. Them fools deserved that asswhooping.

I stormed out and angrily got in my car. On the ride home, Angie called rang my cell.

"Hey, are you still coming over?" she asked.

Hell, no!" I yelled and hung up the phone.

Chapter 7: The Intervention

(Brother Oscar)

Earlier that week, I called in sick at work to do a job search. I wanted to be a journalist again because selling insurance sucked. I'm a writer, not a salesman. And I wanted to work in a market bigger than Atlanta. Maybe Chicago, New York or Philly. But when I searched for gigs, I got depressed. I felt like I was too far behind to catch up to my peers. Every time I thought about how much time I lost in Carolina, it left a bad taste in my mouth.

After I turned down Boston for Ol' Girl, my career options dried up. Was that my one big chance? I didn't know, but I shouldn't have had to make that choice in the first place. How the saying goes? You lose money chasing women, but you'll never lose women chasing money? No shit. It'd been three years since I had a byline. I did a little freelancing, but nothing that looked that good on a resume. But in four months of job hunting, I'd sent out about 400 resume and clips. That had to pay off sometime, right?

Then one day that week, the phone rang. I raced to see the caller ID.

"Aw, shit," I sighed as I answered. "Gent, it's 9 a.m. Why ain't you at work?"

"I took the day off. I'm running errands before I go see my mom." He paused. I was miffed that it wasn't a job, so I missed his cue.

"Oh yeah, that's right. Mississippi. You're seeing your mom."

"*And* Nate, Oscar. It's okay to mention my brother. Did you burn those CDs? I can't make that drive to Natchez without good stuff to listen to."

"I'm not so sure it's good stuff, but yeah, I got 'em ready for you. You coming over?"

"In about an hour," Gent said.

"Cool," I said.

So he came over and I thought he'd grab the CDs and leave. Nope. Gent got to talking. And then a game of Madden broke out. And then we ordered pizza. Before you knew it, Gent was there most of the day. If Carlos would've come over, it would've been college all over again.

But it was good to hang with just Gent. Before the BBR, Gent became distant. Like something was always bothering him. He seemed like he had his shit together, but Gent was wound a little tight. And in all the years I knew him, I never figured out how to handle that. Gent and Carlos were tight because they were roommates since freshman year. Carlos and I became friends our junior year when we took a lot of the same journalism classes. We've all been boys since then, but Gent was a bit of a mystery.

"Why you want all that old school stuff, Gent?"

"Because I like all of that old school stuff, Oscar."

"I like some of it, too. But Alexander O'Neal? Really?"

"Hey, Alex was cool until he got fat and toothless, wore eye shadow, did coke and bucked his eyes like a gay Morris Day. But homeboy had some hits."

"Yeah, I guess."

"Besides, he's from the crib."

"I thought Alexander O'Neal was from Minneapolis?"

"Nah. He's from Natchez. So was Richard Wright's crazy ass."

"*Native Son* and *Black Boy* Richard Wright?"

"Yeah, him." Unimportant historical facts like that arrested most of our attention that day. That and the Madden. And the BBR. "You read that *Sista Girl* piece on Carlos?"

"I read it online," I said. "Carlos doesn't come off well in it."

"Whoever ratted us got us good. They may have killed the BBR before it started."

"Maybe. But I'm beginning to think the BBR is just fodder for Los to write about."

"Can you blame him?" Gent said. "Relationship stuff sells. Problem is, we ain't done much *revolting* since Borders when that copy of *Beloved*—"

"I know, I know—"

"Knocked you *squay* upside the head," he said finishing his thought. "But, Los said some fellas who came to that first meeting are actually doing some BBR shit."

"Like what?" When I asked I got up to make a Hennessy sidecar. "You want one or you about to hit the road?"

Gent hesitated before he answered.

"I didn't think it was that tough of a question."

"Oh—nah," he said, snapping out of a daze. His mind went somewhere and it took a second to come back. "I could really use that drink, honestly. But I better not. But yeah, man! Some brothers are actually doing the shit we talked about! You know, Tremaine? The sweet acting dude with the conk in his hair? Well, he and some brothers filed suits to get money back from chicks."

"Jokers are actually doing that shit Whother Josh suggested? Los down with this?"

"Yep," Gent nodded. "Los thinks we should get down and do the same. But Los said he needed stronger, ironclad cases. These don't fit the bill, he says."

"Well, duh," I said. "I know some women are just using some dudes to get them to spend money, but to sue to get that spent money back? It seems like Indian giving."

"Well, joke or no joke, word is spreading. How else could *Sista Girl* find out?"

"True," I said, as I took a big sip of my drink. It was almost as if Gent couldn't look at me and the Hennessy together. I don't want to act like he had the shakes or something, because he didn't. But he seemed off. "Gent? Is everything alright?"

"Yeah. Why?"

"I dunno. You just seem kinda—distracted."

"Nah. I always get that way before I have to make that drive to Natchez," he said. We both got quiet for a second.

"You don't like going home, do you?" I asked. The question froze him.

"Home...home is tough, Oscar. Every time I go home, I think about my dad. I mean, it's still like he just passed. It's just always hard going home, that's all." And then, after a small pause, Gent tightened back up and got back on topic like he said nothing.

"You know the funny thing is that Los probably should file a big ole suit to get all the dough he spent on Lola. He's Exhibit A of a brotha who got took!

"You know they gonna get back together, right?" I said.

"I dunno about that because—" he stopped when my phone went off.

"Hold up, Gent." I said, checking my phone.

"Is that your girl?" Gent asked, eyebrows raised.

"If you mean Angie, then no. She's not my girl."

"What you doing with that anyways, Oscar?"

"Nothing, Gent."

"You're a nothing *lie*. She's married, Oscar. And you know—"

"I don't want to talk about it," I said. But that didn't stop Gent. When he gets in big brother mode, he can't help himself. "I know she's someone *else's* wife."

"They say you cut your years short messing with other people's wives."

"Who the hell says that?" I asked.

"*They*, that's who."

"What Negro Almanac you read that in?"

A stiff of silence came over us.

"I think I'll have that quick drink. Cool?" Gent said walking toward the kitchen.

"You know how you handle your liquor better than I do," I said.

"Most of the time, yeah." He plopped ice cubes into his glass and poured the cognac. "Negro Almanac? Is that a new one?"

"Yeah," I said. "You like that, huh?"

"Yeah, it's funny. You should use it. It's your kind of humor. So when was the last time you wrote something anyway?"

"For pay? It's been a minute."

"Didn't you have an interview with a magazine last week?"

"Over the phone. They weren't interested. Another rejection."

"Stay at it. Something will happen."

"Yeah," I said. Gent looked at the laptop. I noticed he just held, not drank, the Hennessy. Almost like he regretted pouring it.

"You still think about Carolina?" *Damn it, Gent.*

"Yeah, a little bit."

"You were the man there for a minute. I'm not bullshitting when I say this but, you're a better writer than Los."

"Thanks." *Please stop, Gent.*

"You put out some great stuff. You think you went wrong when you—you know—looked out for everybody else except yourself?" *Fuck you, Gent.*

"What are you getting at, Gent?" He hadn't sipped his drink. He studied it. Stared at it as if he wanted to have a heart-to-heart with it. But no sip.

"Oscar, we can't be caretakers for people until it's time for us to. In Carolina, you jumped the gun and tried to look out for your girl to the point you probably blocked your own blessings. You probably don't know what I'm talking about do you?"

I thought about it for a second. "What do you mean?"

"You made a wrong turn somewhere. We men have to be established sometimes before we can drop everything—like using those gifts to the best of our ability—to make someone happy who probably wasn't the person God wanted you to be with. You passed up Boston that year for Ol' Girl, right?"

"Yeah."

"That, my friend, is called a wrong turn. And it's been five years and you ain't recovered. But when you recover, you'll get your wife; your family. Whatever you want. So I ask again: what are you doing with Angie?"

"I—"

"You don't have to answer because I *know* what you are doing." He sat down at the computer station and looked at the laptop screen. "You may think it's too late, that you've lost it all—that you are too far removed from it to make up for lost time. But trust me. You shouldn't give up." He then looked at a newspaper with Obama's picture above the fold. "He's got to beat Hillary."

"He absolutely has to," I nodded.

As if by habit, Gent raised the glass for a sip, but then stopped himself.

"Remember when we all went to the Million Man March?"

"Yeah. I rounded up the busload on campus."

"That's right, Oscar. You did that. It wasn't me. It wasn't Los. You got us to go to D.C. That was a huge deal. Do you remember what you were like then?"

"Young. Idealist. Naïve."

"Yep, yep and yep. You were weak, man."

"How'd you figure that made me weak, dude?"

"You used to treat all the girls on campus like they were *all* angels. Like they were these 2-D beings wronged by every dude and you carried the guilt of manhood. And a lot of those sistas took advantage and made you their doormats. Remember Tasha Lumpkin? You caked her like crazy, and she pissed all over you. Am I right?"

"I guess so."

"And what about Monica Caldwell? She messed you over too."

"Yeah," I said. And that's when Gent finally put down the glass.

"Just because you're down, it doesn't mean you have to live through other people. Don't be afraid to get *your* success, Oscar. Don't cut short your progress. Men make decisions with the future in mind. I'm talking about *your* future—not Ol' Girl, Tasha, Monica or Angie—but Oscar Ruark's future. Angie digs you and gives you confidence. But there's something bigger for you. God dropped off your blessings somewhere, and you still ain't picked them up. I can't put it any plainer than this: there's more to life than a cheap fuck with a married chick. That's not you, Oscar. You're a good dude."

He took one last look at his drink and made for the door.

"In the end, cheap thrills don't do a thing. I know that much. And deep down you know that too. I'm out, bro. I gotta check on Nate and Mama." He dapped me up and left for Mississippi. And I took a big swig of his untouched drink when he left.

Chapter 8: The Broke Brothers' Night Out: Gent

(Brother Gent)

Carlos and I were on the way to First Friday when I told him the news.

"So your mom is going to stay with you—stay with us—for how long?"

"About a month," I told Carlos as I turned onto I-285. "She's depressed and I don't want her in the house by herself right now."

"She's depressed? You tell me this after I leave Jordan with her?"

"She'll be fine," I said as I thumbed through CDs. "And what's this 'us' stuff? Joker, how long you and Jordan plan to be around?"

"Just a few weeks. I'm waiting for word about a warehouse apartment."

"Apartment? You're letting Lola keep your condo? The condo you're got with your credit? The same condo that has your name on—"

"I get it, Gent," he said.

Fool. He gave Lola two grand when he and Jordan left. Just kick the heffa out!

"You want her back, don't ya?" I asked as I slid a disc in the player.

"No," he paused. Then, "Yes."

"Damnit, Los! You gotta be kidding!" I pressed the buttons on the stereo and music poured out. "You can't be leader of The Broke Brothers Revolution and go back to your trifling girlfriend! That's weak, man!"

"I know that," he said. "Look, I still got my priorities. That's why I brought some of these mini-leaflets to recruit guys to join the BBR tonight." He reached in his coat pocket and pulled out about a good 50 or so index card-sized handbills. While at a stop light, I glanced to look at the leaflets. It was a black silhouette of a man wearing a BBR T-shirt with his fist pumped in the air and his pants pockets turned inside out. Along with Carlos' cell number and email address, it read as follows:

"Tired of sponsoring women's good time just to say hi? Enough is enough! Join The Broke Brothers' Revolution. Broke Power!" The whole flier made me sigh.

"Los, I'm down for the revolution and all, but how you gonna try to recruit people on my damned birthday celebration?"

"Why not? It's a perfect chance for us to get some foot soldiers we can depend on and not any coward bastards like the ones who betrayed us at Borders. C'mon, Gent. It'll be fun! Oh, don't forget we got to scoop up D. He lives on—what the fuck? Is that 'I Can't Go For That' playing? Nigga, why is Hall & Oates on in your ride?"

"You know I don't like the n-word, Los. And you know I don't listen to bullshit."

"Gent, this *is* bullshit. You ain't got any ignorant music to play to get us crunk?"

"Shut up before I toss those damned leaflets out the window!" I said laughing.

I should have known Carlos had an ulterior motive when he said he rounded up Daniel and Oscar to celebrate my birthday. The four of us just happened to be the only fellas who didn't betray the BBR. Still, I reluctantly went along because I just needed to cut loose. Besides, First Friday was usually a big mingling event in Atlanta. It changed locations each month and this time it was at the Westin set up as a *Love Jones*/spoken word deal. But even then, the scene usually reverted to a club/lounge deal.

I pulled my truck into Daniel's apartment complex. We were shocked that he dressed like he wanted to be taken seriously because the brother was wearing a suit.

"You had a court date or somethin'?" I asked with a laugh as he got in the truck.

"Yeah, man," Carlos said. "You look like a fake Lennox Lewis."

"Y'all boys got jokes?" Daniel said. "And yes, I was in court today to deal with something. So shut up Chunky Dr. King and happy 30th birthday, fake-ass Malcolm X."

That wasn't the first time I'd heard that. But I checked myself in the rearview mirror anyway. With my specs on, maybe.

"Why is George Michael playing from your stereo?" Daniel asked.

"First of all, it's Wham! Secondly, 'Everything She Wants' is a classic."

"It's terrible, ain't it?" Carlos asked. "Hey D, did you get with Oscar?"

"I called him earlier and he said he was in the middle of something, but he'd meet us down there. I'm just glad he calmed down about that joint thing at Archie's."

"You feel bad because your ribs feel bad," I said. "I if I were Oscar, I'd still be whooping ass. That was some crazy shit you pulled, lacing that man's weed with PCP."

"And...formaldehyde," Daniel added.

"Formaldehyde?!" Carlos said. "Hell, I wanna whoop your ass now!"

"Yeah, it was stupid," Daniel said. "Yo! That nigga Oscar can fight!"

"Gent, you don't say shit to D when he says the n-word, but you always up in my ass about it," Carlos protested.

"Well, Daniel's a big nigga," I said winking at Carlos. "I'm not fucking with him."

Carlos turned and looked at Daniel, who playfully pounded his fist into his hand.

"Yo, Los, did you ever figure out who dropped the dime on us at the bookstore?"

"Nah, D, I didn't," Carlos said. "But I got some suspicions."

"You mean it wasn't you?" I asked. Carlos did a double take.

"Why would I rat out my own movement?"

"Maybe to get us some face time on T.V.," I said.

"If he did that," Daniel jumped in, "then we would've followed up with more shit to keep us in the news. If Los knew what was gonna happen, he wouldn't have changed up shit if he liked the outcome. So Los didn't rat us out. Right, Los?"

"Damn," I cracked. "Does the suit make you smarter?"

"I know, right?" Carlos said. "All this logic you pulling out your ass is—damnit, Gent! Could you please play something else? This retro shit is killing me."

"You know you feeling 'Caribbean Queen,'" I said. "My car. My rules. My birthday. And why the hell am I driving on my birthday? You do realize you are the DD, right?"

He flipped me the bird. He knew I was gonna get tore up that night.

"I don't know who the rat is, but we can do some things to get a movement going before we try something that big again," Carlos said.

"You know I'm down," Daniel said. "You bring them leaflets?"

"You know about that bullshit-ass plan?" I asked. "I'm gonna hang with you boys, but I ain't passing shit out on my birthday. I don't want another Borders buttwhooping. Y'all don't know how violent women can get when you shake their status quo. Well, actually Los you should know about that. I'm surprised your balls aren't in traction."

"Ha, ha, ha," Carlos fake-laughed as he handed Daniel some of the leaflets. "Well fine, Gent. Leave the BBR to us. But I do have an idea that we should use tonight: a spending cap. Grown men need to spend their money on important things other than shit to draw women's attention. So let's spend no more than $15.

"Fifteen dollars?" Daniel asked. "Jury duty pays more than that. What the fuck?"

"Yep," Carlos said. "That might get them—what?—maybe a beer and a cocktail?"

"Or it might get us clowned," I said.

Johnny Kemp's "Just Got Paid" played and Daniel shook his head. "Gent, this is the gayest ride out with the boys ever. How I'm gonna impress hoes in this suit with $15?"

"Nigga, no one told you to dress like freakin' Prince Matchabelli!" Carlos snapped. This is The Broke Brothers' Revolution, not The Jokers Perpetrate Like They Got Loot Revolution. Let's try to pick up chicks without dough, because that shit gets old."

"I betcha this embargo business won't sit well with Oscar," Daniel said.

"Actually Oscar may like it," Carlos said. "He ain't never got no money."

Chapter 9: The Broke Brothers' Night Out: Oscar

(Brother Oscar)

I didn't have *any* money that night. I had $7 on my debit card and *exactly* $34.07 in my pocket, and that's because I took all my spare change to the Coinstar machine at the grocery store. I was hauling ass because if I got to First Friday early enough, I'd get in free. Balling on a budget sucked, but my brokeitis flared up again. See, there was a glitch in payroll that week and all those who got paid through direct deposit had to wait until Monday for a payout. That meant a weekend of uber-poverty for me.

No matter. My empty wallet wasn't going to spoil my fun. Besides, I looked good in my ocean blue suit, pink oxford shirt and my fly, blue Kenneth Cole shoes. I may have been broke, but at least I looked good.

Anyway, so I was killing time in Lenox Square Mall and guess who I saw. Dominique Dawes. Yeah, that fine as hell, flip/somersault/ split, Dominique Dawes. I spied her shoe-shopping at Saks. And I was only at Saks because I was en route to The Atlanta Bread Company on the bottom floor to see Angie and explain what happened to me the night of Daniel's party. But I dropped everything when I saw Dominique Dawes at the shoe department. So I hung around the cologne counter to check her out from a far. While doing so, the saleslady at the scents counter sniffed me out.

"Can I help you, sir?" she asked. I did a double take. Damn. She was hot, too!

"No thanks. Just looking."

She walked off. She looked nice. But like I said, I was focused on Ms. Dawes. And then Dominique looked up and smiled at me, which totally caught me off guard. Trying to play it off, I hastily looked for and sprayed some random cologne. *Prish!* Ugh! *Carlos Santana Cologne?* Why the hell would anyone want to smell like Carlos Santana? The saleslady giggled as I tried to wave away the foul mist. Carlos Santana must smell like turtle piss. I looked up again. Oh shit! She was 20 yards away.

Then my cell rang. It was Daniel. I hadn't talked to him since I wailed on his cheek and ribs earlier that week at Archie's. I answered.

"Hey, it's Daniel. Don't hang up. I'm sorry about the other night."

I looked up again. Dominique Dawes was checking me out! Whoa! I wasn't focused. I had to get Daniel off my phone.

"That was some real DAN shit you pulled at Archie's, but I'm cool. We have to talk later because right now, I'm in the middle of something." I hung up the phone, didn't say goodbye or anything. I figured I'd only get one crack at this. Then my phone rang again. This time it was Angie. Sheesh! Against my better judgment, I answered.

"Oscar, where are you?" she asked.

"I'm on my way. I'll see you in a minute," I said, hastily getting off the phone. Then Dominique Dawes walked right up to me. *Stay cool, Ruark.*

"Excuse me," Dominique Dawes asked. "Do you like these?"

I thought about lying and saying something like 'I *like* the shoes. But I *love* you, Dominique Dawes.' But that'd be creepy. But I had to say something. Maybe I could compliment her on the shoes. I took a look at them. Them shoes were ugly as hell.

"You're a beautiful woman, but those shoes are awful." Yikes! Was that too much? "I don't like the style or the color. The good news is that you have small feet, and you're beautiful, so I doubt anyone will give two damns about what's on your feet."

A crease formed around her cheeks. I made Dominique Dawes blush! That was a great sign. I extended my hand. "Oscar. Oscar Ruark. It's an honor to meet you."

"Oh, so you recognize me," Dominique Dawes said.

"Brothers followed gymnastics because of you. I didn't know you live in Atlanta."

"I don't. I'm here on business. And please, call me Dominique." *Dope.*

"Dominique—I can't believe we're talking right now. This is really an honor."

"Why thank you. You seem nice man. I don't run across too many nice men when I come in town." *Super dope.*

"We should do something about that." We smiled at each other and paused.

"I'm in town for a couple of days but I don't know the scene here. Any suggestions?" *Supercalifragilisticaexpiali-dope-cious.*

"My friends and I were going to check out First Friday tonight if you're interested."

"I may want to pass on that. I have a lecture to give at Spelman tonight. But maybe we can meet someplace low-key afterwards?" *Holy SHIT!*

"Sure. How about we meet at the top of the Westin? We can have a cocktail and I show you the entire city from there."

She smiled and pulled a pen from her purse. She grabbed the card with Carlos Santana's sweat on it or whatever the hell was in that stuff and wrote her cell number.

"I should be done around 10-10:30. Want to meet a little after that?"

"Absolutely." She walked off smiling as I watched her put the shoes back on display.

I'll be damned. I went window shopping and got Dominique Dawes!

"Congratulations," the perfume saleslady said.

"You watched that whole thing, didn't you?" I grinned.

"I sure did," she said. "You must tell me how that goes." Here's my card. My name is Wendy and my cell is on the back. Call me."

Wow! It was raining so many panties that I almost forgot about Angie.

When I got to the Bread Company, Angie was about to leave.

"Angie, I'm so sorry. How long have you been waiting?"

"Fifteen minutes," she said scowling. She was so beautiful when she was upset. "What do you want, Oscar?"

"I want to apologize for the other night," I said. "I had every intention of coming over. But then I got involved with D's dumbass and before I knew it, I got in a fight. So when you called I was still pissed. But I didn't mean to snap at you. I'm sorry."

Angie got up from her seat and sat in the chair beside me. She leaned over—damn she smelled good—and whispered in my ear: "You have no idea how much I wanted to see you that night. Let's stop playing games. I want you then, and I want you *now*."

I must've fallen in a vat of pheromones. Was it Carlos Santana's stankin' ass?

She walked away and Black Magic furrowed his brow. Yes, one of the finest women on earth, one Ms. Dominique Dawes, had a date with *me*. But Angie wanted to fall under Black Magic's spell. I couldn't let her walk away soaking wet, could I? So I chased after that beautiful, cinnamon-colored woman

"What are you doing tonight?" I asked when I caught up to her.

"I don't know. But Jack's still on his Congressional trip in Iraq."

"I'm going to First Fridays tonight at the Westin."

"With Carlos and company? Why are you part of that BBR foolishness anyway?"

"Maybe we can get into all the whys of that later tonight."

"Maybe I have something better that I want you to get into," she said. She kissed me on the cheek and gave me a devious smile. "Meet me at the Westin. I'll look for you around 10 and we can drink on the top floor."

It wasn't until she walked off that I realized I double-booked my dates. Shit.

Even worse, I had $34.07 in my pocket. I was too broke to romance *anybody*.

Double-shit.

"Hell of a broke-ass situation you've gotten yourself into, Ruark," I said to myself. "Boy. This time I really did nut up."

Chapter 10: The Broke Brothers' Night Out: Carlos

(Brother Carlos)

I was about to nut up.

Gent's my boy, and it was his birthday, so I didn't mind buying his drinks. But the nigga can drink. So like it or not, Daniel and Oscar would have to pitch in, especially since Gent was more occupied with drinking instead of handing out BBR leaflets.

But I felt we were at the right place because frankly, a First Friday in Atlanta is practically Ground Zero for The Broke Brothers' Revolution. Women were huddled with their girlfriends and men were on the move, trying to penetrate those cliques. And when it comes to those cliques, let me be clear: girlfriends and gay guyfriends are dude repellants (Yes, ladies. Straight men aren't as enamored with gay guys like you are). And that girlfriend bubble—that Praetorian Guard women surround themselves with—function as de facto juries against men who approach. And fellas, keep in mind that since girlfriends are often so catty and secretly envious of one another the *paraika* will poison your target against you. Even with the best wingmen, brothers usually must resort to their best tool in the toolbox, and that's bribery, be it food or drink, to satiate the *paraika*.

And yes, we guys know this. But some women don't see how the dynamic of who they hang with could be detrimental to their ability to find a man. In fact, I know women who think if they go anywhere by themselves that they seem desperate and no one will want to talk to them. Bullshit. It's when women are out by themselves and not with the *paraika* that guys feel the most confident in approaching dames. Why? Because hateful girlfriends aren't around.

I'm not saying women shouldn't hang with their girlfriends. It's just that sometimes, your friends are big cockblockers, that's all.

I passed out a few leaflets but it was clear that most of the brothers there were afraid to revolutionize. I even recognized one guy, Ron, from Archie's Pool Hall. We weren't friends but we were cool. Ron pointed out to me some lawyer chick across the way that he'd already spoken to and bought her a drink. But it didn't sound like she gave him all that much play.

"Dude, that chick makes a lot of money," I said to him all militantly like I was Malcolm X talking to congregants of a black Baptist church after service let out. "Pause before you sponsor her. Are you gonna preemptively buy drinks for every woman you meet? Is that really fair? What is that? Eight to twelve bucks just to *talk*? Women don't even appreciate it anymore. They just expect it as the price of us to be *acknowledged*. And Ron, after you bought the drink, what happened?"

"She told me she got a boyfriend," Ron said shaking his head.

"She got a boyfriend!" I parroted. "Isn't that some bullshit? That hank *knew* you were there to kick it with her and she didn't mention shit about a boyfriend until?"

"Until she got the drink in her hand."

"Until she got the drink in her hand! C'mon, my brother. Why don't you come out to Archie's and I can tell you some more about all this. Join the revolution, Ron!"

He took the BBR leaflet, but then looked over again at the lawyer chick. She pointed him out to her other girlfriends, who seemingly wanted to know who paid for the drink. Then she gestured for him to come back over. He looked at me.

"You see that, man?" he asked before stuffing the leaflet back into my hand. "I think you get flies with a little honey. You ever heard of that saying?"

"Actually, I don't think that applies here becau—"

Ron turned and walked away. Jackass.

"I swear, ignorance is an addiction," I said to myself. Then Daniel found me and walked over with a sad face. Apparently, he wasn't having much luck either.

"Man, these niggas stupid!" Daniel said. "They all agree with the BBR concept, but none of them were interested!"

"Nobody wants to take the blue pill," I said, referring to *The Matrix* as I looked out at the desperate sea of men and women trying to mingle with each other. "You seen Gent?"

"He's at the bar, I think," Daniel said.

"Let's go keep an eye on him."

After finding Gent, we posted up at the bar and waited for Oscar. While doing so, Daniel peeped a booth of three women and thought we should holler at them. Now like I said earlier, when men walk up in their personal space and want to converse, some women expect them to pay for *something*. Unless, of course, you had good wingmen.

Well I didn't know how Daniel operated. Gent was usually bright and funny—but Gent was getting bent. And although he's a walking icebreaker, Oscar was a terrible wingman. Remember that *Seinfeld* episode where George hated Jerry because he was so damn charming and made him seem lame by comparison? That's Oscar.

"Some cute women you peeped at that table," I said to Daniel.

"Yeah," he said. "Them bitches are all kinds of hot, too. But they are all wearing those pregnant women tops. You see that?"

He was right. All of them wore those tops that seemed form-fitting until it got to the ribcage, and then flailed out like a pregnant lady dress. All guys *hate* those tops.

"Yeah, I noticed those," I said. "They make it tough to see their shape. Why are all of them wearing the same type of top?"

"Cuz it makes 'em all look the same," Daniel said. "Some hoes want to stand out and look like their girls at the same time. Fuck if I know why. But if they all the same then that makes cracking the table tough."

I never really had to fight the dating war because I was insulated by my long-time relationship with Lola. Daniel knew this shit first-hand. But I knew a thing or two also.

"Should we do a proper table reconnaissance? A PTR?" I asked.

"No, Los," Daniel said dryly. "What the fuck is that?"

No matter what, fellas, conduct a PTR. Why? Because most women are stingier than men. No matter what some say about being equal and how they can afford stuff, many often don't actually pay for shit. And the one time they do, they want a fucking medal for it. Ladies, courtesy is saying 'thank you' and holding the door open or something like that. Courtesy is *not* buying a stranger a $12 Long Island Iced Tea. And what kills me is that most girlfriends won't even pay for each other, yet they hope strange dudes will do it because we're men and want to talk them.

If the shoe was the other foot, and "courtesy" came out of their pockets, women would scream bloody murder. But many of the same dudes who spend like that treat women like objects. A lot of them think, "Well, I just bought something for you, so now you're obligated to get down with me." But these same women think they can keep their money *and* their self-respect. Good luck, dolls.

It's nice to be treated like a queen and not fret about a thing, including the check at dinner. But shouldn't she have to actually be *my queen* to receive those benefits? And to be my queen, I think I should get to know her a little better without losing my shirt in the process. That's why going Dutch should be a legitimate option. I shouldn't have to finance your good time when we're perfect strangers. Shouldn't I spend more as I know you more? Trust you more? Love you more? *That* is a good man. It's not about being cheap. It's about being smart and honest. A good man doesn't throw money at women like whores in his harem. A real man tries to engage her on a deeper level. But some dumb broads just want to look good with their girlfriends, wear Fuck Me Pumps and draw attention to themselves. They keep money in their pockets and look for suckers to spend a grip on them and their girlfriends. And they still find shit to bitch about.

That's why I had a major, super-duper BBR offensive in mind. Yeah, the BBR licked its wounds after the Borders debacle, but I waited for the right time to spring some serious shit on the world. A guy in Savannah wrote me with the idea of suing ex-girlfriends for all the money spent on them while dating. It was a tactic that had been bandied about and I thought had potential, but I wasn't sure it would draw results. So I did a little research and I found a couple of guys—three, in fact—who were doing similar action and all of the litigants said they were interested in combining lawsuits. And these guys didn't care if it was for a trip to Jamaica ($879), or for a trip to Steak 'n Shake ($24), they wanted money back from chicks who manipulated them—their words, not mine—into paying. I didn't know if I wanted to pull the trigger on this. My fallout with Lola was still on my mind. And as much as I tried not to think about it, the specter of being back out on the dating scene in search of a new Miss Right scared me.

"Nigga, you gonna tell me or what?" Daniel said, leaning in.

"Huh?" I said.

"You talked 'bout some PTR shit," Gent chimed in, taking a big gulp from his drink.

"Oh." I hadn't realized my mind had wandered off. "In a nut-shell, PTR is to wait until they've ordered a round. When the drinks arrive, then you approach. This buys time and at least prevents you from buying an extra round."

Daniel pursed his lips and nodded slowly.

"Let's see," Gent said. "There are three of them. Four times 15 is $60. So we got $60 to cake 'em when Oscar gets here. Where is he? And how we should approach?"

"I could think of something," Oscar said, sneaking up behind us.

Now this was going to be fun. Four young, black men were about to rock the worlds of a table of ladies. It had the makings of a great night until I got a text. It was Lola:

"You ain't nothing but a punk Carlos," Lola's text read.

First of all, I was upset with the phone company because I thought I canceled service to her phone earlier that week. Secondly, I wasn't eager to engage in another text war.

"You know what would be a good emoticon?" I asked the fellas. "Just a picture of a smiley face giving you the finger."

"Get out the text war," Gent said. "Just let the ho go, Los." Yeah, Gent was gone. Sober, his militant ass would never call a woman a ho. Still, he got Oscar and Daniel in on a silly chant:

"Let the ho go! Let the ho go! Let the ho go! Let the ho go!"

"I'm trying," I said. "But she keeps firing shots that won't change shit."

"Like America during the last stages of Vietnam?" Daniel said.

"What?" Oscar asked.

"Yeah," Daniel said. "Like the Christmas bombings in 1972. We were withdrawing troops but we still bombed them on the way out."

"Why the hell are you a security guard?" Oscar asked in amazement.

"Okay, this conversation is too deep!" Gent yelled as he headed toward the bar.

Meanwhile, I ignored all of them and tried to think of something smart to text back.

"Is it gay to use an emoticon?" I asked Daniel and Oscar while Gent was at the bar.

"If you got a dick," Daniel said nodding. "Oscar, you heard about the spending cap?"

"Nope," Oscar said. "But since I'm broke, I am all for it."

"Then I can get your first drink," Daniel said. "Least I can do since Archie's."

"How about you just loan me a c-note?" Oscar asked. "I got a hot date later."

"With who?" Gent asked as he handed us each a shot of blue liquid.

Oscar gave it a sniff. "Smells like our doom."

"It's a drink, and don't worry about it," Gent said. "It's a celebration, bitches!"

We turned up our shots and slammed them on the bar.

"Now let's go run these hoes," Daniel said as he turned to table of women.

We shrugged our shoulders, buttoned our blazers, and followed his lead.

Chapter 11: The Broke Brothers' Night Out: Daniel

(Brother Daniel)

And then they locked our black asses up.

I couldn't find anyone to post bail. Josh? Voicemail. Brina? She told me to go to hell. So the four of us were stuck in one little cell for a while.

"I can't believe I'm in here," Gent mumbled.

"You?" Oscar said. "Man, I lined up two women for tonight."

"You were working on a threesome?" I asked.

"Uh-uh," Oscar said. "I booked dates with two different women. Not on purpose."

"How the hell you double-book by accident?" Carlos asked.

"Black Magic," Oscar said. Carlos and Gent scratched their heads.

"He's talkin' 'bout his dick, y'all." When I said that, Gent and Los looked at each other and stepped away from me. "When Oscar was stoned at my BBR gig, he grabbed his dick and called it that and mumbled something about magic tricks." Oscar turned red.

"You *tell* women that, Oscar?" Carlos asked. "That's lame as hell."

"Whatever," Oscar said. "Man, I could be romancing Dominique Dawes right now."

We all did double takes.

"What?" Carlos asked.

"You heard me: Dominique Dawes. I met her at the mall earlier today and we were supposed to meet at the Westin around 10."

"Wait," Carlos said. "You met Dominique Dawes *where?*"

"At the mall," Oscar said.

"Which mall?"

"Lenox."

"Which store was she in?"

"Saks, Los. Damn! Why is this important?"

"Because your broke ass took MARTA after meeting a world-class athlete at Saks Fifth Avenue?" Gent mocked. Poor Oscar. His car was in the shop that night.

"Yeah!" Carlos said, on the verge of tears from laughing. "That was your broke-ass plan? Take the train in Atlanta? This ain't *Beat Street*! You and Ramon had to paint the trains first? *No one* takes the train in Atlanta! What if she wanted to go out after that?"

"Them niggas'll be thumbing a ride," I cracked, flipping my thumb.

We could not stop laughing to save our lives. A guard came over and made a gesture with his hands to lower the noise a bit. We did, but we kept clowning.

"You ignorant, uncouth jokers don't know dick," Oscar said. "It would've been classy and romantic to take a cab."

"Take a cab?" Carlos asked. "You borrowed a C-note from Daniel, chump!"

"You don't borrow money to take out women," Gent said. "Borrow money to buy cars, houses—not to chase ass. Those are diminishing returns. Prioritize, man. If you ain't got the cash, you can't do it."

"Y'all boys missing the point," I said. "It's Dominique Dawes! Choice bitches just don't fall out the sky. I'd blow my wad on that chick!"

"But once she discovered how broke you were, she'd clown your ass and somersault out the door!" Gent said. We burst out laughing again.

"Dominique Dawes," I said. "Double D! The other woman had to be pretty fine to be on a level with Double D and make you forget that shit."

"Thanks," said a woman's voice down the hallway. She walked in slow, and her hips switched from left to right, in sync with the 'clip, clop' rhythm of her boot heels.

"Hello, boys," she said to us. "Hi, Oscar."

"Angie?" he asked. "How'd you know we were here?"

"I walked in the lobby at the Westin and saw the bouncers haul you guys off. Dominique Dawes, Oscar? I guess an Olympian is worth standing me up over, hmm?"

Hell naw. When I last checked, Dominique Dawes was fine and shit, but that Angie? Man, that chick was *King* magazine meets Claire Huxtable.

"You need a ride home?" she asked. "Or do you prefer MARTA?"

✳ ✳ ✳

"Say *what?*" Carlos asked the three chicks at the table. If the talk stayed on this topic, Los would get on some anti-woman rant and sink the S.S. Pussy. But they were talking stupid. Them hoes said they needed a man to make $250,000? Wow.

"Only, like three percent of the country makes that kind of money," Gent said.

"How your drunk ass gonna cite facts?" I mocked. Then I noticed the chick beside me was all up in my mouth with every word I said. Since she was a hottie, I took a shot.

"Damn, girl," I said to her. "You are so beautiful."

"Why thank you," she said. "And you're handsome."

I know, ho.

"What's your name?"

"Gina. Gina Hightower. And yours?"

"Daniel Abercrombie."

"Baby, I just *love* your dreads," she said as she grooved her fingers through my hair.

"Baby?" I asked as I coolly grabbed her hand from my hair and rested it neatly on her thigh. Don't touch the hair, chick. "You a little fresh, ain't cha?"

"Maybe."

Cool.

Gina's crew were wannabe-bourgie chicks, but were really some dick-seeking missiles. I didn't sniff any of that from Gina, though. Her scent was fresh. She was—I dunno—different. So different that I figured she hung with them hoes just to get out of the house. Then my damn phone went off. It was dumbass Sabrina.

"One of your girlfriends, Playboy?" Gina teased.

"No," I said checking the phone message. Brina sent a picture of her with a banana in her mouth. Damn. She wanted it. But later for that. I was on some new booty.

"So," Gina started. "Do you have a girlfriend?"

"No."

"I bet you do."

"Give me your number and I can prove that I don't."

"That's nice, but you can't prove a negative, Playboy."

"Hell, there's a first time for everything, Gina."

I didn't have a girl. Just a few jump-offs I called up whenever. But Gina didn't care. She figured I was a player and she liked that shit. She was curious as shit about me.

"So tell me more, Daniel," Gina said.

"Well, as you can see, I'm the fine one in my crew."

"Right. Maybe more like the full-of-shit one." She said grinning.

"Naw, the *fine* one."

"Or, the thinks-he's-slick one."

"Fine one."

"Slick one."

"Well, if that's true, then it takes a slick ass to know a slick ass. And to be honest, you look scheme-y as hell." She smiled and then wrote her number on a napkin. I'm glad she gave it then because shit got heated with everybody else at the table.

"Don't y'all think your standards are too unrealistic?" Carlos asked the other two chicks. "Does every guy have to be a baller?"

"Look at the Obamas," Oscar said. "He wasn't making big money when they met."

"I don't see how Michelle did that," said Kesha, the queen bee of the group. It was her, Gina and some nondescript girl who hardly said shit. "I guess it's good for her. But I'd want a brother to have more going for him."

"Have more going for him?" Carlos asked. "Barack went to Harvard!"

"But he still wasn't making Michelle-type of money," Kesha said. "That community organizer job didn't pay no money." Dumb ho.

"The brother could be president and you're dogging his job history?" Oscar said. "Michelle saw his potential!"

"Potential don't pay bills," Kesha said. "If he ain't got nothing by 30, then sorry. Not interested." That stopped Gent's sipping and made him put down his wine glass.

"Wait," he said. "I'm 30."

"And what do you do?" Nondescript Girl asked him.

"I'm an accountant."

"That's nice but that's not enough cheddar. *Sorry!*" Kesha laughed as she high-fived the Nondescript Girl at the table. Them bitches.

"Did you just insult my man on his birthday?" Carlos asked.

"It's okay, Los," Gent said tensely. "Kesha, I do fine. I got a condo in Buckhead and—wait, why am I validating shit to you? You're talking out your ass."

"Don't diss 'cause she ain't feeling you," the Nondescript Girl said.

"But she just dissed Gent. Wait, since when did you talk?" Oscar said to Nondescript Girl, as he looked up from sending a text message.

"What's your damn name, anyway?" I chimed in.

"Yeah, girl, you ain't said shit the whole time!" Carlos snapped.

And just like that, the Nondescript Girl got punked and shut up. I don't even think she gave her name. If she did, I don't remember it because the bitch wasn't memorable.

"So I was thinking," Gina said turning back to me. "Maybe you're the *broke* one. After all, y'all came over after we ordered drinks." *Damn! Busted!*

"No way!" I laughed.

"Yes, way!" Gina laughed back. "I saw you and your friend check out our table earlier. But y'all didn't step to us until our drinks came."

Damn, smart bitch picked up on everything!

"Well, shit," I said. "You got me dead to rights."

"I know. It's *Detective* Hightower when I'm not in law school."

"So you were checking me out earlier, detective?" I said as I squeezed her thigh a bit. Hoes love that thigh-squeezing thing if they feeling you. We leaned closer to each other, spoke softly and was in our own little world until the DJ played that stupid Young Mann song, "Gary Got a Little Head." Gina didn't pay it no attention. Instead, she got kinda fast on me and gave an "I want to fuck you" look. I know when they want it, and Gina wanted it. So I slid my hand up under her skirt and palmed the top of her mocha thigh. My fingers felt the warmth between her legs and then her thighs shook.

"What the hell are y'all doing?" Oscar asked us under his breath.

"Don't worry about it, nigga," I said.

"Yeah," Gina said. "You just make sure that sorry mess y'all talking about doesn't come over here, okay?"

"Whatever," Oscar said. "I'm about to leave. Los and Gent can keep this up all night. And I don't wanna hear him ranting about this song." True, because Gent was pissed about "Gary Got a Little Head." Los told me Gent wanted to blow shit up over the shit.

"Hey, anybody got the time?" Oscar asked. "I'm supposed to meet someone."

"Hold on," Gent said. "Seriously, ladies—y'all like this song?"

"Yeah," Kesha said. "Everybody likes this song."

"I don't like this song," Gina said to me with a smile.

"This song sets womanhood back 100 years," Gent said. He seemed so disgusted as he turned to Carlos. "Los, we just talked about this jivey song, didn't we?"

"Hell yeah we did," Carlos said, taking a big swig from his wine glass.

But them hoes weren't listenin' to Gent. He got pissed and mumbled almost to himself, "Just more cheese for the hood rats. Don't let me see y'all come tax season."

"I'm sorry," Kesha said. "What did you say?"

"Oh, you didn't hear me?" Gent said. "This lowly, unglamorous, bling-less accountant will fuck your returns up! And woman, I got money. I don't have to prove that to you. I could probably buy and sell your simple ass a couple of times over if I wanted to. I'm so tired of this stupid shit. *Two hundred and fifty thousand?* You little girls must've pulled that figure out your ass because that logic is *shit.*

"You know how many good, hard-working, decent men are out there—teachers, cops, barbers, mechanics. And your dumbass equates a man's worth at a quarter of a million? I'm so tired of *negroes* and *negroettes* putting so much emphasis on bullshit. It don't matter how much money you make, because in the end, that shit don't get you tickets to heaven. I lost my brother to broke-ass mentalities like yours. Now I don't usually get this upset to women, but, you know what? Fuck it. My own mama would probably kick my ass right now, but to hell with her too, because right now, she's at the crib, possibly dying for all I know and still hating me while she worries herself to death over her evil, jailbird son. Either that or she's eating

Los' daughter's candy even though she's diabetic. But my point is that you, Kesha, have been a stone cold witch since we sat down."

After about five seconds of silence, me, Carlos and Oscar erupted into hooting and high-fiving. Kesha and Nondescript were quiet and had their arms folded like Sitting Bull or some shit. But Gina showed her true colors: "Oh my God!" she said snorting.

"Gina, did you just snort?" I chuckled.

"She did," Oscar said. "I can't believe I just heard a woman snort."

Before Gina could say anything back, *splish!* Kesha threw her red wine in Gent's face. We all sat there in shock. I waited for Gent to Hulk the fuck out. But he had no reaction at all. But as for Kesha, she got to yelling. "Fuck you, ol' punk-ass nigga! No muthafucka talks to me that way! Who the fuck do you think you are?!"

"Hey!" Carlos said. "We paid our good, hard-earned money on that wine and you throw it in my man's face and clothes! What is *wrong* with you?"

"Who do y'all niggas think you fucking with?" said the Nondescript Girl. "You can't come up in our space and disrespect us like that!

"Whoa! You cuss like a sailor!" Oscar said pointing to the Nondescript Girl.

"Is he going to do something?" Gina whispered to me while looking at Gent. "I'm pretty sure he wants to beat her ass. I would."

"I dunno," I said. "I just met him a month ago. I don't think the nigga violent."

The table held its breath to see Gent cut loose on them bitches. But he was chill.

"Y'all crazy asses just wasted the drinks we spent on you!"
Damnit, Los. You had to set it out like that? Really?

"I knew y'all were being cheap," Gina teased me, nudging my thigh.

"If y'all here to think you can fuck with us, y'all tripping," Kesha said.

"Fellas let's break camp," Carlos said to us as he got up from the table.

"Don't have to tell me twice," Oscar said as he got up. "I got a date."

"I can't believe y'all just gonna splash wine on my man like that," Carlos said. Then: *Splish!* The Nondescript Girl splashed her glass of wine in Carlos' face. Gina got pissed.

"Why are y'all showing your ass?" Gina asked as she stood up. In fact, we all got up, but when we turned from the table, Gent stayed behind, grabbed the wine bottle—*Splish! Splish!*—and poured it on Kesha and Nondescript's hair, face and dress.

Then them fools Carlos and Gent dapped each other up and starting chanting—*"Broke Power! Broke Power! Broke Power!"*—like we were at a damn BBR rally or something. And here's what was funny: some brothers at the party joined in!

"Broke Power!"

"What the hell?" Oscar said looking at me.

"Broke Power!"

"Beats the fuck out of me," I said.

"Broke Power!"

I gotta admit that it was kinda cool. Still, Kesha and the Nondescript Girl were ready to fight, so them hoes jumped on Los and Gent. The fellas didn't swing on them, but when the bouncers came over, all they saw were niggas in a fight with some women. Gina tried to square things by flashing her badge, but bouncers ain't cops and they ain't got time to sort shit out. All they saw were some niggas yelling "Broke Power" scrapping with women and shit. So they promptly yoked us up until the cops came to arrest us.

✳ ✳ ✳

"Nice truck, Angie," Los said as we piled into her Acura SUV.

"Thanks for bailing us out," I said. "You didn't have to do that."

"I didn't do it for you," she said. "Is your car still at the Westin, Gent?"

"Parking deck," Gent mumbled as he fell in and out of sleep. As for me, I checked my phone and saw that Gina sent me a text message:

"I hope U can make bail early. Atl PD doesn't mess around. I have to take these fools home. Call tomorrow, Jailbird." And a smiley face. Yeah, I dug her.

"You're smart brothers," Angie asked. "What do you have against women?"

No one really was eager to field that one. But, Carlos took a crack at it.

"We don't have anything against women."

"So why are four college-educated men getting into fights with ghetto girls?"

"Actually," I said, "I never finished and Gina ain't ghetto. But go on."

"Anyway, what is this dumb club you've started? Is it a publicity stunt, or—"

"Angie, please," Oscar said, jumping in.

"No, let her finish, Oscar," Carlos said.

"I just don't understand why you brothers want to embarrass yourselves. And you're dragging your boys down with you, Los."

It got quiet again. Then Carlos dropped a bombshell.

"It was you who tipped off Jacobs, wasn't it?" he asked Angie. Damn. I looked to my left and saw that Gent was sleep. Too bad. He was missing some good shit.

"I have more to worry about than your plot to get out of buying a woman drink."

"I told you, Angie, it's not *just* about that," Oscar said.

"Yeah, you're a smart woman, Angie," Carlos said. "I thought you could see that the BBR can be about more than that."

"Explain it to me," she said. "I've known you since the '06 campaign. I don't think you are a jerk, but there's something going on here that doesn't set well."

I had to get in on this. "Well, I just wanna defend us on what happened tonight because I don't want you to think that we just some fools."

"Uh huh," Angie said.

"Because I can speak for everyone and say that we respect you and women like you."

"I appreciate that, Daniel," Angie said. "Go on."

"Thanks. See Angie: them bitches started it." Apparently, *this* is where I fucked up. Angie pulled the car over.

"What did you say?" she said, looking back at me. Suddenly, I didn't feel a need to participate in the conversation.

"I...I just said they started it, that's all."

"No. The other thing. What did you call them?"

"Bitches. I'm sorry, it sorta slipped out."

"It's three in the morning, I get you clowns out of jail and you have the nerve to call women 'bitches' in my truck to my face? That's it! Get out!"

"Huh, what?" said Gent, waking up when Angie raised her voice and pulled the truck over on the side of the road. We were downtown but were a ways from the hotel.

"I'm sorry Gent, but y'all got to get out." Oscar started to get out of the truck, too, but Angie had other ideas. "Where are you going, Oscar?"

"You just kicked us out!" he said. "I'm getting out!"

"Well not you. You stay." Oscar turned to us and shrugged.

"Sorry, guys," he said as he got back in. "My shoes are too fly for that walk."

"Why not just kick out Daniel and give me and Gent a ride?" Carlos asked.

"Because you recruited fools like him," she said looking at me. "Just making a point, Just like you and your BBR. Call some other 'bitch' for a ride." Then she drove off. And it was cold as hell for April, too. Pissed, Los and Gent looked like they would kill me.

"What is wrong with you, fool?" Carlos asked me.

"Don't say shit else 'til we get to the car, D!" Gent said, as we starting walking. Nobody said shit for a good 25 minutes until we got to the truck. Then Carlos said:

"Fellas, some of these women are out of control. Angie is okay, but those dames at the table were ridiculous. So it's time for the BBR to take the gloves off."

When Los said that, it gave us a boost. Broke power, bitches!

We piled in the truck and rolled to Gent's crib in Buckhead. I asked him if I could crash on his floor and he was cool with it. It was 4 a.m. and Carlos' daughter was wide awake on the living room floor, watching T.V. I walked to the kitchen for some water.

"Jordan?" Carlos asked. "Baby, why are you up? It's past your bedtime, Little Girl."

"Miss Mattie's sleep, so Imma watch T.V."

"Asleep?" Gent asked Jordan. "Baby, where is Miss Mattie?"

"Fellas!" I yelled in shock. "She's here!"

I found Miss Mattie lying back-down on the kitchen floor. Next to her was a spilt-over bottle of Crown Royal. I got on my knees to check her vitals. She was unresponsive.

"Mama!" Gent said. "Oh, Jesus!"

"Daddy!" Jordan cried from the living room. "What's wrong!"

"It's okay," Carlos said, getting her before she could come into the kitchen. It's bedtime." He picked her up and took her upstairs.

"Good night, Miss Mattie," Jordan waived as they moved up the stairs like nothing was wrong. But there was plenty wrong. As a security guard, they train you to do a lot of things including CPR. I'm damn near a paramedic. If there was anything that could be done, I would know what that was right?

"D! Is she alive?" Gent asked.

I didn't have the answer and I didn't have time to try. I just had to act. I lifted her chin, opened her mouth and started CPR. I never gave it to a live person before—just those stupid dummies. Too late for all that. I had to do my best.

"Thirty compresses," I thought. I clasped my hands over her chest plate and went to work: *press, press, press, press, press, press, press...* Was it working? I had no idea.

"Gent, call an ambulance!" I yelled. He ran to the living room to use the phone. I got to the 30th press then put my ear to her mouth to see if she was breathing. Still faint. Fuck! Thirty more presses. *Press, press, press...*Then I checked again. Shit. I sealed my mouth over Miss Mattie's and gave her some breaths. *C'mon. Breathe, Old Lady!*

Gent returned to the kitchen and was damn near hysterical. "Is she alive?!"

"I'm working on it," I yelled. "Quit interrupting and let me do this!"

Blow! Press! BLOW! PRESS! God, please! Help me save this lady!

Chapter 12: Gee Nor Haw

(Brother Oscar)

To break our silence, Angie turned on her satellite radio:

"Get on your knees, bitch / I'm Rick James, bitch / Get yo' neck into it / 'Cause you can suck a mean dick!"

"What! They'll let you say anything on the radio! You hear this, Oscar?" she asked as she merged her truck onto the off-ramp of the freeway.

"I try not to listen to the radio, Angie. But yeah, I've heard this before." The song is 'Gary Got A Little Head,' or something like that."

"And they mean the oral sex kind of 'head?'"

"Yep. This song partly started our argument with the hood rats."

"Let me guess—some more 'Broke Brothers' bull, huh?"

"No, Angie. Gent and Los were wondering how those women could like that song and not be offended. There is some principle behind BBR."

Angie gave an "I don't really believe that" look as she pulled into the Waffle House parking lot. We walked in and got a booth. I checked the clock: 4 a.m. The waitress came over and took our orders: country ham and eggs for me; omelet, hash browns and eggs for her. When the waitress left, I tried to make small talk to break the ice.

"You think Obama puts Hillary away in Pennsylvania? The super-delegates co—"

"I did it. I ratted you and your boys at Borders," she said

"Why would you do that?" I asked as I leaned back in the booth.

"The BBR is so silly, Oscar. Start by looking at yourselves and stop blaming women. You want to chew me out? Fine. But I did it and I'm not sorry. So there."

I wanted to tell her how low it was to drop a dime like that. Tell her that she may have killed a promising thing before it got off the ground. But I honestly didn't care at that point. I was jailed because my BBR friends did tussle with some simple women. But who got us out of jail? Angie. So I couldn't bitch to her. Unlike Los, Gent and D, I knew when to shut up. When the waitress brought our food, I was ready to change the subject.

"I'm hungry. Let's just get through the night without any more drama, okay?"

"So what the hell were *you* trying to pull tonight, Oscar?"

So much for the "no drama" thing.

"Oh, c'mon! It's Dominique Dawes!" I said as I cut my country ham with my fork's edge, stabbed it and dipped it in my grits. "How could I pass her up?"

Angie cut her eyes and salted her food, crisscrossing an invisible star over it.

"You just gonna salt down your food before you even taste it?" I asked her, laughing.

"Homegirl is a cutie pie," she said starkly. "I wouldn't turn down a date with her."

"Wait a minute, you swing both ways?" That made her kick me in the shin.

"Ow!"

"A woman can compliment another woman without it meaning anything, Oscar."

"I wish you had a less painful way of saying it," I said, rubbing my leg.

"Why'd you bother with me when you had a date? What were you up to?"

"I wasn't up to anything. Even after scoring a date with Dominique Dawes, I forgot about her when I saw you. You let me be who

I am. That's why I like being with you. What sucks is that I don't see a future with us."

"What do you mean you—"

"You're married. You don't want to lose him. And you don't have the guts to cross that line. And I hate that I even want to cross that line with you, because it's all wrong."

"So why are we here then, Oscar?"

"Because you drove." That brought a smile to her face. "But seriously, Angie, the old folks say you cut your years short when you sleep with other people's wives."

"Really? What page is that in the Negro Almanac?"

"Hey! Quit using *my* sayings! I'm serious. You're married. That means something. That doesn't go away. I've been through so much that I don't wanna piss off God anymore. I mean that. I feel like I'm tempting fate." We were quiet and then:

"You really worry about pissing off God?" Angie asked, with her head tilted.

"Well, yeah," I said. "You know what I've been through. I don't go around thumping Bibles, but no matter how great the chemistry, it's just not right. What? We'd have flings when your hubby's in D.C. while Congress is in session? Start something we can't finish? What would be the point?"

"But, Oscar, you've become my best friend. I don't see why we have to–"

She cut herself off. We quietly worked on our food for a couple of minutes.

"You've become my best friend, too." Those words crawled out of my mouth and tugged on her dress. "I was so depressed when I came back home. I was beat up and broken. But then I meet you and you make me feel so *able.*"

She lifted her head and gave me a half a smile.

"But if we cross that line, Angie, someone's gonna get hurt."

"I know," she said with a long face. Another damn, awkward silence returned.

"It's like what the old folks say: we can't go gee nor haw.'"

"What?"

"Well, my folks grew up on farms. And the order for a mule to go left was 'gee' and to go right was 'haw.' When the mule can't do either, it's stuck. Like now. We're stuck."

"I see," she said pensively as she nibbled on her toast. "Say, why couldn't the mule take regular English commands like house pets do?"

"Hell if I know," I said. "Even more confusing, my folks said 'gee' and 'haw' could also mean back and forth. Not only can't black folks master English, they screwed up mule-speak, too!" We chuckled a bit at my folks' expense but got serious again.

"Oscar, if they had two meanings, which meant forward? Gee or haw?"

"Haw, I think."

Angie took a deep breath and then she reached for my hand across the table and traced the protruding veins on the back of it with her index finger.

"Haw, Oscar."

"Haw?"

"Yes, Oscar. Let's have the damned affair anyway. *Haw.*"

I don't know if 4:30 a.m. was a good time to break everything you believe in at that late an hour for an affair. My granny said the only things open that late were hospitals and legs. Legs it was. I closed my eyes, took a deep breath and gave in.

"Spend the night?" I asked her.

"Absolutely," she said. "Let's go." We got in her truck and headed to my place.

Now here's where real life differs from T.V. Hollywood would cut to us in bed. But this wasn't Hollywood and we still had a 15-minute drive home from the Waffle House to get to my bed. And as horny as we were, the travel time was long enough to cool us off a bit. When we pulled into my apartment complex, the passion, romance and magic faded a bit. Those surprising April snow flurries

that fell earlier? Gone. Angie's sex kitten gazes? Well, it was so late
her eyes were more bloodshot than anything else. The spontaneity of
requiting unrequited love? Gone. By 5 a.m., and an uneven mix of
alcohol, jail time and greasy diner food, there was little energy for
lusty indulges. Still, there was a will to do it. I held her hand and
gave her a soft smooch as we crossed the threshold.

"It's my first time here," she said, checking out my digs. "I like
the hardwood."

"Yeah, I like it too," I said.

After I slid off her coat, I walked up behind her, placed my
hands on her shoulders, and rubbed away. Then, I wrapped my arm
around her stomach and pressed her back into my chest. We swayed
a little as I held her. It was all a drowsy, trippy affair. Then I turned
her around to me and our lips touched. I felt her feign off sleepiness
for more smooches.

"Go to the bedroom," I whispered to her. "I'll get the wine."

"Okay, baby," she said softly, and then retreated to the room.

I poured two glasses of red and joined her. She was laid across
the bed. I took a deep breath and slid in the bed with her. After an
exhale, I convinced myself that I wanted to do it and we could make
sense of it later. So I leaned over to kiss her.

But she was asleep.

"Shit," Black Magic muttered.

Part of me was relieved. As much as I wanted her, all of the
earlier spells had worn off. I was feeling more sensible. So I did the
gentlemanly thing—I took off Angie's clothes, so she could sleep
comfortably. Like a sleep-drunk kid, she let me help her take them
off. You know how kids are when they don't want to be alert. She
raised her arms as I pulled off her sweater and stripped her down to
her bra and panties. It afforded me a look at her sensational ginger-
snap-brown body and all its curvaceous glory.

"You ain't gonna try nothin'?" Black Magic asked. "You can
still get it."

I gently laid my hand on one of her thighs, and slowly ran my fingers up toward her navel. Then I opened my palm and gently moved it over her breasts up until I ended at her face. Her brown, silky soft skin only made me want her more. I held her hand in my face and kissed her—gently—on her lips. Then I rubbed my cheek against hers.

"Mmm, baby?" she asked in a breathy voice as she lightly kissed my thumb as my fingers touched her full, perfect lips.

"Yes, Angie?" I cooed back to her.

"She wants you to take her, Oscar," Black Magic said.

"I know," I said to myself. I rubbed her a little more and her body responded as if life itself dwelled within my fingertips. She slowly moved. I leaned closer into her and kissed her again. Then my computer beeped. It did that whenever I got new email.

"Ignore it," Black Magic said. "You've got more important things in hand right now."

And I did, notably, Angie's right breast. She still had her eyes closed, but she continued to move sensually with my every touch. I kissed the tops of her breasts through her bra and made small circles around her nipples with my tongue. She took a deep breath. And then my computer beeped again. Who was emailing me at that hour?

"Ignore it," Black Magic said.

I did. Although she responded to all my advances like a woman willing to do it, I didn't want to trick her into sex while she was sleep drunk. That's not the coolest thing to do to a rape victim, of all people. I *had* to be sure. So I turned her into me. Still drowsy, but a little aroused, her eyes stayed closed.

"Do you want me, baby?" I whispered.

"Oh yes. Take me, Jack."

Jack?

Somewhere, a needle scratched off an album. Talk about dousing cold water on a fire. Did she call me her husband mid-coitus?

"Who?" Black Magic asked. If my dick had hands, they would have been on its hips. I slowly let go of Angie's body and she nodded

off for good. As she slept, I was left with my thoughts. *She called me Jack.*

I thought about the conversation I had with Gent. I tried to figure out what it all meant. He was right wasn't he? This whole thing seemed unlike me. What was I doing with her? As she slept beside me, I sat up in the bed with my head in my hands. "She's married," I thought to myself. "This has to stop, now." But I was tired of losing all the time. Tired of restricting myself from what I wanted. So why did I stop then?

"Because this isn't it," I heard Gent's voice say in my head.

"What the fuck does that mean?" I said aloud to myself. Great. Gent had me talking to *his* voice in *my* head. Then the damn computer's email alert went off again. Annoyed, I finally got out of bed to check it. And—oh my God—it was an editor in D.C.

The guy's email stated that he needed to fill a politics reporter gig quickly and they wanted to see more of my clips as soon as possible. I glanced in my bedroom, where Angie laid, knocked out. That was some man's wife in my bedroom. Gent was right: what was I doing with her anyway?

"Fuck this," I said to myself. So I grabbed my files and disks and headed to Kinkos. I hastily scratched out a note for Angie and left it on the bed. Then I grabbed my things and stormed out of the apartment.

When I returned three hours later, she was gone.

After that moment, I made it a point to avoid talking to Angie...again. From that point on, I ignored her calls and her texts. I felt bad giving her the shaft, but I was done. I couldn't do that to myself anymore. I couldn't tell if I wanted her for love or sex or ego or whatever. All I knew was that I finally felt it was time think about me and only me. And no woman was gonna stop me from doing that this time. Not even Angie.

No, I wasn't *going to let* any woman do that to me. Not this time. Not ever again.

It was time for me to get my grown man on.

God willing.

BOOK TWO: Power

Chapter 13: To Sir, With Love

(Brother Gent)

"It's Christmas in June!" Carlos yelled joyfully as he ran down the stairs and into the kitchen where I was making coffee. I had quit coffee about a year before but got back on it out of necessity. Two months had passed since that awful night we found Mama on the kitchen floor. After that, I promised myself I would be as 'round the clock as possible—staying up late and getting up early—to tend to her. She may have survived that episode, but I wasn't sure she could survive another health scare without my supervision.

"Hey, calm down," I said. "It's too early for all that fuss on a Friday morning."

"Man, you sound like your mom," Carlos said as he grabbed two mugs from the pantry. "Anyway, did you hear me? It's Christmas, Gent! I found *the* case study and we're gonna have lunch at Houlihan's today. And the *AJC*'s buying."

"I hate Houlihan's. What is this case study and why is the *AJC* paying for it?"

"Because it's work-related," he said as he poured the coffee. "It's *BBR*-related!"

"What is it, fool?" I asked.

"You know how I've been looking for cases to exploit where guys are suing women to get money back that they may have spent on them, right? Well, those few cases seemed either weak legally or too small to draw attention. But believe it or not, I finally found the perfect case—one that is solid legally and actually captures what the BBR message is about. I found a guy who is suing his ex-girlfriend— excuse me, ex-fiancée—for breaking off their engagement. And he's suing for her share of the bills for a wedding that didn't happen. He even has to sue to get the ring back, Gent!" Carlos then smiled and took a sip of his coffee. Carlos said case study, but he really meant to call the guy a guinea pig. The pig's name was John Rothman. Rothman said his fiancée, Laura Weiberg, withdrew more than $45,000 from their joint checking account. Rothman said that about $29,000 of the money Laura took was his, so he filed a claim in court to get it back, along with $18,000 in rent expenses (they lived together) and for her half of the deposits that were already paid for their wedding this fall.

"Forty-seven thousand?" I asked, stunned. "She straight jacked him!"

"It gets better," Carlos said. "She broke it off with him the same day he lost his job."

"That's cold. So what are you gonna do with this?"

"Dude, I got a twice-weekly column in 125 papers nationwide and an editor in Marty who has my back on whatever I write. So I got him at the ready to get the guys upstairs to approve of an *AJC*-run creation of a website for guys to post their horror stories, electronic petitions for guys to sign—it's going to be great. This is just the start, Gent. Just wait for the press conference we're having on Monday."

"Wait. You're not a lawyer, Los. Why you in the man's press conference?"

"Because I'm gonna make Rothman the centerpiece of The Broke Brothers' Revolution. I'm gonna pimp this white boy and resurrect the BBR. It's publicity gold."

I had to admit. It was kinda bloodthirsty. But damn sure was clever.

"I see. So does he live here in Atlanta? And what kind of work did he do?"

"John Rothman was a stock analyst for Bear Stearns in Manhattan. But he's only in town here a few days because—get this—he's the best man in his friend's wedding."

"Ouch!" I said. "Bear Stearns, huh? Lotta folks lost their jobs when they collapsed."

"So can you come with me to meet this guy in a few hours?"

"I'd like to, but I can't, Los. Mama's got a doctor's appointment. Call Oscar. Maybe he can bond with the guy since his girl dumped him when he lost his job. Then you two can put your journalist minds together to vet this guy."

"Damn, that's a good idea," Carlos said as he got up to leave the kitchen. Before he left, he balled his fist and looked at me with the world's biggest grin. "Broke power?"

"Broke power," I said.

✳ ✳ ✳

"You scared us, Ms. Hawkins," Dr. Avery said as she put down her clipboard and stared at my mom. She had her head bowed.

"I'm sorry, Doctor," she said. "I didn't drink that much."

"It's bad enough that you didn't," Dr. Avery said. "But you went into shock, Ms. Hawkins and could've died. The cancer's enough of a problem, don't you think?"

"About the cancer: when can she start chemo again?" I asked.

"Well, it's been about two months since the diabetic shock. Vitals look good—how about next week? I want us to do this as soon as possible. You ready for that, ma'am?"

Mama raised her head and looked sadly at Dr. Avery.

"You can beat this, Ms. Hawkins. We're going to do everything we can to fight the cancer, but it won't matter if you do something crazy. I can't tell you what to do but—"

"Yeah, you can!" I jumped in. "You're the doctor!"

"Boy, hush!" Mama chirped. "The doctor's talkin' and you runnin' your mouth! Baby, is ya' single? As you can tell, my son ain't had none in—"

"Ma!"

"Ms. Hawkins, we've been through all this. I'm married."
Damn. "Let's stay on topic, here." Doc put her hands on Mama's
shoulder and looked at her sternly. "There's no other way to say this.
If you do what you did again, no doctor on earth can help you."

"Yes," she whimpered.

"I'm a praying woman," Dr. Avery said as she sat beside Mama
on the patient's table. "I know my medicine, but I also know my
Bible: 'He hears us, and if we know that He hears us, whatever we
ask we have it in Him.' Or something like that."

"Yes, Lord!" Mama cried with her hand raised to the sky.

Dr. Avery told Mama what she needed, and I was glad. When I
asked Vanessa months back who Mama should see in Atlanta, I knew
she'd get me a good person.

"I see you have that pendant around your neck."

"Mm-hmm," Mama said as she clinched it. "It's Saint Jude,
baby."

"I see," Dr. Avery said. "Well, don't be afraid to pray, okay?" A
tear fell down her cheek as Dr. Avery held her hand. Mama's other
hand clutched St. Jude. Then Dr. Avery prayed something only the
two of them could hear.

"Amen," Dr. Avery said, completing the quiet prayer.

"Amen," Mama followed.

"We start next Thursday. If there are no setbacks, we can finish
before summer's out. It'll be tough. But remember: it's darkest before
the dawn."

"Don't worry, baby," Mama said as she hugged Dr. Avery. "I'll
be careful. I ain't gonna drink myself to death. That's how Genthaniel's daddy killed himself."

Wait—*what?* I thought Sir died from a stroke. At least, that's
what I remembered. Dr. Avery saw the puzzled look on my face and
took that as a cue to dip.

"See you next week," she told Mama as she walked out.

"I like her," Mama said. "Shame she married. She'd be a good girl for you, Gent. She smart. She pretty. But you cut your years short when you sleep with other men's wives."

"That's what I told Oscar," I said as we left the office and walked to the truck.

"Well, he should stop messing with other men's wives then!"

"You gotta stop eavesdropping before you say the wrong thing in front of folks."

"What your friends gonna do? Get y'all dumb asses thrown in jail like that night—"

"I found you half-dead on the floor?" I tried to catch myself before saying my complete thought out loud. But it was too late. *Whap!* She slapped the shit out of me and I deserved it. I know I say a lot to my ma, but I can't disrespect her like that.

"Sorry, Mattie," I said as we got into the truck. *Pinch!*

"Ow!"

"And boy, I done told you about that 'Mattie' shit! Now let's stop in a store for a minute. We need some greens for Sunday." We went to a store and I got a cart. I know she said she only wanted greens, but Mama in a store meant we'd be there a while.

"You see these collards? They ain't hitting on shit," she grunted. "Mmt. Why we stop in this sorry-behind store anyway?"

"Mama, you're a trip. How you gonna say the store ain't hitting on *shit*, but then you clean it up and say sorry *behind*?"

"Huh?"

"Nothing," I said as I rolled our cart to the meats section.

"Oxtails or turkey wings?" she asked.

"We could have both," I said.

"I don't want both, Genthaniel." Damn, she was in a mood.

"You in a fit, ain'tcha, Ma?"

"M*mt*," She grunted, ignoring me. "No fat back? This place ain't got no fat back?"

"Mama, we're at Whole Foods. They don't have fat back here. And you shouldn't eat that salty stuff anyway. You got cancer!"

"Well, this Whole Foods store ain't hitting on half shit. Can we go to a store with food that niggas eat? Let's put this sorry-ass food back and leave."

So we put back the food, hopped in the truck and went to Food Fair. We didn't talk about Sir while we were there, though. Mama was too busy focusing on her food. It was interesting to see her fight herself. For every unhealthy thing she picked up, she put something nutritious in the basket. For instance, when she got country ham, she also got some bags of spinach. Anyway, by the end of it all, we ran up a grocery bill of $184.23.

"You got any funds to contribute to all of this, Mama?"

"No son," she said as she winked at the woman at the checkout line. "I haven't worked in months. You know, being that I'm sick and all. Besides, that's why I do the cooking. Now when you find a nice young woman, we can talk."

I didn't say anything. Instead I paid for and packed everything in the truck and drove us home. It's not like I ain't got a sex drive or nothing. But I didn't have anything going on in the women department before Mattie's cancer. And then when Carlos and Jordan moved in and a bunch of other stuff happened, a woman would've been a nice distraction. But I didn't worry about that. I was more concerned about what Mama told Dr. Avery. At home while putting away the groceries, I brought up Sir again.

"What did happen to Pop, Mama?"

"Well, your Daddy had a stroke because he didn't take his blood pressure medicine."

That was new information.

"Why didn't he take it, Mama?"

"Because he drank too much. He drank more, stopped taking his medicine and that led to the stroke. Don't make a big deal out of nothing." She went back to the groceries.

"But you never told me it was because he didn't take his pills because of—"

"His drinking!" she said as she dropped a carton of eggs on the floor. "Shit!"

I hit the floor with paper towels to wipe the mess.

"Any them some good?" she asked while placing the other groceries on the counter.

"Yes'm. Looks like about five eggs are some good."

"Mmt! I guess that's enough for breakfast. Whew! *Jesus!*" I stopped wiping to look up and noticed that Mama seemed woozy. She gasped as she found the kitchen chair. "I'm acting like I ain't sick."

It was like she read my mind. But surprisingly, she wasn't done talking about Sir. When I handed her a glass of water, she gave me a little bit more after each sip.

"Your daddy loved y'all," she paused to sip. "Bragged on y'all all the time. Even when y'all kept getting into shit. Especially you, Gent. All them fights you got into."

"I remember, Mama." It wasn't that I was bad. It's just that you couldn't tell me shit. I kicked ass and took names. I even spent two months in juvy because I stole some shit from a store. The parents probably expected me to be the one in prison, not Nate.

"Your daddy didn't talk much after Nate went away. He stopped talking to me. But he talked to that bottle. One day, he left his pills, but he was already on the road in Southaven. That's when I knew he hadn't been taking 'em."

"Was that when we got that call from Earl?" I asked.

"That's when we got that call from Earl," she said nodding her head. "If I had known, I coulda made him take them pills." She stopped and stared off into space.

"Mama?" I asked as I stopped unpacking the groceries. "Mama, you okay?"

"Yeah," she said, slowly coming out of her daze. "Yeah, I'm fine."

Then we heard the key in the front door. It was Carlos as he eased the tension.

"Hey, Gent. Hey, Miss Mattie," Carlos said as he kissed Mama on the cheek.

"Hey there, Carlos," Mama said. "Your crazy girlfriend got Jo Jo?"

"Lola's not my girlfriend anymore," Carlos said rolling his eyes. "But yes. Lola's got Jordan the whole weekend. People should be over here soon for the poker game."

"Oh, that sounds like fun," she said.

"Yeah, I could use some fun," I said. "How was the lunch with Rothman?"

"It was great, Gent," he said smiling. "Oscar went with me and we both agree that this dude got hosed by his girl. It's a perfect case to exploit."

"I guess that's good for you, Carlos. But don't be too happy at other folks troubles," Mama said, rising from her chair and heading to the stairs.

Then the doorbell rang and I walked past her to answer it.

"You need to eat somethin', don't cha, Ma?" I asked before I answered the door.

"No, baby. I need a nap. I just ain't got no appetite right now."

It was Daniel at the door. And he had a guest with him. It was Gina, the detective in law school he met at First Friday.

"Boy, who that pretty girl on your arm?" Mama asked as she stopped walking up the stairs and peeped the doorway. Nosy ass.

"It's me! Daniel, Ms. Hawkins! And this is my girlfriend, Gina." Girlfriend?

"Well, come here and give me a hug! You too, baby!" she said to Gina as they hugged and made small talk. Since Daniel revived Mama the night she went in shock, she greeted him as if he was family or something. I did, too. I mean, he saved her life. And ever since then, The Hawkins loved some Daniel Abercrombie. He was our hero. But I was still stuck on that "girlfriend" thing. No slight to Gina. She was a nice woman who I didn't know much about. Hell, I was still learning about Daniel. But what I did know made him a cool guy for the fellas to hang out with. But if I had a sister, I probably wouldn't let her within four time zones of him.

"You stick with this ol nappyhead boy," Mama said as she headed back up the stairs, "I need to take a nap. Y'all have your fun." Then she vanished up the stairs.

"Your girls aren't coming are they?" Carlos asked Gina.

"They went to the movies and I didn't want another altercation," she said shaking her head. Sometimes I wonder why I hang with them fools."

"Me too," I said. Everyone looked at me like I said too much. "So you play?"

"Hell yeah," she said. "But before I get settled, where's your bathroom, Gent?"

"Second door on the right." We got quiet as we watched her ass twist down the hall.

"Girlfriend?" Carlos asked when the bathroom door closed. "You must need money."

"Ha!" I laughed as the doorbell rang. It was Oscar with a case of beer in hand.

"Could y'all niggas keep it down?" Daniel asked "My girl is in the bathroom."

"Your girl?" Oscar asked. "You must need some money or something."

"That's what I said!" Carlos laughed as he opened up the beers.

"Wow," I said. "A black man named Barack *Hussein* Obama got nominated for president and now Daniel 'Fuck Them Hoes' Abercrombie has a girlfriend. Nothing makes sense anymore!" Carlos handed us beers and Gina walked out the bathroom as the doorbell rang. It was Vanessa. She had her wild, reddish-brown hair pulled back in a ponytail and wore a white tank top and jeans. Her hips were so big she looked like a bowling pin. V looked through me to the kitchen and saw Daniel handing Gina a beer.

"Who's that with Daniel?" she whispered as she handed me a bottle of Johnnie Walker Blue. A $200 bottle of whiskey? I was more mesmerized by the drink than Vanessa's snooping.

"Huh?" I said, fixated on the bottle. I noticed the seal was broken so I twisted the bottle cap. "Oh, that's Gina. D's new girlfriend. V, this smells more like—"

"Hennessey. I just poured what I had left at the house in that bottle."

"Left over Hennessey? Why, that's, um—mighty negro of you, Vanessa," I grinned.

So that night Oscar, Carlos, Daniel, Gina, Vanessa and me played poker for about four good hours. Of course, we didn't just play poker. We ate, drank and talked about a lot of stuff. Well actually, everyone had a drink, but I hardly touched mine. I was still shaken by what Ma said about Pop.

"Gent, I figured you'd play better than this," Gina said, breaking my train of thought.

"Gent usually drinks better than this," Oscar cracked as he turned his beer up.

"Yeah, I guess I'm a little bit off, tonight," I said as I pushed my chips over to Gina since she won that hand. I checked my watch and realized that Mama didn't come back down to eat anything. I needed to check on her.

"So, Gina," Carlos started. "You're in law school, right?" Gina nodded to him. "I need to pick your legal brain. Oscar and I met a guy who's suing his ex-fiancée because she backed out of a wedding and stiffed him with the bills. Can he win that case?"

"Yeah, I think he can," Gina said. "Is that related to y'all's little club?"

"Baby, The Broke Brothers' Revolution isn't a 'little club'," Daniel told her.

With a break in the action, I took it as a chance to check on Mama.

"Great," I said sarcastically. "Now you got the women razzing on us at the table. I'm gonna go check on Mama. Break anything and I'll break y'all's asses."

"Sir, yes sir!" Carlos said and he got back to telling Gina about the Rothman case.

As I ventured upstairs, I got the same sense of dread that I felt when I found her unconscious in the kitchen. My body was flushed with heat and I got anxious. But when I got to her room, I found her breathing (whew!) and asleep. She needed to eat something, but I didn't want to wake her. But then I found a different concern. I noticed something in Mama's hand. I carefully pried it from her grip to see that it was a letter from Nate:

Mama,

I hope you are okay. I'm sorry about how things were when you and Gent last saw me. But I'm okay. I know you wrote me and told me that you were staying with Gent for a while. But I need you here.

You just can't leave me here, Mama. I miss your visits. Don't break away from me. Don't do that. Gent left you. But I always been here for you. Remember, daddy here too. Come home.

Nate

The nerve of that clown to bring up Pop's gravesite like that! I was pissed. It had to stop. Right then, I vowed to purge all bullshit out of the House of Hawkins. I couldn't put my finger on it, but something was jacking up my family. Whatever it was it got Nate, killed Pop, worked on Mama and was gnawing my ass too.

"Not this time, Nate," I mumbled as I took the letter and slid it into my back pocket. I walked downstairs into the kitchen and went straight for the Hennessy Vanessa brought. I poured myself a shot, threw it down my throat, and slammed the glass on the counter top.

"Yo! You alright in there?" Oscar asked from the living room.

"Kool and the Gang, man," I said. "Just pouring myself a drink." Or three.

The shot glass wasn't big enough, so I got a bigger glass and poured myself a much healthier dose of the Hennessey. I quickly downed the drink and grabbed myself a beer out the fridge to take to the living room. But by time I got back to the poker table, things had wound down. Daniel had Gina's purse, Vanessa stood up, Oscar rubbed his eyes and Carlos was in a corner on the phone.

"Who's he talking to?" I asked.

"Lola," Vanessa said. "She says Jordan's ill. She can't stand for Los to have fun."

"It's that bullshit that she pulls that won't die," I said.

"I know, right?" Vanessa said. "Well, I'm gonna take off. Thanks for the invite, sir!"

"Thanks for coming," I said. "Say, V, I know it's last minute, but I need a favor."

"Sure, what's up, Gent?"

"Could you watch my Mom this weekend? I got some business I have to take care of in New Orleans tomorrow and Sunday." Carlos overheard all this and got off the phone.

"New Orleans?" Carlos asked.

"Yeah, man," I said, giving him a knowing look. "Mama trusts you because you referred Dr. Avery. So I was hoping you could watch her while I'm gone."

"But Gent, V doesn't have to do that," Carlos said. "I'll be here."

"No you won't, Los. You're coming with me. And so are D and Oscar."

"We are?" they both said in unison.

"Yeah. Y'all ain't gotta work this weekend do ya?" They shook their heads no. "Good. We'll take my truck."

"Gent, are you sure everything is okay?" Gina asked.

"Yeah," I said. "My boss just sent me a text that reminded me that I needed to be in New Orleans to chase down a client for the firm. I'm just trying to make a trip of it."

"Sure, Gent," Vanessa said slowly. She seemed confused.

"Thanks so much V," I said. "And fellas be ready. The truck pulls out at high noon."

Chapter 14: The Broke Brothers' Road Trip

(Brother Daniel)

"So what's this trip really about?"

"Nothing," Gent said to Carlos calmly as he steered the truck onto the interstate. Because I liked my leg room, I sat in the front and Los and Oscar sat in the back.

"No way," Oscar said. "What business could pop off during Friday night poker?"

"Yeah!" I added. But I didn't care. I had other things on my mind. Like making rent. My landlord set me up on a payment plan in eviction court. But I fell behind and I needed $1,900 or I'd get kicked out later that week.

"Truth?" Gent said. "I need a break from Mama and her situation. It's been intense since she's been staying with me."

"I know the feeling, bruh," Carlos said. They got quiet in the car.

"Well, I don't know what the hell either one of y'all is talking about," I said.

"Me neither," Oscar said laughing and then giving me a fist bump from the backseat.

"I don't care if you clowns understand," Gent said. "We're doing New Orleans on me. Just don't piss me off this weekend and enjoy. That okay with you broke jokers?"

"Yep," we said like little kids at the same time.

But it still didn't make sense. Los said that Gent had a hair-trigger about shit. But I ain't figured him to be no impulsive type of dude. Somethin' else must've been up. But what did I know? As long as no money came out of my pocket, I was down for a trip.

When we stopped to fill up on gas in Alabama, Gent turned to me.

"Can you drive?" he asked "I didn't sleep well and I'm tired. You mind?"

"I guess I got to," I said, looking in the back seat. Them fools Oscar and Carlos were knocked out. So I got out to talk to Gent. We never really talked one-on-one before.

"Your girl is pretty sharp, D," he finally said, breaking the silence. "I overheard some of the advice she gave Los about the Rothman case last night. She's a catch."

"Thanks, Gent. Say, about that case: it's good publicity for Los, but what's the rest of us supposed to do? Sit around and wait? What's the next step for the BBR?"

"I don't know, but Los says he has a plan. And right now, I don't care. I just want to have some fun this weekend. So dig this: can you push this whip? I could use the nap."

I smiled. He tossed them to me and we were off to Nawlins.

As I drove the truck and the guys slept, I had time to think about stuff. When I think about all the time I spent dicking around, drinking, smoking and spending what little money I had chasing ass, it made me mad. I wasted a lot of time fucking around. And look where it got me. Close to eviction.

And still I score a chick like Gina. You know she did a background check on me and that shit didn't piss me off? Made sense though, since she was a cop and all. Actually, the shit made me feel kinda special. I mean, she was going through a lot of hoops to see if I was legit. That means that she didn't just want my dick. She wanted me. I figured somewhere I'd fuck it all up, but I was gonna try to hold on to her as long as possible. It made no sense for Gina to be with me. But I was gonna try to keep her anyway.

Gina made me feel good. As I steered the truck to our hotel, I had another thought. Nothing makes me feel better than when I palmed a bitch's booty after I laid it down. Being in a woman makes you feel like a man. So I reckoned that the cure for all that ailed Gent was booty. So what if I found him some in New Orleans?

"That's a horrible idea," Oscar laughed as he tossed his duffel bag in the closet.

"Go ahead and laugh. I'm just saying Gent is y'all's boy, and he needs some ass. If he don't bust a nut soon, he's gonna bust some heads wide open. Watch."

"D, could we not talk about people bustin' nuts, please?" Carlos asked.

The three of us were in the hotel, unpacking our shit, while Gent went to get booze for the suite. And it was a pretty sweet suite. The hotel was in the French Quarter, had flatscreen T.V.s, two king beds, two bathrooms and a sofa. Gent's job hooked him up.

"What kind of work Gent does again?" I asked while checking out the bathroom.

"Corporate accountant," Carlos said.

Well, shit. Gent wasn't rich, but he was clearly the least broke of the Broke Brothers. It got me to thinking: maybe Gent could come off the money I needed for the apartment. Hell, it was the least he could do, right? I saved his mom's life!

"Must be nice," I said as I jumped on a bed and grabbed the T.V. remote.

"Yeah, Gent's doing well for himself," Oscar said. "Hey Los, you buy what he said?"

"You mean on why we're here?" Carlos asked. "I think so. When we were in school, we made a lot of trips here. This is where he cuts loose. It's his second home."

"Cut loose?" I asked. "Like how?" Almost on cue, Gent charged in the room with booze and four of the most fantastic hoes on his arm I'd ever seen.

"Hey, boys! It's time to drink!" he said. "Y'all get any ice?"

"I'll get some!" Oscar said springing off the bed, grabbing the ice bucket and out into the hotel hallway. What wolf tickets Gent sold to get those girls up there?

They couldn't have been older than 23, 24. There were four black girls with nice, quality weaves and either wore thigh-high shorts or some skin-tight booty-tastic jeans. There was a light one, brown one, dark-brown one and a brickhouse, blue-black bitch who looked like she *built* the Amistad. She was dark, lovely and I wanted her. The other chicks were 5'4 to 5'7, which was nice, but Amistad? She was about 5'16, 5'17. Okay, she was about 5'11, but you get the point. Pretty, thick lips. White-ass teeth. Pretty cheek bones. Skin smooth and rich like chocolate fudge Snack Pack pudding. And man, was she thick. Big hips, big ass, big titties, NO WAIST. Unbelievable.

"Gent, what liquor store you went to?" Carlos asked with bucked eyes.

"Vino's," Amistad said, smiling at him. "And your boy started drinking without you."

Gent smiled at us when she said that.

"Aw shit," Carlos said. "Has he been bothering y'all?"

"Oh no," Amistad said smiling and turning to Gent. "Besides, he's cute."

"No more questions!" Gent proclaimed with a fun yell. "We got beautiful women to entertain! Get comfortable, ladies. Fellas, introduce yourselves."

So we greet the girls and all of that. I'd give you names but honestly, I forgot them.

"I'm sorry, but your body is ridiculous," I said to Amistad. "What's your name?"

"Thanks," Amistad said. "I'm Gina." Fuck!

"Damn!" Carlos joked. "If anyone of y'all is named Lola, you gotta go. Either that or get tetanus shots." Gent and Carlos laughed at me as Oscar returned with the ice.

"What's funny?" Oscar asked. "What did I miss?"

"Don't worry about it," Gent said. "Let's have drinks!" He pointed to each one of the girls and filled their orders as they chirped them out to him. Then he got to Amistad.

"Crown and Coke," she said to him, licking her lips.

"What you know 'bout that Crown?" Gent said. "That's my Old Man's drink."

"Sounds like a cool dude," she said. Yeah, Amistad was really sweet on Gent.

"He was," Gent said. "I guess that makes me cool because it's my drink, too."

"Really, Gent?" Oscar asked. "What isn't your drink?" The rest of us laughed but Amistad and Gent weren't studyin' us as they clinked their glasses.

"My God she's thick," Oscar whispered to me and Carlos. "I bet she got some high-ass blood pressure." I nearly spat up my drink, laughing when he said that.

"Hey, y'all niggas better not fuck this up," Carlos whispered to us. Then he turned to the women. "Did I overhear y'all girls say you gotta work tonight?"

"Yeah, we're part of a marketing company that travels across the country to promote liquor brands," the Brown Bombshell said. Damn. Gent hit the jackpot, didn't he?

"So where are you working tonight?" Los asked.

"Donkeys," Amistad said.

"Donkeys?" I asked. "What the hell is Donkeys?"

"Donkeys is like a brother's version of Hooters," Gent said. "But instead of breasts, it's about—ahem—the donkeys." We looked at the girls' big donkey asses and then looked at each other. The girls saw us ogle their booties and then smiled at us. *Yes.*

"We're meeting the girls at Donkeys later tonight," Gent said. It was like he was a different cat altogether. Then Amistad tapped him on the shoulder. "Oh, and the ladies said they'd bring some liquor back to the hotel afterwards." The girls nodded to us.

"That…is…*awesome!*" Oscar said.

"Well cheers to that!" Carlos said as we raised our glasses to toast that awesomeness.

So we all drank 'til about 7:30. They had to be at Donkeys at 8 and said they got off at midnight. The plan was to meet them there and head back to the hotel for an after party. When the girls left, we looked at Gent in awe.

"What?" he asked as he poured another Crown—a double this time. "Like I said, I'm here to have a good time. And they look like a good time, right?"

We nodded quietly as we turned up the three Crowns he poured for us. Still in awe at the sexy goodness that had left, we gladly decided to do whatever Gent said. Afterwards, we went to different corners of the suite to change into fresh clothes.

Now I'm the biggest nigga of the crew, but I wasn't the most ripped! Oscar was in good shape. He had a basketball player's body. Sorta looked like Michael Jordan. Carlos had the worst body. He had a gut and needed to do a few sit-ups before it got out of hand.

But then I looked at Gent. He was inch shorter than Oscar, so he was about 6'1. But his body? Dude looked like he was in prison and lifted weights the whole time there. He was all cut and buff. And he had a mark on his upper right pec—like he had been cut there or something. And it wasn't no damn tattoo either. The other fellas didn't see what I saw though. Oscar was over the sink, shaving his head, and Los was going through his bag for a belt. After he changed his contact lenses, Gent caught me staring.

"What's that mark on your chest?" I asked walking up to him.

"That? Oh, that's a birthmark." It didn't seem like a birthmark, but I got a text from Gina at that moment so I let it go. I looked at the text:

"Glad you made it. Vanessa called and I may hang with her and Miss Mattie."

"Cool. Gent will like that," I texted back.

"K. Won't bug you rest of trip. Hav fun w/the boys. And look out4 Gent. He needs u guys. He just doesn't know how to ask."

I don't know what came over me but I couldn't help but send her one last text: "Miss you." She texted me back a smiley face. Fucking emoticons.

"So where to first?" Oscar asked as he tossed Carlos a spare belt.

"Dinner at G.W. Fins," Gent said as he poured a round of shots.

"Shit, Gent, we just had a dr—"

"Hush, Los! We're home in Nawlins, baby. You know how we do, C'mon now!"

Bottoms up. And I felt that one. It made me a little woozy. Okay, a lot woozy.

We had a bomb-ass dinner at G.W. Fins and everything was cool. Carlos and Oscar kept bugging Gent about splitting the bill but he wasn't having that. Me neither. I was broke. Gent said he'd pay for the weekend, so I let the nigga pay for the weekend.

After the meal, we tried to hang around the dinner table a bit because we felt too full to get into anything else. But instead of taking it back to the hotel for a nap before we got up with the Donkeys girls, Gent was fresh as a fuckin' daisy and was crunk as hell. He bought us cigars that some Latin-somethin' dude hand-rolled on the street although no one lit them. Instead we stepped in a bar and all four of us got hurricanes. But as soon as we finished those, Gent moved us to *another* bar. At that place, tequila shots. Oh boy.

Los was holding up okay, but Oscar was fading. I tried not to relapse because when I drink, I try to chase it with some weed and/or some booty. But Gent? Dude's an alcoholic athlete. He got stronger as the night went on. And the dude talked to anybody. Other dudes were cool with him and hoes loved him. Speaking of hoes:

"It's 10:20, Gent," I said to him. "What time we supposed to get up with them girls?"

"Midnight," he said. "Let's check out one more spot real quick first." Well, fine, fool. So I went to Oscar, who was seated at the bar, looking like he was about to fall asleep.

"Yo man, look alive," I said to him. "We got bitches at the end of tonight's rainbow."

"D, we got bitches at the end of this bar," Oscar joked, pointing at Carlos and Gent.

"Ha!" I laughed as I got him off the bar.

So this last bar we went to was in the Quarter and was a little seedier than the others. It had a few pool tables and dart boards. It was a lot like Archie's back home, really. Oscar saw a jukebox and headed there to play some songs while we headed to the bar.

You know that hot redhead from *Mad Men*? Yeah, I know—it was one of the shows Gina liked and she got me watching the shit. Anyway, you know the thick redhead with the big-ass titties? The bartender looked like her. In fact, Red looked like Jessica Rabbit.

"Your breasts are absolutely beautiful!" Gent said right out the box to Red. "I bet they are absolutely perfect! Can you show them to us?"

"Sure!" She pulled up her shirt and flashed her big, strawberry-nippled titties to me, Gent and Carlos.

"Good Lord!" Gent howled. "I'm all out of beads, Red. But those are lovely! That did it for me! You're my new favorite bartender! Can I get four Jamesons neat, baby?"

"Baby, with a smile like that, the first round's on me," Red said.

"You keep it up and *I'm* gonna be on you," Gent said. Carlos and I froze to see if that damn line was too much or not. Gent was on a roll but he was close to harassing hoes.

"That could be arranged," she smirked as she walked away to tend to other barflies.

"Did I miss anything?" Oscar asked as he returned from the jukebox.

"We got more drinks," Carlos said.

"Oh, and the bartender lifted her shirt and showed us her big-ass titties," I said.

Oscar made a sour face at Gent, who smiled and downed his drink.

"We can go back to Atlanta now," Oscar sighed.

But we didn't go home. We stayed there drinking. I checked the time: 11:35. Seated at a table near the bar, we got into some drunk conversation about the BBR.

"But seriously, Los, we ain't done shit!" I said. "After this thing Monday, then what? And why you set the shit up at noon? You know I gotta be on the desk then."

"I know, but it was the best I could do before Rothman left town," Carlos said. "Gent can't make it, either. Oscar will be there though." Gent waived at Red.

"But I can't stay long," Oscar said. He stopped talking when Red came over.

"Yes, sir?" she asked Gent as she came to the table.

"Vodka shots and then the check," he said. When she walked off to fill the order, he said, "And have your number ready for me when you get back."

"I don't think she heard you," Oscar said, obviously drowsy.

"I think she did," Gent said as he pulled out his cigar, lit it up and began to puff. I think it was okay for him to smoke in there. If it wasn't, Gent sure didn't care. "So fellas, about Rothman: what y'all need to understand is that the BBR isn't all about stunts."

"Right," Los said. "It's just a way to tell women that some of them are requiring too much from guys. Take the Rothman case. This man made good money but he got engaged to that woman because he thought he was getting a partnership. He was investing in her. But now it's like some women expect to do whatever they want to a man and it's a man's duty to just take it, no matter how wrong she may be."

"Some of these chicks are crazy, man," I said. "Most of them, actually."

"And they make excuses for their craziness, too," Oscar said, waking up. "When men do something crazy, we're evil. When they act crazy, there's always an excuse. There's always an excuse why they cheat or show out in front of girlfriends or why they leave you at your lowest point. I feel for Rothman. This dude lost his job and his fiancée dumps him the same day and robs him! What kind of bullshit is that?"

That's when Red came over with the vodka and the check. But Oscar was steaming. He was awake now, and he had stuff to get off his chest. And Red heard all of it.

"Women are good at telling us what a 'real man' is. But what do they know about a real man? Especially black women. Most of them grew up without a father in the house so what the hell do they know about manhood? And then they wonder why no one wants to be with their ass. If nice Jewish boys like Josh Rothman are getting treating like shit, what chance do non-rich, regular brothers like us have? What man you know can afford to miss tens of thousands of dollars like that?"

"Dude, you're shouting," I said, trying to calm Oscar down.

"Women and their chickenshit expectations. Men ain't perfect. Men ain't no two-dimensional blank slate. We think. We have feelings. We got hopes and dreams just like their asses do. And they don't think for one damned second about what *we* want. They don't think about us at all. All these dames just think about themselves."

"Man, Oscar, I agree, but why you going off now?" Carlos asked.

"Because I'm drunk, tired, bloated and pissed that I keep missing all the cool stuff on this trip, including inside jokes and sexy, strawberry bartender titties!"

Oscar turned and realized Red was still there waiting for Gent to sign the check.

"Wait here," she said walking to get someone. Oscar quickly turned up his drink.

Then Carlos got up from the table. Me and Oscar got up with him.

"Fellas, we better book it," I said. "I can't get locked up again. C'mon, Gent!"

Gent just looked at me like I was crazy and shook his head. Instead, he stayed seated at the table and took a few more puffs of his cigar.

"Y'all boys, calm down," Gent said.

Then Red walked back to the table with a large, big, bald, black *Green Mile*-looking nigga—in a tan And since my fighting skills weren't all that (although I say Oscar got the drop on me at Archie's because I was high), I didn't want to take on a bouncer.

"Who's the leader?" Red asked Gent.

"He is," Gent said as he pointed at Carlos and sold him out immediately.

"I'm LeVander Mitchell," *Green Mile* said to Los. "I'm assistant press secretary and special assistant to Mayor Nagin. Ramona said you guys could probably use my help."

"Tell them about the Revolution," Red/Ramona said to Carlos. Stunned, Carlos started talking to LeVander. Meanwhile, Red looked at Gent and smiled.

"Eavesdropping, Red?" Gent asked.

"Ever since you guys walked in the door," she said. "That's what good bartenders do. LeVander is one of my regulars and I wanted to introduce him before you guys left."

"Ramona told me that your organization needs exposure," LeVander said to all of us. "You know that rant Nagin went on after Katrina hit? That wasn't out of thin air. It was totally planned. Everything he said was scripted. The media ate it up."

"And you made that happen?" Oscar asked. LeVander nodded.

"Because of that—and the hurricane disaster, of course—we were on every major program in the country. Even Oprah's staff got in touch with the mayor. And because of me, Oprah to do her show here in New Orleans."

"Oprah?" we all said at the same time. Oprah would change everything. Seriously.

"So, you have an in with Oprah?" Carlos asked.

"Essentially, yes," he said with a smile. "I know one of her con-
tributing producers. Not one of her main producers on staff, mind
you, but I know a guy who knows a guy."

"So why would you help us, LeVander?" Carlos asked.

LeVander put his big hooks on Carlos' shoulder. "I'm a divorced
father of two and my woman is the coldest, meanest bitch you'd ever
know."

"Is her name, Lola?" Oscar joked before Gent shushed him.

"I just want to be a part of whatever you're planning, brother,"
LeVander said. "But whatever you do, you got to do it big or else
Oprah won't be bothered."

We all looked at Carlos.

"Well, Los," Oscar asked. "You think you can do it big?"

"Broke Power," Carlos said with a huge grin. "LeVander, you
are the man."

✳ ✳ ✳

"Why?" Gina asked with a balled-up fist.

"Why what?" I asked. She then opened her fist and showed me
Amistad's bra.

"Why'd you fuck her, Daniel? I thought you stopped that
shit!" She hit me in the chest, but spread her legs and straddled on
top of me. I was confused as hell.

"Let's go to the hot tub. I got some weed. You wanna smoke
in the hot tub?"

"Bitch, I ain't smoked in weeks!" Gina ignored me and started
to ride, and then we got butt-ass naked on the sofa. And she kept
slapping *and* choking me.

"Fuck you, Daniel," Gina said. "Nigga, you ain't shit, you
know that?"

"I know. Wait…*what?*" She rode harder and squeezed my neck.
Her hips were out of control. She rode me so hard and then–

PLOOSH!

We were in the hot tub! I was underwater and she was on top, choking me. Okay, this didn't make me feel good 'cause the shit wasn't sexy no more. But still, I was about to come. Who busts nuts when they're being drowned and strangled? But then–

"Gurggglglegggggggllllllllll...cough! Cough!...Argghh! Ah! Ahhhh! Ohhhh!...Cough! Cough! Ahhhh!!! OHHHHHH!!!"

Then I woke up in a cold sweat.

It was daylight and it was punkass dream. Whew! I looked around the room. Carlos was in the bed under the covers and someone was in the shower. There were liquor bottles, half-empty cans of soda and plastic cups all over the room. I got up and checked the mirror. I looked like shit. Hell, I felt like shit. I grabbed my bag for some fresh clothes. The clock read 10:19 a.m.

"Oh, *you're* up," Oscar said as he got out the shower. He poured some cups of coffee and handed one to me. "Heard from Gent?"

"Naw, man," I said. "Damn, my head hurts. Dude, I can't keep up with Gent." Then all our cellphones went off the same time. It was a text from Gent: "Be there in 30."

"Well, I'm glad he had a good time," I said. We started packing our shit to get ready for check out. The door clicked and fidgeted, and then it opened. It was Gent.

"Where you coming from?" I asked.

"Church," Gent said.

"*Church?*" we all asked together.

"Yeah, I went and sat in the cathedral down the street to pray a bit. I left before mass started though. I hate mass." He looked at me as he got his overnight bag and started to pack stuff. "You don't remember late last night do you, D?"

"Uh-uh," I said. "What else happened last night?"

"Well, the Donkeys girls hung out here for about an hour and then Los and Oscar passed out. So you and me talked to the girls about going to their hotel across the street and getting in a hot tub with them. But damnit, D, you passed out! They were tipsy, half-naked, and ready to go." The hot tub talk explained the dream with Gina.

"So, you saying you got down with one of 'em, Gent?" Carlos asked.

"Who said it was just *one*?" All our mouths got wide open.

"A threesome?" Carlos asked. "What?" Gent shut his eyes and nodded.

"Damn," Oscar said. "And we passed out like some busters. That's lame as hell."

"The other girls got tired and went to bed, so Ramona texted me to see what I was doing. I told her to join the chocolate Donkeys chick and me at the hotel and—"

"I can't believe you had a Neapolitan threesome while we were sleep," Oscar said. "Wow. Everything good on this trip, I missed. This is the worst road trip ever."

"Gent, you got any aspirin?" I asked. He tossed a box of Goody's Headache Powder.

"What person born after World War II uses Goody's Headache Powder?" Oscar asked. "Do you use Tussy deodorant too?"

"I'm gonna take a shower," Gent smiled as he headed to the shower. "You know, to wash these two women off of me. Be ready when I get out. Check out is in 25 minutes."

So we grabbed something to eat and hit the road back to Atlanta. Even with all the fun he had, I couldn't tell if Gent had fun, if that made any sense. I mean, it seemed like he got what he accomplished on the trip, but you never could tell with Gent. We still had to stop to Natchez to get some stuff from the house for Miss Mattie. When we got there it seemed like a simple enough stop as Gent reached in his picket to look at the list of items she gave him. We set foot in the house and the moment we walked in with Gent, I could feel him change. He picked up a cardboard box and walked down the hallway.

"Y'all have a seat," he said. "This won't be but a minute."

So we waited in the living room and had a look around. It was a small, country house. All the pictures were still on the walls and Gent and Nate's school trophies and medals were on the bookcases. But then we heard a faint sound. It sounded like a guitar was playing. So the three of us walked down the hall toward an open bedroom door to check it out. Once we arrived there, we saw Gent sitting on the bed holding an electric guitar with a box of clothes and trinkets on the floor. He kept plunking the strings and smiled.

"This is my dad's guitar—Sir Lee Hawkins' guitar," he said. Gent smiled again and answered me by plucking some strings. He played something slow, and then he switched up and picked up the tempo for about five good minutes.

"What was that you just played?" Oscar asked.

"*Blue Orleans*—my pops wrote it. You know Mama don't know I can play?"

He put the guitar around his shoulder and picked up the box. "Let's go, fellas."

As we were leaving the bedroom, I saw a picture of a man on the dresser. It was in black and white and the man had a square jaw, strong cheeks and narrow eyes.

"Gent," I said, as I picked up the picture and showed it to him.

"My God, man, is that you or is that your dad?" Carlos asked.

"I look just like him, don't I?" he asked.

"It's scary how much you favor him," Oscar said.

"People always said me and Nate looked like our dad," he said.

Gent grabbed the picture and put it in the box. We left the room and walked out of the house with Gent carrying the box to the truck. But once we got to the truck, Gent had one more surprise. He slid a FOR SALE sign out the back of the truck with his cell number on it. He stabbed its pointy edges in the ground. Then he got into the car and looked at us. Had that been there the whole time? We didn't say anything. He was going to sell his mom's house. Wow.

It must have been his plan all along. Maybe wildin' out in New Orleans was his way of psyching himself up to put that sign out.

Good for him, I guess. Something like that had to take a lot of balls. But after seeing that, though, for some strange reason, I didn't want to ask nobody for shit on my rent.

Chapter 15: Haw or Gee?

(Brother Oscar)

I had never seen so many people at Archie's before.

Honestly, I didn't think Carlos could get any kind of media worth their salt to show up for the press conference, especially since it was held the Monday before the Fourth of July holiday. The actual holiday was that Friday, but reporters try to work ahead and finish features so they could take off and enjoy it.

But Los apparently cashed in every favor he earned as a surprising 10 media outlets showed up to the BBR press conference at Archie's: three TV stations (one of them public access); three radio stations (two urban and one public stations); two newspapers (the black weekly, *The Atlanta Tribune* and, of course *The Atlanta Journal-Constitution*) and two magazines (one which included *Sista Girl Magazine*, which creamed Carlos in an interview back in March). All of them showed up to hear what the BBR had to announce to the world. I have to admit it was pretty exciting. The revolution only had six official members if you included new guys John Rothman and LeVander Mitchell, and only Carlos, Rothman and I could attend the presser, as LeVander couldn't leave New Orleans at the last minute and Gent and Daniel both had to work.

"You ready?" Carlos asked Rothman in the holding room where the three of us waited. Rothman looked like a Wall Street guy. Handsome cat. Lean white guy, about 5'10, neatly cut black hair in a coal-colored suit, black tie and white pocket square. And although it was a hot, sticky June day outside, I doubt that John Rothman ever broke a sweat in his life. The guy was that smooth.

"I think so," Rothman said. "All this attention is amazing." Carlos winked when Rothman said that. Carlos had amazing swag when it came to all things BBR. He was audacious, he was confident, he was on. I had never seen him with such an arched back.

We walked out and took our seats before the media at one of Archie's tarped-over pool tables with a couple of mics on it. Rothman sat in the middle, and Carlos and I flanked him. To start things, a male TV reporter asked Rothman why he sued his ex.

"Laura and I were together for three years," Rothman started. "You know, calling off the wedding is one thing. I'm a big boy and I can accept that. But raiding bank accounts, stiffing me with wedding bills and keeping the ring is another thing. That's not right."

"Are you suing for the money, or are you just angry?" a female radio reporter asked.

"Both. I'm angry and I'm out of work. I need my money, simple as that. I can't eat expenses alone for a wedding that isn't happening. And I can't ignore that tens of thousands of dollars were stolen. So I'm glad Carlos reached me."

"So what role do you play, Mr. Tyrone?" a TV reporter asked. "Is this just fodder to get people to read your column?"

"Well, first, let me say that I feel for John," Carlos said. "Some women feel so entitled that they've put men in an unreasonable posture, which gives them license to be selfish, inconsiderate and totally irresponsible. When I reached out to John, I told that him about The Broke Brothers' Revolution, and that I've been writing columns to highlight the growing disparity in relationship expectations for men and women. After talking to John, I thought his plight was ideal example as to why the BBR exists. Let me be clear: John Rothman is our rallying symbol. And we hope folks will visit our website—TheBrokeBrothersRevolution.com—where they can donate to John's legal fund. And yes, that is a serious request. Lawyers are expensive, and, like he said, John is out of work. This is a landmark case, in our opinion, and quite frankly, we want him to win it."

"I want me to win it, too!" Rothman joked as the media collectively chuckled. "I think Carlos should be commended for talking about the shifting dynamics in male/female relationships. It's not an easy thing to challenge conventional thinking. Especially if what you challenge threatens to not get you laid."

The press corps *really* laughed at that one. Rothman had a sneaky sense of humor.

"I'm not lock-step with Carlos on his views," Rothman continued. "But we both agree that modern chivalry is out of whack. It's one thing to expect a guy to be a provider. That's inherent to men's natural sensibilities. But it's another thing to take advantage of those sensibilities to bilk him. Unfortunately, I'm a victim of that mindset, and it's cost me my life savings and—to be frank—probably three years of my life with a woman I thought loved me for me. I guess I was wrong."

I *felt* the press corps give a collective "Awww" to sympathize with Rothman's plight. That was the genius of Carlos hitching his ride to this guy's story. Rothman had the charm and the personality to take the edge off Carlos and the BBR's flinty disposition.

As the presser continued, I looked down the table and saw Carlos nod at everything Rothman said. I used to be ambivalent to the BBR and sometimes saw it as Angie saw it: a frivolous enterprise for cheap guys. But over time, I got its gist. The BBR wasn't about paid gestures. The BBR was about male frustration. It was the frustration that good, decent, honest men felt when engaging women who were so empowered that there seemed to be no pleasing them. The BBR was the fight for the good guys, not the conquerors, captains of industry or playboys. Instead, it was for the common man who had the fiber, fortitude and grace to be real, but was rebuffed by today's imperialistic women who want the world, even when the world would never be enough. Carlos was a son of that anguish. And he found an equally-wounded casualty of fate in John Rothman.

"And your role, Mr. Ruark?" a reporter asked, turning to me.

"Ah, yes," I said. "I will track all petitions on the website as we look to advance a concept that will take place in New Orleans. There, the Honorable Mayor Ray Nagin—a friend of the BBR—will soon proclaim August 18 as 'Going Dutch Day.' Mayor Nagin hopes this will remind people of all genders that even after Katrina, New Orleans is open for business and both genders are encouraged to patronize the city's shops, restaurants and bars. Mayor Nagin's proclamation is designed to show appreciation to The Netherlands for its assistance to the city in the aftermath of Katrina. But he is specifically putting in strong wording to support the practice of going 'Dutch,' as men and women will be asked to pay their own tab that day."

"It will be a guy's version of Sadie Hawkins' Day," Carlos added.

"Right," I said. "E-signatures collected for petitions on the website will be used to lobby mayors across the country to proclaim Going Dutch days in their towns. I will coordinate this activity. Also, the site will also feature blog posts from Carlos and me, and will allow guys to post their dating frustrations on the site." (What the media didn't know was that my blog posts were technically for the *AJC* since they owned the site. Having AJC credentials were a welcome addition to my journalism resume.)

"So, Mr. Rothman," the same reporter asked, "you're okay with all this activity surrounding your case?" Rothman then smiled and looked at me and Carlos.

"I have only two words to say about all of this." Rothman then stood up, loosened his tie and unbuttoned his shirt. He then opened up his shirt like he was Superman to reveal that he wore a BBR T-shirt as an undershirt, with the logo prominently shown.

"Broke power!" he said pumping a fist in the air. Carlos and I got up and stood beside Rothman and pumped our fists as well. Since we were all smiles, it was the perfect photo op and was the perfect way to reboot the BBR.

✳ ✳ ✳

"You nervous?" Carlos asked as he rolled up his sleeves.

"A little," I said, handing him a beer. It was now early August, and a sleepy Tuesday night at Archie's meant $2-pool games and a bucket of beers for $10. I'd been so focused on BBR stuff since that press conference that my big interview in D.C. snuck up on me.

"Man, don't sweat it," he said as he knocked the 6-ball in a side pocket. "Editors don't know what they want. Newspapers are struggling. So talk blogs, taking pictures and posting video. They've read your clips and your blog posts. They know you're talented. They just want to know if you're the future. Even if they don't know what that future is."

"I guess so." I said. "Hey, you see the hits on the site? We're up to 7,000 visitors. I think the BBR is getting somewhere."

"Yeah," he said smiling. "Guys are finding the site, signing petitions and all that. It's coming together. It really is."

"Well I hope we can keep it up," I said as I downed my beer and then lined up my shot: 12-ball, corner pocket.

"So how's Angie?"

"She's married, Los. That's how she is." I crouched to take my shot.

"I've known Angie for a while now. Ya know she married into those dealerships?"

"Can I please shoot?"

Carlos finally shut up and when he did, I ran the table. I knocked in five balls in a row with only the 8-ball left. When you've been out of work, lived in your piece-of-shit car and suffered broke-itis, you gotta have a hustle. And mine was pool. But in mid-stroke:

"Gent told me that 'Lola' means 'sorrows' in Spanish."

Laughing, I stabbed my stick into the felt, missing the shot. "What? It really means 'sorrows'? Ha! Gent's a nut! What's he up to tonight?"

"Out grocery shopping with his Miss Mattie. Jordan wanted to go with them."

"Jordan loves them," I said. "Whenever y'all move out, she's gonna miss them."

"That's sooner than you think. We're moving back into it in September."

"Lola's moving out?"

"Yep," he said after missing his shot. "Kinda weird. Lola and I moved in that house *together*. Now in two weeks, I'm going to move her out so I can live there without her."

"Wait. You're helping her move?"

"Oscar, I won't believe that heffa's out unless I physically move her out myself."

"Well, congratulations," I said as I looked at the table. It was my shot and I had to knock that damn 8-ball in. "Two banks before I knock it in that corner pocket."

"You're crazy, man. You got it straight up. Just take the easy shot."

"That's no fun, mate," I said as I chalked up my stick and leaned over to square it up. "I feel like this interview is like my last chance to get back on track." I lined up the shot but paused. Carlos made a face that assured he wouldn't distract me this time.

I focused back on that black-ass, punk-ass ball at the end of the table, and I suddenly had this evil, malicious, desire to knock the shit out of it—take out the last five or six years of bullshit on that ball: Monty, Ol' Girl, Carolina, the sorry-ass insurance job I had, my defaulted student loans, the credit card debt I built while out of work, living in my car, the plasma I gave to get a few dollars in my pocket, my gutless cracker boss who fired me—all of that bullshit. I even wanted to knock it out because I couldn't have Angie. I wanted to hit that 8-ball so hard it'd bust through Archie's walls, go on to smash through the windows of Atlanta's skyscrapers, burrow through the alabaster or stone or whatever-the-fuck Stone Mountain was made of, travel another 180 miles up the freeway and fire a big hole through the Confederate flag hanging at the South Carolina state capital in Columbia. I wanted to take everything out on that ball.

And *that's* when I learned that it's about how you play the game. All my life, I thought I was too good to play games. But I kept getting played. Everyone played me. Everyone beat me. But to quote football coach Herm Edwards, you play to *win* the game. I needed a win, and I didn't care how I did it anymore. With my thumb splayed upward, I grooved the stick in there and then: *CRACK!* Doink, doink, *knock*! 8-ball fell in the corner pocket. Just like I called it.

"Whoa!" Carlos said as he nearly spit up his beer.

Damned straight, Carlos: *whoa*. Take notes, World. Oscar Ruark had arrived.

The next day, I was full of nerves. The flight to D.C., the cab ride to the office—all of that stuff just built up this anxiety in me. I had to calm down before I talked to those people. So I stepped in the restroom to collect myself and splash some cold water on my face. I was careful to not mess up my James Bond suit though—a gray jacket and slacks, white oxford shirt and a black tie, complete with a white pocket square.

I ducked into a stall to say a quick prayer. Then I checked my watch: It was time. When the receptionist guided me through the newsroom I felt what I hadn't felt in years: the constant buzz, the ringing of phones in the distance, the tap-tap of the keys—I missed all that energy. As I took in the atmosphere, a short, balding white guy in his '50s—sorta looked like Charlie's Grandpa in *Willy Wonka And the Chocolate Factory*—greeted me with a handshake and a smile.

"Oscar Ruark? Stu Gregory, politics editor. Welcome to D.C. How was the flight?"

"Well, the plane landed, and that's all you can ask for, right?"

We laughed good-naturedly as he guided me to managing editor Dan Lewis' office. Lewis had a huge corner office at the other end of the newsroom. A tall, white guy with a great head of silver hair and some tortoise-rimmed glasses greeted us at the door. He had a white dress shirt with a yellow tie and looked like a Just For Men hair dye model.

"Oscar Ruark? Dan Lewis! You guys come on in and have a seat. Nice suit."

"Thanks."

The conversation went well. Even when they asked me about my time at the old paper in Carolina, it was cool because I didn't bullshit them.

"So they *did* let you go?" Stu asked.

"Yes. But I considered a job at the Boston Herald, but I turned it down."

"Turned it down?" Dan asked as he looked at Stu. "Let me guess: a woman?"

That drew a wry smile. "You *are* in the news business," I said.

"But judging from your clips, Oscar, you were no slouch," Dan said as he flipped through my clip file. "They gave you the keys to the store and you took full advantage of it. Lifestyles, entertainment, TV, sports—this is all over the place, but you did it well."

"Were there any lessons you learned from your time with the paper?" Stu asked.

Yeah, I learned that being the only black guy on a white staff sucks. I also learned what it was like to have a lot of crap to do, get it all done, and when that workload wore you down, then that's your ass. I knew better than to say that though.

"Well, I'm fortunate I grew as a reporter there. They gave me room to work my beats and experiment with my style. So I chalk it up as a learning experience."

"Good," Stu said. "So let's get to it. You know the saying that politics is celebrity for ugly people? Well we're looking for someone who can cover D.C. like it is Hollywood. But we compete with the Post so we can't put out crap. We're the second newspaper in a one-paper town! But because of this election, readership is up and web hits are soaring. People are thirsty for news on Obama, McCain and Hillary."

"It's a politics beat, but you could make it your own and have fun with the coverage," Dan said. "You write humor well, and you can still handle the issues."

"You can appeal to the 18-34 demo," Stu followed. "And your looks work for D.C." The T.V. talk was the first of three things that caught me off guard in the interview.

"T.V.?" I asked, perking up. "I don't understand." Dan and Stu looked at each other.

"There's a small detail we never posted in our ads about the position," Dan said. "We're in negotiations with cable networks to use some of our staffers on camera."

"That's right, Oscar," he said, nodding. "Who we hire will be on television."

"That is so cool!" I said, trying to contain my excitement.

"We would've been flooded with resumes of a lot of pretty T.V. people who can't write dick," Dan said. "Our copy has to be strong. And we know you can write."

I was overwhelmed. It all sounded so awesome.

"Now briefly—The Broke Brothers' Revolution: what is that about?" Dan asked.

Now I don't know why but I didn't expect any questions about the BBR. So obviously, that was the second thing that surprised me.

"Oh, that's just something that my friend who writes for the *AJC* is trying to get off the ground," I said. "He's had some woman issues of late and he's used that as great inspiration for copy. The *AJC* hired me to write blog posts for the BBR site."

"Well," Dan started slowly, "if you were to get this job, we'd have to ask you to relieve your role in the group. At least end your work for the site. It seems fun, but we have a political post and we need the writer to seem as credible as possible."

"No problem," I said loosing up my arm to throw Carlos under the bus. Bye, BBR.

"Now when we spoke to Mrs. Ridenour she told us about your work for her and the congressman Ridenour," Stu said. "She said you were key to some of their events."

Angie? This was the third and final shock of the interview. How did get in this?

"We even wondered why you didn't list her as a reference," Stu asked.

"Because she's not—um—she's not...well, I didn't want to namedrop," I said, trying to play it cool. "I, um, wanted to earn this job on the merits of my work."

"That's admirable, Oscar," Stu said. "But political connections go a long way here. Some of our staffers don't have the connections Mrs. Ridenour said you had."

I had no idea Angie was pulling strings for me. I didn't even know how she found about I was up for the job. I mean, she straight lied to those people and I was flatfooted on my own interview. I couldn't wait for the interview to end.

Thankfully it did end and soon enough, I was on my way back home. As soon as my plane touched down at Hartsfield, I texted Angie because I needed some answers from her. She invited me to come over and talk, and as usual, curiosity got the best of me and I hopped in my truck to see her. While I was driving, I saw a weird looking billboard. Was that? No, it couldn't be.

But oh yes it was! It was a big huge billboard with a close up of Carlos wearing a beret and a comic strip-like word balloon that read "Broke Power." I pulled the car over to a gas station so I could study the whole thing. Aside from the word balloon, there was a slogan in big letters: THE BROKE BROTHERS' REVOLUTION: THE REVOLUTION WILL NOT BE TELEVISED...WE CAN'T AFFORD IT!

What the fuck?

I shook my head and made a mental note to clown Carlos later. But I didn't have time to do that then. I was on a mission to get some answers from Angie. When I pulled into the driveway of the Ridenour manse at the Atlanta Country Club, I felt déjà vu. When she answered I was smitten again. Same honey-glazed brown skin. Same full, burgundy lips that curled into a full pearly white smile. Her jeans hugged her short, compact curves well. Orange tank top. Perfect breasts. Big coal-colored eyes. And, oh—that was new.

"You changed your hair."

"Yeah, do you like it? I thought I'd try the short twists."

"I do," I said as I walked through the doorway. The place was immaculate. Then she suddenly ran into my arms, gave a huge hug and squeezed me tight. Damn it felt good.

"I've missed you, Oscar," she said with her head pressed into my chest.

Thanks to the closeness, Black Magic broke onto the scene and reared his big head. Angie must have felt him too, because once he firmed up, she slid her hands inside my shirt and rubbed my pecs. Then she tilted her head up and we kissed. Our hands and arms got crazy as we rubbed each other wildly as our lips stayed locked. Angie's hands got more familiar as one loosened my tie and the other unfastened my belt. But the *clink, clink* of the belt snapped me out of the spell.

"Wait, wait—no!" I said. When I stepped back, Angie stepped up. *Shit!*

I pulled her into my body and vampire-kissed her neck. Subconsciously, I snatched the back of her head, cocked it back like a Pez dispenser and licked and nibbled her neck. But unlike a vampire, I saw myself in the huge mirror over the fireplace mantle where pictures of the Ridenour family were. In one was 50-something year-old Jack Ridenour, a husky, strapping white guy with his hair graying at the temples alongside his 34-year old, beautiful black bride Angie on their wedding day. The pictures beside the wedding pic featured Jack, Angie, and two college-aged blond women in a family portrait.

"Angie, this isn't right. Even worse, this isn't me." I pulled away from her to fasten my belt and button up my shirt. The silence filled the room better than the smell of seafood she picked up for dinner.

"I'm sorry," she said. "I guess I misread your signals?"

"What?"

"Yes, you said you wanted us to meet in private! I thought you wanted to—"

"Well you thought wrong, Angie!"

Silence. Damn, those things *are* deafening.

"Maybe you should go."

"Oh, I am going to go, but not before you talk to me."

"Talk to you? You're right and I'm wrong, okay? What else is there to talk about?"

"Uh-uh. You don't get off that easy. I'm talking about what you did."

"You mean putting in a good word to get you a job?"

"How could you do that and not tell me? And now some in the Beltway could think my politics are the same as your jackass husband. Do you see the bind you put me in?"

"Wait, *how* is this bad for you, Oscar? People fudge their resumes all the time." I just stared at her, fuming. "Let's both calm down for a second, okay? I'll make us a drink."

I nodded my head as she made two whiskeys. Angie never saw me upset and it stunned her a bit. It takes a lot to get me upset and Angie had gotten me there. She handed me my drink and then sat beside me on the ottoman for the chair I was in.

"Angie, how did you know I was up for that job?"

"The last time we saw each other, I didn't know where you went. You left me that stupid letter, and—" she sighed before continuing. "I read the email Dan Lewis sent."

"You spied on my computer and checked my email? Angie!"

"I didn't know where you ran off to and your computer kept beeping."

"So you told them I worked for you and your hick husband? Are you crazy?"

"Oscar, I did it to help you. Can't you see that I was only trying to help!"

"Help? What if people figured you helped me because we're fucking!"

"But we aren't fucking, Oscar!"

"No, we aren't! But it's D.C., and rumors like that float all the time there. It's a position to write on politics! This is my credibility, Angie!"

She sighed heavily. "I hadn't thought of that, Oscar. But still—"

"You couldn't call or text to give me a head's up?"

"If I had told you, would you have gone on the interview?" I got quiet.

"Exactly. You wouldn't have. Your ego would've kept your ass here. You'd be upset that I pulled strings to get you the job. And that'd just kill you, wouldn't it?"

"But if you knew all of that, Angie, why did you do it anyway?"

"Because I want you to get your life back. I wasn't trying to manipulate you. I thought you'd be grateful or at least happy about it. You've become my friend and...and...I don't know how we reconcile all this attraction we have for each other, but I want you to be happy. And I want you in my life as a friend. Can we try that?"

I walked to the mantle and I picked up the wedding photo.

"As long as he's your husband, *he* has to be your best friend. Angela, I appreciate you, but we took this thing too far. I can't be whatever you need me to be anymore. I can't be your crutch anymore. I gotta be what I need to be."

Her silence confirmed to me that she finally got my point. Then she stood up.

"Wait right here," she said, as she walked into the kitchen. I waited, but I wanted to walk out of there. Since I found my spine, I didn't want to lose it. But she soon walked back in—with Tupperware.

"I picked up food at Pappadeaux anyway. I can't eat all of this. It'll go to waste."

"Thanks, Angie," I said shaking my head. "Still looking out for me, huh?"

"I would look out for you," she said. "I really would if you'd let me. I wasn't trying to manipulate you, Oscar. I swear it, babe." Some tears rolled down her face. I walked over to her and held her.

And then we kissed, deeply and quietly. No sexual wildness or hair-pulling or anything like that was involved. Just a sweet, soft, long, passionate kiss.

"I met you because I needed to, Angie."

"And I met you because I needed to, Oscar"

"Let's thank God for that much."

"Okay." We stood there and held each other some more.

"You want to know why I needed to meet you?" I asked her.

"Why?" she asked. So I leaned over and whispered:

"Because I'm the new politics writer for *The D.C. Herald*."

"AIIEEEEE!!!" she screamed in joy as she hugged me. "I'm so happy for you!"

"I *am* grateful, Angie. You caught me off guard, but you saved my life. I owe you."

"You don't owe me anything, Oscar. You deserve it."

"I'm gonna miss you, Angie." I wiped the tears from her eyes and whispered, "I'm so glad you drove my piece of shit car to the dealership." That made her laugh. And at Monty's expense, Angie and I shared our last laugh.

And then we finally said goodbye.

Chapter 16: The Goodbye Guy

(Brother Daniel)

"Why am I helping you move this shit in your Mom's crib again?" Josh asked.

"Because no one can help this time of night," I said.

We grunted some more and finally got that heavy-ass sofa bed off the back of Josh's truck. It was good that Ma wasn't home 'cause she woulda dug in my ass with Josh there. Not because he's white, but because I could tell he blazed up before he came over.

"But for real. It's nine o'clock on the day before the Fourth of July. We should be at some cookouts. Where your BBR boys? They can't help?"

"Well, I was gonna ask 'em for money in New Orleans but—"

"How much you short, anyway?" he asked.

"About $1900. The shit ain't changed. What, you got it, now?"

"Hell naw, motherfucker! I ain't got ends like that!"

Whatever, Josh. Josh was getting on my nerves.

"So is the revolution over? Cuz y'all fools ain't done shit."

"Shit, Josh! What *you* care about the BBR for? Your monkey-ass dipped while me and the fellas faced a barrage of books!"

"Barrage? When you use words like 'barrage'? Nigga, please!"

"Since when you think you can just call me nigga like that?"

Josh paused at my response and then took a drag of his cigarette.

"I'm just playin' with ya' like I always do. Damn, you actin' like your boy, Gent."

"No, I'm starting to act like *me*. So chill on the use of 'niggas,' okay?"

"I'll make sure to whiten up for you, D. Just remember that you the one who been ghost, but it's my white ass that's helping you move now, you grouchy motherfucker."

I didn't mean to fuck with Josh so much. But I was pissed. Seemed like my sugar turned to shit fast and I was feeling bad about myself again. And that feeling just reminded me of every stupid day at work, wearing that stupid uniform, sitting behind a big ol' stupid desk watching other mufuckas walk through the building getting paid.

"Hey, look man," Josh said. "I got some green. Wanna take a break and smoke?"

We get on the back porch and take a break to blaze and drink and other shit, right? And mid-toke, a car pulls up. And you could tell when someone pulled up even when you were out back, because Ma had a short, gravel path and the tires made crunchy sounds when cars rolled on it. Also, the headlights go through the house all the way to the backyard. So we ducked behind some bushes below the porch. And then we started shout-whispering—you know, hissing—while we passed the blunt back and forth.

"Dude! *Cough!* I thought your mama—*Cough!*—was at work!"

"Just pass that shit—*Cough!*—and keep your voice down!"

"If she at work—*Cough! Cough!*—then who the fuck is it?" Then the doorbell rang. But we kept our black and wannabe-black asses behind them bushes by the back porch. I crawled on my knees with the blunt in my mouth and reached the wooden fence. When I slowly rose up, Gina was on the other side staring dead at me.

"What are you doing? Is that what I think it is?"

"H-h-hey, baby. This? This is Josh's. He brought it over. Right, Josh?"

I turned to Josh but he hauled ass through a neighbor's yard and dipped. Again.

"Baby, what are you doing here?" Gina asked. "And I thought you quit that shit!"

"I did. My bad," I said as I unconsciously puffed the joint. She looked at me like she was gonna slap the black off me, so I tossed it, which sucked because it was good shit.

"Why you didn't tell me you were getting kicked out, Daniel?"

"I don't know what you're talking about, Gina."

"I know what's going on, Daniel," She grabbed my hand and led me to the back porch's rocking chairs. I sat down and she eased her ass in my lap. "When I ran your background in April, your eviction popped up. It said you went to court for a payment plan. So I monitored the situation. Now it's July and we're here." She got on top of me in a power position and put her fingers through my dreads. "Were you trying to make this move and disappear from me?"

"No," I said. "Well, maybe. I just—you know—you are doing thangs and I...I panicked. So what? You done with me now? Well, Daniel Jupiter Abercrombie has some rude boy pride in me!" She kissed me to shut me up. That got me going. I squeezed her soft thighs, moved my head into her titties and slid my hand under her top.

"Daniel, you were born in Tennessee. So don't give me that 'rude boy' stuff."

"Yes, ma'am," I said as I unbuttoned her top and put my mouth over a nipple.

"Do you know why—*oooh*, that feels good—why I got into law enforcement?" She had told me one time but I forgot so I just shut the fuck up and kept kissing and sucking. "I grew up knowing lots of good brothers get screwed by the law. *Sissss...mmm*! And when I made detective, baby—oh *damn*!—I really wanted to help brothers. So I'm your girl. Are you listening?" She stopped my kissing and held my chin.

"Yes, ma'am."

"You're 27 and I'm 31. You don't get to call me 'ma'am.' Dig?"

"I dig."

"I know you feel bad right now. That's why you kept it from me. But it's okay. I'm here for you. You're nobody's dummy. You read everything. You're curious. You got potential. And I want to love a man with potential. Will you let me do that?"

"So what you saying, Gina? You gonna loan me $2,000?"

"What? No! I'm not saying that at all!"

"So what's with the "Love and Happiness" stuff, Al Green?" She laughed and hair from her short cut moved over her eyes. She moved it away from her face and leaned over me again. I'm amazed we didn't break our ass in that rocking chair.

"I was thinking of another Al Green tune: 'Let's Stay Together.'"

It's only been three months. Live together? Ain't that shit too soon?

"What you thinking, Daniel? You think it's too soon, don't you?"

Bitch, get out of my head. There were so many positives. I could split rent, Gina would try to cook and the sex was great. A win/win right? But once you move in, you either gonna love the woman, or she gonna give you sore nuts. Just ask Carlos. But I wasn't gonna let that bullshit happen to me. So fuck it. I dove in head first.

"Let's do it," I said as I finished unbuttoning her top and slid it off. We kissed some more until we rocked out of the rocking chair and fell on the porch floor. I was flat on my back with Gina on top of me the same way she was in that dream I had of me drowning.

"Is this a dream?" I asked. She held my face and kissed me.

"Better not be," Gina said, smiling. "Because you're hard. And I'm wet."

That's my girl.

✳ ✳ ✳

"You ready for this?" Oscar asked as he placed my flatscreen T.V. by her stereo. He helped finish my move to Gina's since Josh bailed. "This is *you* we're talking about."

"I don't know. But it's a place to stay for now. Just don't tell the fellas, okay?"

"No sweat. I know how it is. You wanna keep stuff to yourself for a while."

We took a break and I poured two glasses of Hennessy and handed him one. He took a sip. *"That's* what I'm talking about. Hey, ever thought about going back to school?"

"Man, I ain't like college the first time. Why should I go try that shit again? But I got a question for you. If you were me, would you have moved in with Gina?"

"Nope, because I'd be *you*. She's a detective and you're a semi-reformed weed-head with a Ho-Trail of Tears up to your dick. And you can't throw piss out the window."

"I can't throw what?"

"Piss out the window. I heard Gent's mom say it once."

"Ha! That old lady is a trip." We got quiet, sipped our drinks and marinated on that shit for a second. I thought about Miss Hawkins and how the few times I was around her, I dug her. And then I thought about that night when we found her on the floor and how Gent worried about her. That shit would freak me out if that was my mom. Or Gina.

"So what does 'Can't throw piss out the window' mean any-way?"

"It means 'You ain't hitting on shit,' that's what it means."

"This is one fucked-up pep talk you giving right now, Oscar."

"Yeah, well listen, Young Buck. I got a few years on you. So let me tell ya what Gent told me a while ago: Quit worrying about what she doing and get *your* shit together. You know, in school, I was, like, a male feminist—always apologizing for being a man."

"You were an emotional tampon? A Captain Save-A-Ho?"

"Sigh. Anyway, my problem was that I focused too much on what women wanted and ignored *me*. Like when I listened to Ol' Girl and didn't try to get that Boston gig, that has messed me up to this day. You follow?"

"I think I do."

"Really? Okay. Tell me what I just meant."

"Okay, I lied. I wasn't really paying attention."

"Anus! Dude, can't you see? I'm playing catch-up, D. Who knows if I blew my one big chance in life trying to please a woman who didn't have my best interest in mind? All I'm saying is the only way to feel like a man is to be a man. Get a better job and make a better life for *yourself*. And when your act is together, it won't matter what Gina is doing because you can hold your own and not be a deadbeat."

"Yeah, I think I'm getting it. For real this time, I do."

"Good," Oscar said. "By the way, you've been missing out on some things, man. The BBR website has gotten thousands of hits since Carlos has been writing about John Rothman. Carlos is even looking to get us back in action in the field again."

"Cool. Shit 'bout time some BBR popped off. I hate I missed that press conference. But if Rothman wins his case, it's a whole new ballgame for the BBR ain't it?"

"Yeah," Oscar said. "You should meet him. He's a cool guy. And we're getting lots of donations and publicity because of him. We are a long way from Borders. You've seen that big Nazi BBR billboard with Carlos' face on it on Memorial?"

"I did!" I said. "I think that shit is tight to def. Made me wanna go march or some shit! This Rothman case is like, the fucking gift that keeps on giving."

"Well Rothman gets the big BBR picture," Oscar said as he put down his glass and turned to me. "We have to get the big picture too, D."

"What you mean?"

"I mean guys like you and me—we've got to forgive ourselves for our screw-ups. I talked to my dad last week and he said we have a God of second chances. He even reminded me of the old Sunday School lesson."

"Cool," I said. "Okay, so what was the Sunday School lesson?"

"We have a God of second chances. That *was* the lesson. Duh! And we have to look at the guy that made those mistakes and say we're not that guy anymore. The man who did that dumb stuff? Say goodbye to him."

Say goodbye? Shit. I hated looking at that guy in the mirror. When I thought about the shit I done—to hoes, to friends, to myself—I was shame as hell.

"Tell that dude goodbye, huh? Just like that?"

"Just like that," he said.

We downed our drinks and finished the move into Gina's. The whole talk made me think. I wasn't ready to say goodbye to that old guy. I mean, I wanted to, but there was something that had been nagging me for a long time. And while I rearranged the furniture with Gina that night, I think I was ready to make a change. And by bedtime, I was ready to give my new commitment a shot.

"Gina, what if I told you I wanted to play again?" I asked while we were in bed.

"Who ya playing for, babe?" she yawned as she turned into me.

"Well, I gotta get my ass back in shape, but I think I can make the Georgia Force. You know, Arena Football? What you think?"

Gina squirmed around a bit and mumbled some sleepy talk, then finally got herself together and laid her head on my chest.

"Sounds like—*yawn*—a lot of work. Been so long since you played, babe."

"About seven years."

"I hope this isn't something you think you got to do for me, Daniel. You don't have to play ball to feel useful. I mean, you fine and all, but you gonna take some hits, Boo."

"I plan to do the hitting, Gina. What? You doubting me?"

"A little. I should give you a tryout. Maybe you should show me what you got."

"Oh, I'm gonna show yo' ass, too," I said, rolling on top of her. She wrapped her arms around my back and opened her legs. I placed my hands on her thighs and slid inside her and we got down, real nice and slow. And on that night, in that apartment full of moving boxes, pizza boxes and half-rearranged furniture, I felt like a Super Bowl champ and not the chump I'd been most of my life.

※ ※ ※

The Monday after the Fourth of July, I was back on the grind. I spent more time in the gym, but other than Oscar, the fellas didn't know what I was up to. Hell, Carlos and Gent still didn't know that me and Gina lived together. But it was good that Oscar knew everything, because I think he could relate to me a little more than the other guys. Plus, I needed the workout partner.

"Joker, how is playing football a fresh start?" Oscar asked while standing over to spot me on the bench press. "Most people turn over new leafs by going to college or something. C'mon! Give me three more!" I counted the final presses and yelled in pain:

"ARRRRGGGGHHHHH!" I got that set of 15. But I still had three sets left. Shit.

"Good job, D. I got worried you were taking on too much."

"Shit, I probably am," I said, panting. "Gimmie a second— *gasp*—so, Oscar: you think this is this a waste of time?"

"Well, I already said that football at this stage is something you should let go. But then last week, I got a phone call. It was the editor of the *D.C. Herald*. They're flying me up to D.C. for an interview August 30."

"That's that shit there!" I said dapping him up. "You getting up outta here, huh?"

"I hope so. When I got that news, I thought about you. I know our situations are different but I know it's tough to give up what you do best. I sell insurance now, but I'm a writer. Maybe football is what you do best. It's a long shot, but you've been working hard. And if you had a trainer pushing you, maybe you could make the roster. So I found someone for you. Do you know who Ricky Harrison is? He's plays defensive back/wide receiver for the Force, and y'all were on the same roster at Chattanooga."

Oscar pulled out his cell and showed me a picture of a short, muscular dude with dreads. The hair was different and he didn't have the goatee in school, but, yeah, I remembered him, alright. Gay ass.

"Aw shit. That's gay-ass Ricky Harrison. How the hell did you find him, anyway?"

"It's called Google, man. I emailed the team's PR staff and they connected me to him. He's a trainer in the offseason and he's already *in*, D. I ain't saying sleep with the guy. Besides, if he is gay, he seems to be tamping it down pretty well. D, he can help you."

I stayed quiet and did a second set on the bench. I knew I had to swallow my pride and get help from that in-the-closet fruit Ricky. But I swear, that was all I'd swallow.

By time I got up with Ricky, it was August and I had him meet me at work. At first he wanted to come to the house, but I didn't want Gina to see me with him. I don't like strange people coming into our place. Especially Ricky's gay ass.

It was quitting time and I changed into my gym gear early— Ricky told me to be ready because we were gonna get a quick jog in before we started anything. So Ricky walked up to the security desk and—damnit—Vanessa was there.

"Hey, Daniel! I haven't seen you with the fellas lately. What's up? How's Gina?"

Vanessa meant well, but she swore she was part of the crew. But the BBR was dudes only. No girls allowed. Not even hot chicks like Vanessa. Besides, I was so nervous about being seen with Ricky I wanted to get the hell up out of there with the quickness.

"Hey, is that Daniel 'The Dan Train' Abercrombie?" Ricky said walking up the desk wearing tight-ass workout clothes. Shit. "I haven't seen you in a month of Sundays."

"Um, I gotta go, V," I said as I damn near ran to the exit to stop Ricky from getting deeper in the lobby. You'd do the same if you saw a mufucka wear that shit at your job.

"Good to see you, Rick. What the hell you wearing?" I asked as we left the building.

"My workout clothes. All the fellas on the Force got the same Under Armour gear. I even brought you some if you wanna change—"

"Nah, I'm good. All that tight shit on in public? Niggas'll think I'm fighting crime. You know you look like the twisted preacher at NewBirth."

"Ha! Boy, you still a trip!" he said as we got to the parking lot.

"Where's your car, Rick?" Then Ricky pushed the car alarm button on his keys. Would you believe that little nigga drove a fucking PT Cruiser? Oh hell no. "Are clowns and a ladder gonna come out this mufucka? I'm 6'5, 250! How am I gonna fit in this?"

"You're not," he said. "You're gonna run your big ass to the gym and I'm gonna follow you with my cautions on. Then we gonna work some more at the gym." Run? Oh, hell naw! It was hot as the Devil's balls outside and I ain't feel like running shit. Yeah, I *told* V I was gonna run, but that was to throw her off my scent.

"Man, fuck this," I said as I started walking back to the office. Then my cell rang.

"Yo?" I answered.

"Yo?" Gina said. "Who are you? Rocky? You punching sides of beef yet?"

"Not yet," I said looking back at Ricky, who sat on his car bumper.

"I don't want to interrupt. I just want to wish you well on your first day. I'm headed to Zumba. I'll have dinner ready when you get in, okay?" Lord, she was killing me.

"That sounds good."

"Love ya, babe. Bye."

"Love you, too."

I got off the phone, took a deep breath and slowly walked back toward Ricky.

"You might want to wear the 'superhero' gear I brought you." Ricky said with a smile. "It'll help with the heat."

That fucking gear didn't help at all. It was so hot and humid that it felt like I had steam in my lungs. And my damn dreads were lashing me all over my face and body. Let me tell you something: running sucks and I hadn't run like that in years.

And when I finally got to the gym, Ricky fucked me up. He ran me through a battery of bullshit—jumping jacks, bodyweight squats, squat thrusts. And dude had a drill for every fucking thing. Speed drills. Sprint drills. Mobility drills. And he gave me a taste of the strength drills with medicine balls and other shit I ain't ever used in a workout. And after all that, he wanted me to hit the weights. By time I got home, my whole body ached.

But when I did get home, however, I saw the pork chops, mashed potatoes and green beans on the stove. But where was Gina? After a small search, I found her in the bedroom, laid flat on the bed in her white Zumba gear. She was asleep with her iPod on and earphones in her ears. She was face up in a 'T' formation, with her arms stretched from her body and her legs straight and together. My sore ass kneeled down at her feet and lower legs, which hung off the edge of the bed. I laid my head on her lower body. And then:

"What the—?" she jumped up and got in whoop-ass mode.

"Gina! Gina! Calm down, baby. It's me!"

"Oh, Daniel! You scared me!" she said yawning while waking up. "You hungry?"

"I can eat. But I need a minute."

"Aw, my poor baby got hazed. Maybe it's payback for all those gay jokes."

"Hell, naw, Gina. No one on the team, said that shit to his face."

"Whatever. Daniel, you can't even keep stuff from the BBR."

"Yeah I can. Except Oscar, the fellas don't even know we live together." Oops.

"What?" she asked sitting up in the bed. "Why don't they know about us, Daniel?"

"Baby, it's not like that."

"Then what is it like?"

"Nothing. It's like nothing, Gina. Don't worry about it." I sat up on the bed and my muscles felt like someone beat them with a hammer. I was too sore and too tired to explain shit. I just wanted to lay there with my back to the headboard and drift to sleep.

"Wake up, Daniel and talk to me." Fuck!

"Why? You just gonna jump me anyway. I mean, can't you see I'm tired as hell!"

"Why haven't you told anybody about—"

"Because I'm afraid I ain't gonna make it, that's why." Didn't seem like she expected that answer. She calmed down and sat beside me.

"You talking about football or you talking about us?" I looked away. "Talk to me."

"Gina…what if I'm gonna always be a fuck up? I just don't know sometimes."

"Baby you're not a—"

"I almost quit today. I just started this shit and I almost quit. Maybe all of this is a bad idea. You know, sometimes I don't wanna deal. Sometimes I don't want to be responsible to nobody. Not even you, Gina. I wanted to quit today and go back to being me. Without all these expectations and shit."

She got quiet. I guess she tried to figure out how to respond to the shit I laid on her.

"Yeah," she said quietly. "It sounds like you got a lot on your mind and things are moving too fast for you. I'm sorry to put this on you."

"It's okay, Gina." We both laid there on the bed and stared off. I didn't like the feeling I gave her then. But I was being honest and just getting some stuff off my chest. She may not have wanted to hear it, but at least I told her. That's better than what I usually do. I usually don't tell women shit.

"So why didn't you?" she asked

"Why didn't I what?"

"You said you wanted to quit. So…why didn't you quit.

"Gina, are you cross-courting me?"

"Cross-*examining*, man. And here's what I think: I think you don't want to admit that you've started something that you don't know how to finish."

"Yeah the hell I do. I can tell Ricky to go to hell and—"

"I'm talking about us, this time, Daniel. Not football."

"Oh." Gina moved closer and rubbed my shoulders.

"You don't wanna quit. You just don't know how to keep going, do you?"

"No. I don't."

"Let's talk about this later. Right now, I'm hungry and I'm curious to see how much salt the food needs. I'm still kinda new at this cooking thing." She kissed me on the cheek, took my hand, led me to the kitchen table and we had dinner.

It was then I knew what I had. It was then I knew I really loved Gina.

After dinner, I laid in the hottest bath possible. As I soaked, I got a text from Oscar:

"Hallelujah! They offered me the job today! I'm movin' to dc! BBR gotta celebrate! Oh, last night shot pool and lied to Los bout not knowin' what was up with you. I h8 lying. C'mon man. We fam. Talk 2 ur boys!"

I hate dudes who use numbers in texts like they Prince. Then Oscar sent this one:

"Los n jordan gonna move out of gents and back into twn-home. Los said he'd throw me a going away party. You gotta come. hope ricky aint kickin yo ass yet. HA!"

"Gina!" I yelled from the tub. "Oscar got the job! He's goin' to D.C.!"

"Really?" she said talking before she walked in. "Damn!"

"What's wrong?"

"Nothing. Just checking out your big, sexy black ass in that tub!"

"I know that look, Gina. Daddy can't rock you tonight. I'm too sore."

"No. What I'm thinking is that's *you're thinking* that you can't do nothing. I'm thinking that maybe I can slide in that tub witcha..."

"Gina, don't play. I'm sore for real."

"...And take the booty from you! *Mmm hmm!*" She slowly walked closer to the tub.

"Careful, Gina. I'm serious. The water is—"

"Shush! I don't bite!" She got on her knees, slapped her hands on my chest and slid it down to grab my dick. But when that hand hit the water—

"OHHHHHH! Shit! My God, that water is hot! How can you stand it?"

"It has to be real hot if I'm gonna heal, sugar."

"Well, fine then. I'll leave you in your hot-ass water. You'll probably be negro stew in a few minutes. But I know where you sleep, Abercrombie. And know this: I'm taking that booty!" She twisted her ass out the bathroom. I couldn't stop smiling.

When Gina left, I thought about Oscar. That man's been through a lot and I could tell how happy he was. He was gonna get back to being himself. Good for him. That shit—well—I guess it encouraged me. Oscar's job and Gina's ass. Maybe not in that order, but they were both on my mind. I dried my hands, grabbed the phone and texted Ricky:

"I'm sore now, little Nigga. But I'll see yo ass, Thurs."

Mufucka.

✳ ✳ ✳

"You don't need me anymore," Ricky said after a workout in late September. "If tryouts were today, you'd make the squad, Dan Train."

"What?" I asked. I didn't think I heard him correctly.

"Yep," Ricky said. "I'd bet my life that right now, you can get a roster spot on Force. When camp starts next March, you should show up."

Oh, hell yeah!

That night, I got a bottle of champagne and a big box of Popeye's Chicken, and beat Gina home by about two hours. I couldn't wait for her to get home. Then I heard a key click in the door. And as soon as she walked in I handed her a glass of champagne.

"Guess what, baby!" I said raising my glass for a toast. But she had a worried look on her face and gave me back her glass.

"I can't drink this. And we need to clean up around here. And when was the last time you went to church? I used to go back in—"

"Gina! Fruit Booty thinks I can make the Force! Ain't that great?"

"Well, I guess so," she said taking my hand and leading me to the sofa like she did when she asked me to move in with her. Uh oh.

"Baby, what's wrong? This is the news we been waiting for! Drink up!"

"Well...I guess it means more money, right. That's a good thing."

"Hey, don't give me flack. I pay my share around here!"

She grabbed my chin and turned my face toward hers. "Get the clues, Daniel."

"Clues?"

"Yes, man. The clues. I turned down champagne. I tell you we need to clean up our act, go to church and I mention more money." She took my hand and put it on her belly.

"It's your turn to play 'Guess what?' now," she said smiling.

So I thought about it. And then I looked at her.

Oh shit.

I was speechless with my mouth open.

"Yes, Daniel. I'm pregnant."

"G-G-Gina! Are you serious? Oh my God! A baby? You? Me?"

"Us?" she asked then anxiously biting her lip.

"Of course, us, Gina!" I said as I hugged her.

"I want to be sure you're okay with this. I mean, I still have school and you have football now and...well...I know we have options if you—"

"Uh-uh, Gina. Not a chance. No kid of mine is an option. Oh my God. Wow!"

As we sat on the sofa rocking back and forth in each other's arms, I thought about me being someone's dad. Years ago I woulda hauled ass outta there. Hell, months ago I probably wouldn't have been shit like my old man. And I didn't feel I was shit then and deep down I thought I didn't deserve shit. But for some reason I got it. And I was happy.

❋ ❋ ❋

It was September when the bottom fell out and everything turned bad in a hurry. Meanwhile I kept a busy schedule. I was worked out two times a day: once during lunch and then after work. And on some nights, I pulled double shifts. With Gina pregnant, I knew we'd need every nickel, especially after the stock market crashed. Them white boys fucked up shit so bad, it looked like America was actually considering electing a black president. So you know the shit must've been really bad.

The BBR was doing okay. But since I started training and Gina got pregnant, I didn't have time to do much with them. But Oscar kept me posted on their activity though.

Wednesdays were my rest days so my body could heal from the two-a-day workouts. So on my day off, I had a date with the couch. So I grabbed the last of my real beers in the fridge, laid up on the sofa and waited for Gina to get in. And then I got the call.

"What's up, Rick?"

"Turn it on channel 2. Quick."

I changed the channel and caught the back end of a story on the sorry-ass Hawks. I've hated them ever since they traded Dominique for old, biscuit-jaw Danny Manning.

"Ricky what's this about? I hate them punk ass Haw—"

"Shh! Look. There it is!" I turned up the volume to listen:

"...Arena Football League owners have decided to cancel the 2009 season. The decision means that all league personnel, including all players, coaches and staff will be out of work for the time being. Reporting live, I'm Scott Hartman. Channel 2 News."

"What? Ricky, how am I supposed to play for a team that ain't playing no games?"

"You're not, Daniel. None of us are. Maybe I can get picked up by a Canadian team. Maybe my boy in Edmonton can hook me up."

"Ricky, you ain't hearin' me. There gotta be something else. A whole league just can't shut down! They been around, what? Ten? Fifteen years? You don't fold up 'cause some white boys fucked up stocks and houses and shit! There's gotta be—"

I then heard a door close behind me. It was Gina and she had heard everything.

"Fuck this," I said hanging up the phone and she extended her arms to me. I ran to her and we held each other.

"I'm sorry, baby," she said. "It's gonna be okay. I know how much you wanted this."

"I'm trying, Gina. But I don't know what else I'm going to do. And every time...it just seems like I get so close and then...damn it! My life is a big tease."

"Hey," she said. "I'm not a tease. I'm here for you." She put my hand on her belly. "We are here for you. As long as we stick together we will be fine."

I used to think that football was the only thing I loved in my life. But with Gina and the baby on the way, I knew I was wrong.

That's when I got Oscar's message. I had to start fresh. Let my fuckups stay in the past. Yeah, the old Daniel didn't deserve Gina or a son or daughter. But the night I lost football was the same night I said hello to my new life and when I finally said goodbye, once and for all, to the old me.

Chapter 17: Lola the Wonderful?

(Brother Carlos)

"How's it going, Carlos?" It was John Rothman on my cell. I was upstairs in my room at Gent's as I loosened my tie to settle in from a long day at the office.

"John! My man!" I put him on speaker to change out of my work clothes. "Let me give you an update on stuff. The Going Dutch Day in New Orleans got more buzz than we expected. The BBR is trending well on Twitter. E-signatures have picked up and proceeds from T-shirt sales have raised about $12,000. And get this: I'm trying to arrange some sit-ins at clubs on Ladies Nights across the country. I got the idea from—"

"She wants me back, Carlos," John said, cutting me off. When he said that, it wiped the smile right off my face and made me take him off speaker and pick up the phone. I thought I heard him wrong, because my cell gets spotty reception in Gent's house.

"What was that?" I asked, hoping I heard him wrong.

"Laura got laid off earlier this week. We talked and—we might give it a go again."

"John, you got to be kidding," I said. "Why? When we first spoke back in July, you said yourself that she'd pull something like this and you told me if that happened to talk you out of it. Well, that time is now. She stole from you, John. She probably thinks you have money because of your higher profile."

"Carlos?"

"Or, maybe she just wants to get you to drop the suit against her."

"Carlos?"

"I mean, c'mon, John. Everybody knows that you can't trust Lola!" Shit.

"Lola? Her name is *Laura*, Carlos. Don't make this about you."

"Right," I said, settling down. "You're right. So, I guess you're dropping the suit."

"I hadn't made up my mind yet. I'm still out of work and I don't know her angle yet. But after all those years, I have to see. C'mon, dude, admit it: wouldn't you like the chance to reconcile with Lola?"

"I dunno," I said like a dejected little kid. "Maybe."

"Give me a week or two, okay? I'll let you know what I do for sure."

"Thanks, John, I appreciate it."

"I want you to know that no matter what I decide, you're a real mensch, Carlos."

"Oy," I said sarcastically. I felt so defeated after that call. Losing Rothman meant losing the attention-grabber of the BBR. That was one thing. But the other thing was that he was right about Lola. If I had my way, I would make it work with her. So in that respect, I was oddly jealous of John. Puzzled by this weird mix of feelings, I walked downstairs to the living room where Gent was watching TV.

"I just spoke to Rothman," I said. "He's thinking of dropping the suit."

"What?" Gent said as he muted the T.V. "Why?"

"He said his ex-fiancée lost her job and came back to him crying."

"And now she wants to work things out," Gent said. "That'd mess up the BBR!"

"To say the least," I said with a slight pout. "My columns, the T-shirt sales, the petitions—we need the national attention his lawsuit provides so we can take advantage of LeVander's connections with Oprah's producer. Damn it, Laura!"

"What kind of work did Laura do?"

"She was an analyst or something at AIG," I mumbled.

"AIG? Well, anybody who worked at that place was a pink slip waiting to happen. But then again, lots of folks are gonna lose their jobs, Los. Coming into the year, our biggest clients were Bear Stearns and Lehman, right? Bear Stearns, where your boy Rothman worked, tanked in April, and Lehman could go any day now. And once Lehman's gone, let's just say it'll be raining people from Wall Street skyscrapers."

"What are you talking about, Gent?"

"I'm lead on one of Lehman's accounts, right? So my boss tells me that Lehman overleveraged and their mortgage-backed securities are junk. He tells me this because once Lehman goes belly up, folks will get canned here at Atlanta office. Including me."

"You're gonna lose your job? No way! Lehman's just one company...right?"

"No." He sipped his soda and shook his head. "It's the whole system, Los."

"The whole system? It can't be *that* bad...can it?" Then the doorbell rang.

"No," he said as he got up to answer the door. "It's way worse."

"I got the job!" Oscar yelled as he charged through the door and broke our conversation. Then the fool popped a Champagne bottle and drank from it. "I start in October. So...I'M GOING TO D.C.!" We cheered as Gent grabbed the bottle and poured some champagne over Oscar's head like he won the NBA Finals.

"What's this fuss?" Miss Mattie said as she walked in from the kitchen. Giggling, Jordan followed with a jar of Vaseline in her little brown hands. Half of her hair was braided, while the other half looked like she stuck her finger in a socket.

"Hey, Unka Ok-ska!" Jordan said with a smile.

"Oh, I see someone's missing a tooth!" Oscar said as he kissed Jordan on the cheek.

"Hey, Ma!" Gent said to Miss Mattie. "Oscar got a new job in D.C.!"

"I brought food to celebrate, Ma'am. Ever had Pappadeaux? It's some good seafood."

"Oh, well that sounds good to me!" she said as she took the bags of food. "That nappy-headed boy coming over, too?"

"You mean Daniel?" Oscar said. "He told me he's working a late shift."

"Well. I'll set the table. Genthaniel was 'sposed to help fry this chicken but his black ass was on the phone. So I started braiding Jo Jo's hair."

"Tee hee! Black...*ass!*" Jordan said as she followed Miss Mattie into the kitchen.

"Jordan!" I yelled as she ran off. "You don't say that word, Little Girl!"

"Mmmm *mmt!*" Miss Mattie said as her voice faded as she made it to the kitchen. "You a mess, Jo Jo! Ya'll boys come on and eat!"

"We'll be there in just a second!" Gent said. He stopped us before we walked into the kitchen. "Don't mention what I told you earlier," he whispered.

"What? You ain't told her you selling her house? It's going on three months!"

"No, not that, Oscar, and hush!" Gent said to him.

"Is it about Los and Jordan moving?" Oscar whispered. I wanted to kick his ass when he said that. Being that it was the first he heard of this, Gent gave me a puzzled look.

"Oh my bad, Gent," I said looking at Oscar like the clown he was. "I forgot to tell you: Lola's moving out on Labor Day and Jordan and I are moving back into the condo. I hadn't told Jordan because I want it to be a surprise."

"Genthaniel? The food gettin' cold!"

"We're coming, Ma!" Gent called out. "Damn, Los. I actually hoped y'all would stay a bit and help me with the mortgage since I'm losing my job."

"Wait—you're losing your job?" Oscar asked.

"Yes, man," I said. "That's what Gent wants us to be quiet about."

"That and the economic world is about to come to an end," Gent said.

"Y'all going too fast," Oscar said, trying to keep up. "So Gent, you've been hush about losing your job, selling your mama's house and the end of the world—whatever that's about. And Los, you're gonna move your baby mama out, move you and your daughter in, and you haven't told the girl her mama won't be there. Y'all niggas got a lot of shit going on!"

"Oscar, I told you about using the n-word up in here."

"Y'all niggas come eat!" Miss Mattie yelled to us. Oscar laughed.

"That's not funny, Oscar!" Gent chided.

"Tee hee! Come eat…nickels!" Jordan piped in.

"You better get your daughter," Gent said laughing, poking Oscar in the side.

"You better get your mother," I snapped back.

"Man, *you* get my mother."

"Oh, Los, I meant to tell you: I gotta stop my BBR activity since I got my job. My new bosses think it could make people not take me seriously. I'm sorry, man."

"I understand, man," I said. "But I'm not going to lie: the BBR is getting its asswhooped tonight. You quit and John Rothman is probably dropping his suit."

"What?" Oscar asked. "Why?"

"His girl came back," Gent said. "Why else would that happen?"

"Well, at least I got Gent and—if he ever hangs out anymore—Daniel," I said. "You do D.C., man. Hopefully, LeVander can work some *Oprah* magic. But we'll manage."

"Actually, Los, I'll be spending a lot of time looking for work and tending to Mama," Gent said. "I have no idea what the job market will be like when this shit hits the fan."

"Well, hell," I said, disgusted. And like that, I was out of foot soldiers. My friends.

"C'mon, man," Oscar said. He then held up his balled fist. "Broke power, right?"

"Broke power," Gent and I said. It was the first time the cry felt empty to me.

We then joined Miss Mattie and Jordan in the kitchen and sat down at the table. Then I went over and pinched Jordan on the arm and pulled a coin out my pocket.

"Ow! That hurts, Daddy!"

"*This* is a nickel. But you weren't trying to say 'nickel' were you?"

"No, sir."

"I figured. Look: you're gonna start talking like five year-olds talk, understand?"

"Yes, sir."

"I don't want her cussing, Miss Mattie," I said sternly to her. Gent and Oscar grinned.

"I'll do better, Carlos. I'm sorry," she said. "Let's bless this food and eat: Lord God, we come here to celebrate your blessing a good man. We understand that we may not know why, Lord God, but you giveth and taketh away. Gent learned that with his job..."

Huh? How did Miss Mattie know about Gent's job? "... so thank ya for this food we 'bout to receive. Nurse our bodies for Christ's sake. Amen."

Miss Mattie gave Gent a disappointed look as the two sat across from each other at the table. What was up with that? Had she overheard us? What else did she know?

"I thought she didn't know about the job," Oscar whispered to me.

"She didn't," I whispered. "Maybe, the old lady has good ears."

"Who you calling old, Carlos?" Uh oh.

"Let's eat, Daddy!" Jordan said, as the cute little squeak in her voice cut through the tension. Miss Mattie plopped shrimp and potato salad on a plate for her.

"Put a few green beans on that plate for her, too please, Miss Mattie," I said.

"You got it. So, Mr. Oscar, how your folks feel about you leaving?"

"Well, ma'am, they knew I'd take the job if I got the offer, so they're okay."

"Oh that's good," she said. "Hand me your plate, Los. Is it good, Jo Jo?" Jordan nodded then sipped her Kool-Aid. Miss Mattie kept loading up plates with food as we passed them around the table. "Well, you found a place to stay yet, Oscar? 'Cause if ya ain't, I hear my house is for sale, ain't that right, Gent?"

Holy shit. She knew! Oscar coughed and I winced as we both looked at each other and then at Gent. Meanwhile, Miss Mattie stopped fixing plates and looked dead at him, too. I wasn't even her son and I was scared. But to his credit, Gent didn't flinch.

"I guess if you lose your job, you could use the money from the house. That money could tie us—well, *you*—over for a while."

"That's not what I was thinking, Mama" Gent said.

"So how much is me and your daddy's life worth to ya' anyway?"

"It's not like that, Mattie. I just thought—"

"Boy, I done told you 'bout that 'Mattie' shit!" she said angrily with tears in her eyes as she pounded her fist on the table.

"Mama, I-I-I just thought—"

"It's alright, son. You got to do what you got to do, huh? I may not be around long no way, right? I'm sorry y'all. I done lost my appetite." She threw her napkin on the table. "Congratulations Oscar. Jo Jo? Come upstairs when you done and I'll finish yo' hair."

"Okay, Mith Mattie," Jordan said. She then—and this was cute and sad at the same time—*wagged her finger* at Miss Mattie. "Stop all dat crying and futhing, okay?" Miss Mattie smiled and went upstairs. We then turned to Gent, who held his head in his hands.

"Crap!" he said.

"Kwap!" Jordan mimicked with her hair flopping about comically.

❋ ❋ ❋

Lola had shit everywhere in the living room.

I had time to move her out but I didn't have time to help her pack. I had a date with Vanessa's girlfriend later for drinks, and although I hated blind dates, I agreed to it because I had nothing else going on. At any rate, I was on the clock. So I grabbed my tools and began to unscrew the wall mounts on the grandfather clock. As I worked, I felt Lola's wolf-gray eyes trained on me.

"Where you got to go, Carlos?" she asked out the blue. "It's Labor Day. I know you're not bringing any nasty-ass skanks around my daughter are you?"

"Oh, five months later and *now* you remember you got a daughter? Save it, Lola. I'm glad you're enjoying your freedom, but excuse me for not taking your shit right now. When I'm done with this clock, I'm getting the hell up out of here." That shut her up.

I finally unhinged the clock, moved it from the wall and laid it on the floor. That's when I headed for the door. But then Lola got in my way and had a soft look on her face.

"I finally read it," she said to me. "The story you won the award for? For *Essence*? You really felt that unappreciated the whole time we were together?"

Why she bring that up? She really caught me off guard with that shit.

"I didn't know how to tell you," I said. "I felt like you wanted me to take care of it all. As if I had all the answers. You compounded this by not being a help to me."

"Really?"

"Yeah, really. We've been together, what? Five, six years? All that time and you still didn't get me." And that's where I messed up. Couples get themselves in trouble when they start thinking of all the time they spent together. Human nature won't let you throw those years away and start fresh. Human nature wants you to try to salvage them. Even if salvage is an unwise strategy.

"I'm sorry, Carlos," Lola said as she sat on the base of the staircase. "I never thought we'd be this way. I just think it all moved too fast for me. I love Jordan. It's just that—um—I'm 27, Los. I didn't want to be a mother so soon. I'm sorry."

"And then she said, 'I'm sorry I was a bitch to you,'" I told Vanessa as I signaled the bartender to get us two more beers. "She started crying, V. Can you believe that?"

"Oh, please," Vanessa said sipping her beer. "The bitch was faking, right?"

It was a later than the usual happy hour at Archie's as Vanessa and I had to work late. Why? Because a week after Labor Day, Lehman Brothers went belly up and the stock market crashed. So on Black Tuesday I had to scrap my BBR piece because the world's economy was on the brink of collapse. As a finance writer, Vanessa had tons of copy due, too. So we didn't leave the office until 10 p.m. It was our toughest news day since 9/11.

Unfortunately for Gent, he was right about everything. His firm, as he predicted, gave him the axe. The bright side—for me, at least—was that he could pick up Jordan from school because she felt sick. Ironically, he was already out with Miss Mattie for what she unilaterally called her final doctor's visit. Gent wasn't so sure. Either way, I made them promise to keep their drama to a minimum since Jordan was with them.

"She probably was faking," I said as I looked up at the TV screen above the bar. "Can you believe the Dow lost, like, eleventy billion points today because of one company?"

"Yeah," Vanessa said. "But anyway, you missed your date with Stacy for Lola? You didn't miss anything. If she weren't my soror, I wouldn't hang with her bourgie ass."

"If she's bourgie, why you try to push her off on me?"

"She needed a date and she's kinda a ho. So I figured you could use the quick fix."

I looked at her and she sipped her beer and smiled. I'll be honest about this: I've always dug Vanessa, and not just as a friend, either. But I never made a move because all the time I knew Vanessa, I was dedicated to Lola.

"Everyone can use a quick fix," I said and I turned up my beer. "And just because I didn't see Stacy doesn't mean I got that fix with Lola, if that's what you're getting at."

"Uh huh," she said with narrowed eyes. She didn't believe me and was sniffing me out. "So what did happen, Carlos? I feel there are gaps in your story."

"Well, we did get worked up. Lola helped me take off my shirt. I really didn't want to because I had put on some weight since we had broken up. She straddled me on top of the stairs. But before we got to into it, I remember that I didn't have any condoms."

"What? You mean to tell me that you, a man..."

"Yes, V!" I said rolling my eyes.

"...Didn't have any condoms. And Lola, also a man..."

"Very funny."

"...Had no condoms!" Vanessa chuckled. "I guess it has been a while for you."

"Yeah, I guess so." I sipped my beer then turned to her. "When was your last time?"

"I ain't telling you that. You'll never look at me the same."

"Bullshit, V. Anyway, I'm tired of talking. The point is that Lola and I are cool."

"Y'all cool? This story doesn't make sense, Carlos." Vanessa said while looking at the T.V. monitors. Then the bartender came with the check.

"I got this one, okay?" she said as she tapped my hand.

"You don't have to do that, V. I can get it."

"No, Los. It's been a rough day and I'm buying. 'Broke Power,' right? You're a good man, Carlos. Jordan knows it and I know it. Who cares what Lola doesn't know?"

"Thanks, V."

We got quiet as we both looked at Suze Orman on *Larry King Live* talking about the economic crisis. We stopped talking to read the closed captions:

"This situation is only going to get worse before it gets better. If you are planning your retirement don't look to the markets. This economy has taken a turn. There is so much uncertainty, I'm afraid that this is the new normal. It can only get worse."

"Damn! Suze just said 'The world is coming to an end,'" I said. "This shit is scary."

"All of a sudden, too," Vanessa said. "The BBR may have more members because the country is officially broke."

"You think any of this will affect us at the *AJC*?"

"It shouldn't. But you never know," she said, finishing her drink. "Let's go, Los."

"Wait. I need to use the restroom," I said as I put my blazer over the back of the stool. "I'll be right back." As I walked away she called out to me.

"By the way," she started with a smile. "It was Williams!"

"What was Williams?"

"Williams? The jackass we work with? He's the guy that I last—*you know*. But seriously, it meant nothing. But I thought I'd share. You may pee now."

That made me walk into the restroom blushing.

"Williams?" I said to myself. "No wonder he always butted in on us at work."

I washed my hands and looked in the mirror. I had a huge grin from ear to ear as I replayed my scenes with Vanessa. Since my time away from Lola, I couldn't deny the closeness with her. And that's why I started to feel low. Why? Because I lied to her.

Lola and I *did* sleep together that Labor Day. Twice.

I splashed some water on my face and headed back to the bar. But when I returned, V had a drink waiting for me.

"You got another story to tell, Los," she said, nudging the drink toward me. She then placed a ring box on the bar and opened it to reveal a simple, elegant diamond ring. "Your blazer fell off the stool when you got up, and this fell out your coat pocket."

"It was my Mom's," I said. "I took it to a jeweler to get it cleaned." She didn't buy it.

"Who were you going to ask to marry you?" she asked in a suspicious tone. I took a sip of my whiskey and got my thoughts together. I was out of hiding places.

"V, um, remember when I told you that Lola and I got worked up on the stairs, but we didn't do anything? Well, that's not true."

"I thought you said you stopped because you had no condoms."

"I didn't have any condoms."

"But you guys did it anyway?" I turned up my drink. I knew she got me.

"One more?" I motioned to the bartender. Out the corner of my eye, I saw her shake her head in disgust. The guy brought me a Jameson neat and I quickly took a sip to let its smooth heat numb me. I wasn't a big whiskey guy, but it tasted like a confessor's drink.

"No condom, then," she said still shaking her head. "Alright. Well—did you come?"

"Unfortunately, like a geyser."

When I said that, Vanessa pounded her fists on my arms and chest. She was pissed.

"Stupid! Stupid, stupid, stupid, *stupid*!" Something told me that she thought I was stupid. "You stupid man! What is wrong with you! You can't trust her and you know that! What if she gets pregnant? What if she has some disease? You think she had you by the balls last time, well she *really* got them bad boys now!" She called the bartender. "I'll have what he's having." she said, clearly disgusted at me. "And he's buying this time."

She tried to get playful with me as she stuck her tongue out and gave me a comforting squeeze of the hand. But despite all that, she was really pissed at me.

"How about this: I'll be quiet. You talk. Then I'll kick your ass after the story. Deal?"

"Deal."

So I told her how it all went down and Vanessa frowned as I revealed everything. Not all the gnarly details, but enough for her to get the picture.

"I still had a few hours before it was time to meet your girl at the W. So I helped Lola break down furniture and did all the hard stuff for her. But it's time to go and Lola starts hugging and kissing me. And when she did that, it all felt so familiar, V. Like everything I prayed for was coming true." Vanessa gnashed her teeth.

"I'm sorry. I hate to interrupt but what exactly have you been praying for?"

"For my family to come together, V. I prayed that Jordan, Lola and I would be under one roof. That's something God owed me. I hardly knew my Mom because she died when I was real young. My dad was a good man, but he worked so hard that I hung out with my aunts, uncles and grandparents more than I saw him."

"I see. Okay. Go on."

"So we kissed and said goodnight and everything, and I raced back to Gent's to get ready to meet your girl. Anyway, I hopped in the car and headed to the W. But then I just turned the car around and raced to Gent's."

"Why Gent's place? I thought you were headed back to Lola?"

"The ring, Vanessa. I couldn't see Lola without the ring. So I've psyched myself up to spring the ring on her, thinking that we finally had a breakthrough and then I get back to the condo and I see another car in the driveway. And when I walk to the door, I hear something—a sound coming from inside the house. And it wasn't music."

"Oh no," Vanessa said. "Don't tell me she had a guy in there and they were—"

"Fucking," I said with venom "I remembered I removed the drapes from the glass sliding door to the back patio. So I went around back and I saw her on all fours taking it doggystyle on the carpet. On my goddamn carpet, V! They didn't see me, but I was so mad, I nearly went back to Gent's to get Miss Mattie's gun and shoot everybody."

"Betsy? That sorry Barney Fife pistol she got? That thing ain't gonna do nothin', Los. Squeeze that trigger and a rolled up flag with BANG on it would pop out the barrel."

"I didn't care, V. I wanted to act out and do something. I was pissed. Hurt. Embarrassed. I still have a key, you know. I coulda charged in and got rough in there."

"Jesus, Carlos. That would have been a mess. What stopped you?"

"I thought about Jordan. And 15 to 20 years in prison for a no good heffa."

Vanessa didn't say anything. She sensed that I just needed to vent and let my angry words breathe. So we sat quietly for a moment and looked at the T.V.s above the bar.

"You know, I know you have this hope of having this nuclear family under one roof and picket fences and all of that with Lola, but I gotta tell you what you surely must know after seeing her on all fours for another man: Maybe it's time to find a new dream."

I nodded my head at her point as she grabbed my hand. It was a tender, quiet, bittersweet moment. And I don't know if I was just emotionally raw or if I was on some sort of rebound or what, but I couldn't help but think that Vanessa was the woman I wanted, needed and should have been with all along.

Then my phone rang and it broke our mood.

"Hello?"

"Fuck her, Carlos!" It was Rothman and he was one pissed white boy. "Fuck Laura, man! The bitch ain't shit. You were so right. You were right about everything!"

"Right about what?" I lip synced "Rothman" to let Vanessa know who I spoke to.

"She didn't want to work anything out," he said. "She just wanted to cozy up to me so I could drop the suit. Well, fuck her. I'm going to the courthouse tomorrow to re-file."

"*Re*-file? Why re-file?"

"I pulled the suit last week. Because I did that, my case goes to the back of the line. So instead of this year, it may be early next year before it goes to court. But I don't care. This bitch has to pay. Fuck her, Carlos! Fuck her, fuck her, FUCK HER! I'm all in, now man. I got no job. I got no woman. I got no money because the bitch stole it from me. So fuck it. I'm down for whatever. Let's fucking march, man. Sit-ins, boycott *Cosmopolitan* or some shit. Let's get your man, Evander Holyfield on this motherfucker"

"His name is LeVander, not Evander Holyfield," I said laughing.

"LeVander, Evander, whatever the fuck his name is. Let's do this, shit! Now, I gotta go because my boys are here and they're gonna get me shitfaced. Broke power, Carlos!"

"Broke power, John!" I shouted back as we ended the call.

"What the hell was that all about?" Vanessa asked laughing.

"That was Rothman, V. He's back. He's back and so is the BBR."

"You happy now?" she asked.

"Not quite. I'd be happier if he made that phone call last week before I fell back in to the Lola trap. I think when he said he was getting back with his girl, it made me consider getting back with Lola."

"Well, obviously that was a bad move."

"Yeah."

We sat quiet again and finished the last of our drinks.

"God, please don't let that bitch be pregnant," I said.

Chapter 18: Jordan and Uncle Gent Take Over the World

(Brother Gent)

"I'm ready, Gent," Mama said walking down the stairs with her purse in one hand and her short cut wig in the other. She stopped at the mirror near the doorway and placed her hair on top of her head. Since the chemo, her hair was falling out and I had shaved the last of it off with my clippers. Damnedest thing I ever did, giving her that cut.

"You okay, Mama?" I asked her as she adjusted the wig.

"Let's just go, son."

"Okay."

As we headed to Dr. Avery's office, I tried to play out whatever she'd say in my mind. And Mama didn't want to let on, but I could tell she was scared, too.

"I was thinking we could get some breakfast. You up for a few Krystal sunrisers?"

"Who the hell told you to sell my house, Gent?"

Oh yeah. I forgot she hadn't chewed me out yet.

"Mama, I just thought—"

"No, you *didn't* think! It's my damn house! You may control it, but I live in it. That house is everything me and your daddy worked for. And your brother's down there!"

"But Mama, Pop's gone and Nate got years to go. We need to sell and start fresh."

"Start fresh? I can't leave home and make like I got a new life like you did. The life I have is the life I got. And that's in Mississippi. Now you gonna pull that sign up, Gent."

"I can't do that, Mama."

"Yes, you can, Gent. You can't just sell my home."

I pulled in the Krystal drive-thru and ordered. Everything I said made stuff worse, so I shut up and handed her the food. She put the coffee in the cup holder and the bag of little square sandwiches in her lap. I glanced at her in the passenger seat and saw she had her hand over her forehead. And I didn't see them, but I heard them. Tears. Very. Quiet. Tears. I pulled over and parked the car in the Krystal's lot.

"Why you stopping, Gent? We gotta go see the doctor."

"We'll get there. You're scared, ain't you?"

"Aw, shit, son," she said with her hand still covering her face. "Why you asking me this now? Eat your food and let's go."

"Mama, you don't fool me. I know you're worried. But I brought you here because I wanted to look after you while you were sick."

"Lord, Gent," she said with a faint sniffle. "Not now."

"But no matter what Dr. Avery says, I ain't giving up. And I'm selling the house because I want you here in Atlanta with me. Your home is with me now."

"My home is in Mississippi in me and your daddy's house. My home is back—"

"With Nate, huh?"

"Well, I don't want him to think that I'm leaving him."

"But what about me, Mama?"

"Well you got some money, Gent. Look like you doin' alright, ain'tcha?

"Ma, I lost my job. And Nate's gone. He ain't *him* anymore. The prison got him. Nate made his choice, and I'm done blaming me for Nate. And you're done blaming me, too. Let him go. Nate don't want anyone to have nothing. And he don't want you close to me, either. He's trying to pit us against each other, Mama, and he won't be happy 'til–OW! Why you pinch me?"

"Because this ain't the time for this! Your brother is doing time for—"

"For something *he* did, Mama. Do you understand that?"

"I know that, boy! Shit! You think your mama's stupid!"

"No. But quit acting like Nate's mess is *your* fault, then!" My voice got a bit loud in the car. "I'm sorry."

"I wish your daddy was here," she sobbed.

"I know, Ma. But it's just me and you now. We're the only ones left. As much as I miss him, Daddy's gone. And Nate's not right while he's in that place. It's just us now."

Mama sniffled. "Well, it ain't my fault that we ain't that close, Gent. I couldn't up and leave like you did."

And then a light bulb went on in my head. Mama didn't blame me for Nate. No, she was just pissed that I left home. I reckoned she had a point. The year after Nate went away, Pop died. And just a few months later, I left for college. I could've gone to school closer to home. I could've visited more. But I didn't. I got ghost. And the closest person for Mama was Nate. With Pop dead and Nate gone, I was the man of the house. But I didn't want to be and I didn't act like it. I had blown it.

"I could have stayed closer and I didn't. I ran away. I'm sorry, Mama."

"I hated that you left, son. I love Nate, but I needed you home."

Then, in that very casual and unconscious way of hers, Mama broke the ice. She grabbed one of the little square Krystal sunrisers and started to munch.

"Mmt!" she grunted as she munched. The little lady got hungry and her eating made me smile. No matter what Dr. Avery had to say, I knew Ma and I were cool again. *Thank you, Jesus.* I'd been carrying that mess—that guilt—for close to 15 years. But I didn't care anymore. I had my Mama back. Then my cell rang. It was Carlos.

"Go ahead, Los. I'm here with Mama and I got you on speaker."

"Oh, okay. Have you guys seen the doctor yet?"

"No, we're on our way there, now. What's up?"

"Well, the market's crashed and I can't get away to pick Jordan up from school. She's not feeling well and the school's thinking it might be the flu."

"Where's that heffa baby mama of yours, man?" Mama asked as we laughed together.

"I can't find Lola and I don't have time to find her. All I know is Jordan's sick."

"I understand, but you do realize this is a really sensitive time for us because we don't know what the doctor's gonna say. You sure you want Jordan to be around us now?"

"Honestly, no, because I don't know how many Crazy Flakes you Hawkins ate for breakfast. But you're her godfather and I need you. Godfathers do this type of stuff."

"Don't worry, Carlos," Mama said happily. "We'll get Jo Jo."

"But Mama, your appointment is in 30 minutes."

"Just drop me off at the hospital and you get her. You hear he's in a bind. You lost your job. Let's make sure he keeps his."

"Thanks, y'all!" Carlos said. "Jordan has her insurance card if you need it. Bye."

He quickly hung up as I pulled the car up to the hospital's front entrance. Mama grabbed her bag of sandwiches and coffee in one hand and her purse in the other.

"Go get my grandbaby," she smiled as she slammed the door and walked toward the hospital entrance. I rolled down the window.

"Hey, Ma! Grandbaby? Since when you claim folks who ain't blood?"

She smiled, turned to the hospital and walked off. I checked my watch. If I could get Jordan in good time, I could get back in time to hear what Dr. Avery had to say. But I missed the exit to get on I-20 from 75/85, and traffic was a nightmare. When I finally got to Jordan's school, I parked the car and stormed into the main office.

"May I help you?" greeted a cocoa-colored sister. She was about 5'7, 5'8 with her dreads pulled away from her face.

"Um, yes, I'm Genthaniel Hawkins. I'm here to pick up Jordan Tyrone in Ms. Felder's kindergarten class. She's not feeling well."

"Oh," she said. "Mr. Tyrone indicated on the phone that he would pick up Jordan."

"Yes, but I'm Jordan's emergency contact. I'm her godfather."

"I understand, but I was led to believe that Mr. Tyrone would be able to get her."

"Well, unfortunately, only Jesus is able." She gave me a blank look. Gulp. I guess she didn't like that joke. "I'm sorry. Just a little Jesus joke."

"Yeah, that's the best kind at a Christian private school," she said dryly as she pulled back a single dread that strayed over her eyes.

"But seriously, can't you check Jordan's files? Just check my ID to see if I am who I say I am. Or maybe we can call Carlos to square this circle?"

"I can't do that," she said smiling. "I don't know how to access student files yet. I'm new here. You can wait until our secretary returns, which should be any second."

"Secretary? Then who the hell are you then?" She showed teeth this time when she smiled. White, bright, beautiful teeth. She tiled her head and extended her hand.

"Yolandra Arceneaux. I'm the new principal here at Calvary. I'm sorry, but I'm intentionally giving you a hard time. Mr. Tyrone did say you were coming. It's just you walked in pretty hardcore and I needed to vet you before I release a student."

"Ah. I'm sorry. Where'd you get that Creole last name, Mrs. Arceneaux?"

"*Miss* Arceneaux. And you do know your names. Slidell, Louisiana."

We smiled at each other a bit. Nice.

"So are you still vetting or am I good to go?" I asked, cleaning my glasses.

"Oh no! I'm just waiting for the secretary to get back. We escort adults here and I don't want to leave the office unattended. I

216 J. Shawn Durham

like your glasses, by the way." We smiled a bit more as a stocky older woman walked in with a banana and a yogurt. That meant Arceneaux could take me to Jordan's class and we could jam out of there.

While walking down the hall, I wondered how I could ask her on a date. I hadn't been on a date in a while and Arceneaux seemed like a candidate to break that streak.

"You always wanted to be an educator?" I asked.

"Actually, yes. I love kids. You ever thought about teaching?"

"I'm not really one to deal with other people's kids."

"But Jordan is someone else's child."

"That's...well, yeah. You got me there."

"You have a strong presence, Gent. The kids would respond well to you."

We stopped short of Jordan's classroom doorway.

"How can you figure that when you just met me?" She smiled without answering and knocked on the classroom door.

"Jordan?' the teacher said. "Your uncle is here." When we entered, Jordan's little brown face laid on her desk. I waived at her and she looked confused. Her hair was in two shiny plats and laid down her ear sides like a sad bunny.

"What you doin' here, Unka Gent?"

"Your daddy said you were sick so I came to get you, okay?"

"Okay."

Jordan got her things, walked up to me and leaned on my thigh. I picked her up and we and Ms. Arceneaux left the class. At the school's exit, Arceneaux touched my arm.

"Thanks for picking her up," Arceneaux said. "Bye, Jordan. I hope you feel better."

"Thank you...um...Yolandra."

"You're welcome, Gent."

From there, Jordan and I skedaddled to her doctor who was able to see her on short notice. Turns out she had swine flu. He gave her a prescription for Tamiflu and after that we left and hauled ass to get to the hospital. Jordan sensed my urgency all the while.

"So…Mith Mathie sick, too?"

"I can't wait 'til your teeth grow back in. Yeah, she's still sick."

"Do you mith your mommy?" I keep forgetting you have to lay things out for kids.

"No, baby. Miss Mattie *is* my mom. We don't look alike do we?"

"Uh uh." *I thought you were sick, Little Girl. All of these questions…*

"How you feeling, niece?"

"Still sick. Will Mith Mathie be okay?

"I hope so, Jordan." It got quiet as Jordan nodded off. But then she woke back up was still in a chatty mood. Shit. She talked more sick than she did when she was well.

"I wish I was home."

"You'll be home soon. Right after we pick up Miss Mattie."

"No. I mean my home."

"Oh. You don't like staying with me and Miss Mattie?"

"I like it. But I mith home. Maybe you and Mith Mathie can stay with us…and mommy, too! But Mommy and Daddy futh a lot. And they futh loud, too!"

If she wasn't saying "fuss" Carlos would kill me and Mama.

"Okay," I said, leaving it at that. That was a talk I figured she'd have with Carlos.

Anyway, so we get to the hospital and I'm anxious. Since Jordan couldn't keep up with me, I carried her and even had to slow down ("I'm dizzy, Unka Gent!" she said). I opened the office doors, sat Jordan in the waiting area and marched to the receptionist.

"May I help you, sir?"

"Yes. My mother Mattie Hawkins was to see Dr. Avery this morning. Is she there?"

"I'm sorry, but I can't really give you that info without—"

"Lady, don't give me shi—" I looked and Jordan shook her head.

"Daddy said no bad wordths, Unka Gent!" she warned. At least *she* was learning.

"Thanks, niece," I sighed. Satisfied, Jordan nodded as I turned to the receptionist. "Look: I just want to know if my mother is fine."

"Here I is, Gent. I'm fine," Mama said walking in behind me and then over to Jordan. "How you feeling, Ms. Jo Jo?"

"Eh. I'm okay. How you feel, Mith Mathie?"

"Yeah, Mama. How you feeling?"

"I feel fine, son," she said, walking toward the office exit. I picked up Jordan and the three of us left the office. But Mama's silence made me more anxious. We reached the truck in the parking garage. I opened up the back door and strapped Jordan in the seat. She had nodded off.

"Okay, Mama," I whispered to not wake Jordan. "Spill it. What did she say?"

"She said it's gone, Gent." I turned to see that Jordan was sleep before I started again.

"Mama, are you sure?"

"Yeah. She said it could always come back. But from what she could tell, the cancer—it's gone, son." She teared up. "The Lord did it. You hear me? The Lord done did it!"

"Oh, Mama!" We ran toward each other and hugged. Mama cried in my chest. It must have lasted almost a good, long minute in that parking garage. I couldn't believe it. The nightmare was over. But was it really over?

"Maybe my hair will grow back and we can get on with our lives."

"Mama...you wouldn't just be saying this to–?"

"Look, here: you ain't got to worry about nothing because I done made up my mind to stay here so you can bug the Sam shit out of me, just in case anything else happens. Now boy, get in the car and let's leave this damn hospital!"

She was gonna stay with me? I couldn't believe *that*, either. Wow. I motioned her to get into the car as I walked over to the driver's seat. We pulled out the garage and drove over a speed bump, which woke Jordan up.

"You feel okay, Mith Mathie?" she asked drowsily.

"I do, Jo Jo. How do you feel?"

"Badder."

"Did you say 'better' or 'badder' Jordan?"

"Badder, Unka Gent."

"Badder isn't a word Jordan, okay? Your dad would kill me if you pick up stuff like that. Go back to sleep. We'll be home soon. Ain't that right, Ma?"

"Yeah, son. Let's go home."

✳ ✳ ✳

"Eat your soup, Jordan."

I got some ginger ale and soda crackers out the pantry when the house phone rang. The cordless was on the table and within Jordan's reach.

"Phone, Unka Gent!"

"Well, my hands are full, Sugar. You answer it." And she did. "Hello?"

"Say 'Hawkins residence,' Jordan."

"Hock-ins res-a-denths."

"Good," I said as I poured the soda in a glass. "Who is it?"

"This is Jordan...Da docta said I'll be okay..." Then Jordan stuck the back of her hand up to her forehead. "Ima lil hot but im okay!"

"Who is asking all this about you?" I grabbed the phone. "Who is this?"

"Hi, it's Ms. Arceneaux. Is this Mr. Hawkins or Mr. Tyrone?"

Jordan tugged my pant leg and I stooped down to hear her.

"It's Ms. Arcee, Unka Gent," she whispered in my ear.

"I know that, now," I said as I gave her the soda and crackers. "Oh, Ms. Arceneaux! This is Mr. Hawkins. Jordan's dad is working late."

"Oh, I was just calling for a diagnosis, if you had one about Jordan."

"No problem. Doctor says that Little Miss Jordan has the swine flu."

"That's what I was afraid of. The CDC told us to monitor these things this year."

"Yeah. She's eating now, and I'm about to pump her full of meds and put her to bed."

"I see. It's just that we have to let the other parents know about these cases to prevent spreading and all to their kids."

"Right." It then got quiet. Like she was waiting for something.

"Okay, then," she said. "Well, it seems like she's in capable hands. We can make arrangements to get her the schoolwork she'll miss while she's out."

"Um, yeah. Absolutely.

"Thanks again for checking up on Jordan."

I hung up the phone and slumped into the chair next to Jordan. I wanted to ask her out but I clammed up. Jordan looked at me with saltine crumbs all over her mouth.

"You okay, Unka Gent?" Then the phone rang again.

"Hold that thought. Hello?"

"How's my baby doing?" It was Carlos. Dang it. I hoped it was Arceneaux.

"Fine. She's right here. Wanna speak to her?"

"Yeah."

I handed the phone to Jordan. "Hi, Daddy!"

Jordan and Carlos was all white noise to me. I was pissed that I punked out with Arceneaux. Jordan interrupted my stewing and poked me in the arm.

"Daddy wanths to thalk to—"

"Don't talk with your mouth full, sweetie," I said taking the phone. "Your daddy is going to worry me to death. Yeah, Los?"

"What's up with you? I thought it was all good with your mom."

"Yeah, I'm just trippin' off of something else. What's up?"

"I need to talk to Vanessa about something so we're going to get a drink after work. Can you watch Jordan a bit later tonight?"

"If by watch, you mean drug her and put her ass to bed, then yes."

"Leave your love life out of this."

"Very funny."

"I think I'm gonna throw a party for Oscar at my place. What do you think?"

"Yeah, I guess. So you guys moving next week?"

"Yep. The Tyrones will be gone soon. Don't tell Jordan, though. It's a surprise. I'll see y'all in a bit." I hung up and looked at Jordan chomp away at the crackers. My mind went back to Arceneaux. Boy, did I feel like a chump. I looked at the phone.

"Screw it," I said aloud.

"Screw what, Unka Gent?"

"Don't repeat that, either." I picked up the house phone and scrolled the caller ID for her number and called it back.

"Hello, Ms. Arceneaux?"

"Yes?"

"Unka Gent?"

"It's Gent Hawkins. I was wondering if you'd like to have dinner sometime?"

"Unka Gent?"

"Oh! Well, that sounds nice. I think I'd like that."

"Unka Gent!"

"You hear her?"

"Ha! It sounds like you have your hands full, so I'll let you go."

"We'll talk soon. Good night, Yolandra."

"Good night, Gent." When I hung up, I almost hit the ceiling fan I was so high.

"Unka Gent?"

"Yes, child?"

"Was that Ms. Arcee?" I looked at her and smiled.

"It's time for you to go to bed, Little Girl."

✳ ✳ ✳

"I botched the date. I'll spare you the details because—well—
I'm not into recounting my awkwardness. It's the damnedest thing:
I can be so on when I'm liquored up in New Orleans and running
threesomes, but I suffer foot-in-mouth disease at the dinner table
with a woman I actually take seriously. I mean, the date wasn't bad,
but it wasn't great either. I just didn't have my cool on. I hadn't been
on an actual date in years and the rust showed. And by date's end I
felt her feel what I was felt: that it was damn shame.

"Well...get home safe, Landy," I said as she got in her car. "And
take care."

"You too, Mr. Hawkins." I wanted to kiss her or something.
But no way after all that goofiness. I jerked up big time. What happened to my charm? "Good night, Gent."

She stared at me for a while before she cranked up the car.
When she drove off, I stood there in the parking lot and watched the
car get smaller in the distance. I went to my car and went home. And
when I got there, Mama was at the kitchen table eating.

"Mama, why you still up?"

"I had a hankerin' for some boiled eggs and souse meat."

"I'm sure none of that will come out in in a bad-smelling way."

"Boy, hush up. You know you want some. Get them soda
crackers."

I got the saltines from the cabinet and a beer out the fridge.
I poured it in a Mason jar, sprinkled a little salt in it, spread some
souse over the cracker and sat with Ma.

"How yo' date go?"

"Well, it was goin' alright for a second. In fact, we were getting
along pretty good. And then we got into her age and I just kept saying all the wrong stuff."

"They say you ain't supposed to ask a woman her age."

"But I didn't ask. She wanted me to guess."

"Oh. You gonna lose that one anyway, son. But women get old too. How the hell you s'posed to find out if you don't ask? Don't fall for some of the bullshit these girls be tellin' you. It ain't impolite to ask shit. Especially if you gonna make grandbabies."

"Oh, so that's what this is about?" I smiled. "You getting grandbabies?"

"Of course, son," she smiled back as she playfully pinched me on the arm. "I want you to have some pretty chillum like Jo Jo."

"Where is Jordan anyway? She's usually up late on Fridays."

"Carlos is upstairs in her room, having a big talk with her."

"Why? Is she in trouble?" Mama put down her egg and looked at me.

"Now listen, Gent: Carlos is gonna ask you if he and Jo Jo can stay a little bit longer."

"But I thought they were moving out. What happened?"

"Foreclosure is what happened," Carlos said emerging from the kitchen doorway.

"Who's foreclosing what?"

"I went to the house tonight after work and found notices from the bank," he said as he joined us at the table. "Lola ain't paid the note since July."

"In three months. Are you serious?"

"I told you that fool girl wasn't no good," Ma said.

"But Los, you gave her money when you moved out right?"

"And we agreed I'd pay half the mortgage while we figured what the next move would be. But I get home and I find them in the mail drawer—first notice. Second notice. Final notice—and she kept them all from me. I trust her to do something as simple as pay the damn mortgage and she can't even do that. What a damn fool I am."

"Are you gonna lose the house, Los?" I asked. He didn't say anything. No one said anything for minute. We just collectively shook our heads in disgust. So I do what made sense to me. I went to the cabinet to grab a bottle of Crown Royal and three glasses.

"If there is a time to drink, Carlos, this is it."

"I told you long ago I can't have none, baby."

"Whatever, Ma. I know you been in my liquor."

"Now how you know that Carlos ain't been in it?"

"Because Carlos don't drink brown liquor."

Carlos looked at her and shook his head to confirm that. Mama nodded in concession and I poured the drinks. And the three of us sat there with our heads down, trying to make sense of the bind Lola got Carlos and Jordan into.

"They been sending these notices and Lola ain't said a word?" I asked.

"Ain't said a word, y'all. I helped her earlier this month and she hadn't said a word! And now I can't get in touch with her. When Jordan was sick I couldn't find her. And when I called today, it said her phone was disconnected."

"So where is that fool?" Mama said as she sipped her drink and looked at me. "Boy, what you give me this for? It makes me want a cigarette."

"We know that ain't happening, Ma. "So Carlos, why didn't the bank call you?"

"I never gave them my new numbers. Remember when I first tried to cut off Lola's phone when I first moved out? Well, the company gave me grief because we had a special plan. I was so pissed at them that I left them so I could cut Lola's service and—"

"That's right! You got a new phone! You never gave the bank the number here?"

"No. I didn't think I'd be here this long. And I didn't give them my work number."

"Damn," I said.

"You know, all this real life stuff is really messing with my revolution," he said.

The three of us got a chuckle out of that but got quiet again. The thought of Carlos losing the house was awful. Worse, it meant

Jordan would lose her room. And that meant more instability for that little girl. Jordan didn't deserve that. Something had to be done.

"How much is it?"

"They want three months of house note, and they want the fourth in advance. Plus late fees and stuff. It's easily over $5,000.

"Good Lord!" Mama and I said at the same time in disbelief.

"I don't have that money right now. I don't want to lose the house. But I just don't have it. I don't want her in public school yet, so I have to pay for the girl's school, my car note, student loans and all that—I just can't do it."

We all sat quietly again.

"Carlos, I would help you, but I'm out of work and—"

"No. You've kept a roof over us. I wouldn't take your money anyway. I'll figure out something, y'all," he said, shaking his head in disbelief. "How could Lola do this to her own daughter?" He turned up his drink and stared down at the table.

"We'll come up with something, man. And y'all can stay here as long as you need. At least you didn't marry that fool or have more kids with her. Thank God for that."

Carlos looked at me and poured another drink.

"You need a lawyer. You think that V knows someone?"

"The boy with the hair?" Mama asked, snapping her fingers. "The one who saved me."

"Daniel," Carlos and I said at the same time.

"Yeah! Ain't his girl in law school?" Carlos and I forgot about Gina. And maybe she could advise him for free.

"You shole do give yourself away when you eavesdrop, Mama."

"But she's right," Carlos said. "I can get some ideas from Gina."

Mama gazed toward the doorway. "Why you up, Jo Jo?"

Carlos and I looked back toward the kitchen entrance and sure enough, Jordan was there in her pink pajamas. She went to Carlos and sat on his lap.

"I had a bad dream about Mommy."

"A dream about Mommy?" Carlos asked, rubbing over Jordan's plaits. We all looked at each other but no one dove in and said anything. "Baby, don't worry about Mommy. I'm sure she's fine. Tell Miss Mattie and Uncle Gent what you told me when I said we were staying here a while?"

"I said 'HOORAY!'"

"Since you're here a while longer, your dad and I got a surprise," I said. "How about we get up early tomorrow, paint your room pink and make over your room just the way you'd like it? Then afterwards we can go to Chuck E. Cheese. What do you say?"

"YAY!"

Jordan hopped out of Carlos' lap and gave me a huge squeeze on the neck. As she did it, Mama smiled and Carlos looked at me. But I tried to not look in Carlos' direction because if I did it'd make me cry. I know he must have felt defeated. I know my friend. It killed him to be dependent on me, but Carlos was doing whatever he felt was best for Jordan. And that was all that mattered. That's what men do. It's what Pop did for us.

"Thanks, Unka Gent! Is Ms. Arcee comin' to da Chuck E. Cheese with us?"

"Oh right!" Carlos said turning to me. "That was tonight. How did that go?"

"Don't ask," Mama said shaking her head.

"Ahem," I said clearing my throat to the adults before answering Jordan. "Well I saw her tonight and she said she can't make it. She has a hair appointment."

"She literally has to wash her hair? That's the oldest excuse in the book."

"I guess so, Los. But I'm tired and I don't care anymore," I said as I got up from the table. "I'm beat. It's been a long night and I'm going to bed. I'll see y'all tomorrow."

The next day the four of us went to Walmart and grabbed some supplies. Gent and I told Jordan she could pick all the designs and frilly things she wanted, so Ma took Jordan to another part of the store to look at stuff, which gave me a chance to talk to Carlos.

"I'm impulsive. You know that. You sure you okay with this?"

"I am. I don't want Jordan to feel like some latchkey kid. I don't know what's gonna happen with this foreclosure mess, but I can't move the girl back into her home just to possibly have to move out weeks later. That would crush her."

"Yeah. So what the hell is going on with Lola?"

"Man, I don't know. And I have no idea where she is."

"You think something's wrong?"

"There could be. I don't want to alarm Jordan. When I last saw her, she was with this dude at the house. That was the day I helped her pack."

"You have to report that, Carlos."

"I already have. And this morning I called D. He said Gina will do some digging."

"This is crazy. I can't believe this."

"Exactly. All I know is I got to protect Jordan. And please don't dog out her principal. I may need that connection if I'm a little short on her tuition in the spring."

"That's very negro of you, Los. But I was so off my game with Landy that I don't expect there will be a second date. I dunno. We'll see."

"I need a break somewhere because hell is breaking loose. Lola is God knows where, and could be pregnant, I may lose my house and the country has gone broke."

We got quiet as we checked out the wallpaper.

"What was that about Lola being pregnant?" Carlos gave me a sour face.

"I may have messed up. Lola and I got down on Labor Day.

"What? That's your idea of a mess up? Too much paprika in potato salad is a mess up. Knocking up your psycho ex is an abomination. If Lola's pregnant, that kid will be Damien. What the hell were you thinking, Los?"

"I wasn't," he said. I wanted to tear into his ass more, but we cut the convo short as Mama and Jordan rejoined us with some girly-looking drapes, so we bought our stuff and headed to Chuck E. Cheese.

When we got there, Carlos had a small surprise for me and Mama. The gang was all there. Oscar, Daniel, Gina and Vanessa showed up and what was going to be a small cheer-up for Jordan turned into an actual party.

And there were lots of reasons to celebrate. It was a going away bash for Oscar, a toast to Daniel and Gina's pregnancy and cheers for Mama being cancer-free. What made me feel good was that Vanessa called Dr. Avery, who couldn't be there, but put her on speakerphone as the doctor congratulated Mama. When that happened, I knew for sure that Mama wasn't telling any tales. She really was cancer-free. What a relief!

But two hours into the fun, I had to get out of there.

"Can y'all get Mama, Jordan and Los home okay? I got some-where to be."

"What? Where you got to be, Dude?"

"Don't worry about it, D. I'll be home soon. If y'all like, you can crack open the liquor cabinet and we can play some cards or something tonight."

"You leaving Unka Gent?" Jordan asked. I leaned over to talk to her.

"Are you having fun, Jordan?"

"Yes, sir. Where ya' goin'?" I whispered in her ear and then she laughed. Then I got the hell up out of there. I hate Chuck E. Cheese anyway. Their pizza tastes like ketchup on a Trapper Keeper.

I went to The Asia House, where I sat down and ordered some real food: spring rolls, General Tso's chicken and fried rice. I hadn't really had time to myself since Ma and the Tyrones moved in so I needed the time to myself. I love everybody, but things were a bit claustrophobic for me. While at The Asia House I kept checking my watch, but had no place to be. It was 5:30, so it wasn't too soon for a

McCallan's neat. But the time alone got me to thinking about a lot of things. It got me to thinking about me.

I decided that I wanted to be happy, but I wasn't quite sure how to do that. Ever since Nate got put away, I'd been good at being miserable. My twin brother ruined his life. And for some reason, I thought it was inherent that same storm cloud over me, too. But I didn't feel the need to have that outlook anymore. With Mama and I being cool again, I was hungry for more breakthroughs in my life.

I was down to a final few sips. "Fuck this," I said to myself. I downed the last of the scotch, took my food, got in the car, and drove off. I drove to Lois and Clark's Hair Salon and when I opened the door, all the women stopped and stared. I walked to the far booth in the right hand corner where Landy was getting her hair done. Landy had about two-thirds of her hair newly twisted up. The other third was a frizzy mess that hadn't been tamed yet. I looked to the stylist and quietly motioned her to give us a moment alone.

"Hi, Landy."

"Gent?! What are you doing here? I thought you were at Chuck E. Cheese?"

"I was, but then I thought about how you were here all day getting your hair done with nothing good to eat. So I brought you an order. Are you hungry?"

"Actually...um, yeah. I am. Why thanks."

"Good," I said as I handed her the food. She looked stunned. "Let's get you a drink."

We walked to the vending area and I stuck a dollar in the machine.

"You always give women food when they are getting their hair done?"

"Hell no. This place scares me. You think I don't see all these women staring at me."

"So why are you here?"

"Because," I started. And that's when I pulled her close to me and gave her a deep, soft, slow kiss. Stunned at first, I felt Landy's once-tense body relax as she melted in my arms. When we stopped, I knew we had an audience watching us, but I didn't care.

"Because I want a do over," I said. "There's something to you, Landy and if I could stop being weird maybe I could show you that there is a lot to me too."

"You sure you can do that?"

"I don't know. But I bet you want to find out now, don't you?"

She looked at me with her mouth open. I'd taken her breath away. Awesome.

"I had no idea you were this kind of...*impulsive* man." I smiled when she said that.

"You have no idea. Call me later?"

"Yes, sir."

"Sir was my father," I said, smiling. Then I kissed her one more time and then I slowly walked out of there with my father's swag. I hadn't felt that cocky in a long time. I had left Landy and the salon, in a swoon, just like I hoped I would. Ballgame.

From that point on, I was in a happy place. The weeks that led up to Halloween were wonderful. Mama's hair started to grow back and her energy was up. And Landy and I worked on a nice slow burn as we dated and had potential for something serious.

In other news, the Mississippi house hadn't had many bids. The economy created a credit freeze and banks weren't loaning any-one money to buy anything. I was still living off my severance pack-age and I decided to use the layoff as a chance to prepare for a job I really wanted. Problem was, I didn't know what that dream job was.

I felt so good that I even decided to give out candy for Hal-loween. That's something I never do. But with Jordan in the house, I decorated a bit and had some fun with it. Jordan was dressed up as a princess, and Carlos, who was gonna go out with her for trick-or-treating was dressed as—

"A broke dad," he said in the kitchen as he reached in the bowl of candy. He then put on a ball cap to match his UGA sweatshirt and jeans. Then the doorbell rang.

"Mama, you got that?" I asked as I yelled toward the living room from the kitchen.

Mama stopped helping Jordan with her dress to get the door. "Son? Carlos?"

"Who is it?" I asked walking to the living room. The Jordan's scream said it all.

"MOMMY!" Jordan leaped to the doorway, where Lola Angelique Mayberry stood.

"Lola!" Carlos yelled. "What the hell are you doing here?"

So much for my happy place.

Chapter 19: Tricks, Treats and Lost Causes

(Brother Carlos)

"Where's the money I gave you for the condo?"

"Los! Keep your voice down and count to five," Gent pleaded.

"One, two, three, four—FIVE GOD DAMN THOUSAND IS GONE!"

"Damnit!" Gent yelled in fit. Still positioned between me and Lola, I should've known he'd only take so much foolishness. He stared me down. "Sit down, Carlos!"

"Lola, you got some nerve coming up in here and—"

"Carlos! I said sit!"

He pushed me down on the sofa with one arm while bracing Lola's bicep with his other hand. That man-shackle was pretty awesome. I couldn't move and Lola couldn't either. Damn. I need to get my ass to a gym.

"Gent, you're going to bruise me! Carlos is the one getting wild in here!"

"Really, Lola? And your showing up out of nowhere don't make folks cut the fool? Now sit down and be quiet!" When Gent's pissed, his neck tightens to the point you see the veins. "Los," he snarled through gritted teeth. "A word in the kitchen. And I ain't asking! And Lola, stay here. Do *not* go upstairs. You set one foot anywhere in my house without my say so and I swear I'll toss your red ass out of here. Do you understand?"

"Yes."

"Good. Carlos? Kitchen. Now."

I felt like I was being bossed by my dad. Except when your dad does it, you don't feel like such a bitch. Still, I followed him to the kitchen.

"Yes Gent, Negro Ranger?"

"You got to chill in here or you'll have to take this Lola shit outside."

"If we do that, I'm getting in the car and running the bitch over."

"Whatever. I can't have y'all actin' a fool here. You gotta calm down and talk this thing out. Now y'all did it almost two months ago. Wouldn't she be showing already?"

"Jesus, you're right. Does she look pregnant to you, Gent?"

"I can't tell." I looked out from the kitchen, gazed at Lola and shook my head. I knew I had to calm down but the sight of her drove me crazy. But I needed a little liquid courage, so I walked to the liquor cabinet and grabbed his bottle of scotch.

As I poured two scotches, Gent looked out again to Lola.

"She looks nervous," he said as I gave him the drink. "But she can follow instructions. Her ass is in that chair and ain't moved."

"You scared the shit out of her, that's why."

"Good. It means she responds to authority. Why couldn't you do that?"

"Because, Thor, you pushed the shit out of me."

"I mean while y'all were together. Couldn't you show some authority?"

"She was my girl, Gent. Not my Labradoodle." I stared at my drink. "Ain't it sad when a man has to drink to face a woman like her?"

"No one told you to fuck the Antichrist. But she really gets to you now doesn't she?"

"She gets to me too much," I said. "Can you keep watch in the kitchen?"

"Yeah I'll be here. Makes it easier to eavesdrop that way."

"I bet." I turned up the rest of my Scotch and braced for a showdown. I smiled at Gent before I walked into the living room. She stood as I entered.

"I want to say I'm sorry, Carlos."

"You're sorry? Do you know what you've put us through? I gave you money for a mortgage that you ain't paid since June? It's Halloween, Lola! Where's the money?"

"Los! Not so loud!" I took a deep breath after Gent's kitchen yell and turned back to Lola. Shaken, she sat in a chair and I sat on the sofa across from her.

"You came to talk, Lola. So talk. Where've you been?"

"Chicago...I've been staying with my mom."

"You were at Gloria's all this time? But she told me—"

"She was covering for me. I was there when you were on the phone with her. Oh God, Carlos. I've fucked everything up. You're losing the house and now you're pissed."

"Lola!" I said trying to stay calm. "Just tell me what happened."

"You remember when we first moved here and I promoted Zeke Austin's club?"

"Yeah?" I said through gritted teeth. Austin was who Lola boned that Labor Day night after I helped her move. The asshole with the Audi.

"Well, Zeke is connected with some people. You always said I looked like Tyra Banks and could be a model. So he thought he could help my career."

"Are you kidding? Lola, you're a writer! You came out the J-School like I did. Is this modeling bullshit why you fucked Austin after we did it on Labor Day? After I helped you move? Huh? You gave that nigga Austin my money? Say something!"

She looked mortified when I let her know that I was hip to her triflingness.

"It's not what you think, Carlos. When you left, I used some of the money on things like food, clothes, make up—I spent a lot of money hanging with Zeke, getting pretty for photo shoots and stuff as I waited to meet Tyler Perry."

"Tyler Perry? Why the hell is he in the story? Ha!"

"Gent, be quiet!" I yelled to the kitchen. He stopped talking, but he was still laughing. Embarrassed, Lola headed for the door. But I gestured for her to sit back down.

"You mean you spent all this money—$5,000 in five months—on bullshit? You didn't once think to pay bills? Tell me your ass got a drug problem or something. But don't tell me you spent the money partying! Is that what the fuck you're telling me?"

"I paid them the first few months. But I didn't think you'd stay gone so long. We've argued before, Carlos, but we usually worked it out. So I figured you'd be back."

"You blew all that money? You ain't think about your daughter? Huh?"

Gent must have heard the anger in my voice, so he made himself visible from the kitchen to check on me. But I gave him a glance and he took a small step back to the kitchen. This was my bag. I didn't need Gent to step in.

"Yes," Lola said lowly. "That's what I'm saying. I lost it partying."

"God, I hate you, Lola! You silly little girl! If you gonna whore around, then at least make sure the man you're hoeing pays for some shit and you get something out of it!"

"Okay, a little bit lower, Los," Gent said, fully out in the living room now.

"You can't even whore right, Lola! What happened? After me you lost your touch?"

And with that, Lola got up and slapped me. It was too quick for Gent to prevent it because he never saw it coming. She then grabbed her purse to leave. But I wasn't done.

"Oh, you're leaving? *There's* a shock. Why the hell you come here anyway?"

She stopped. Then turned and walked to me until we were a foot apart.

"Because, I'm sorry!" she said with tears in her eyes. "I love you, I miss you and I need you. And I'm sorry. Can't you forgive me? Please?"

The words stung me. I looked at Gent and he knew the score.

"I'm gonna go upstairs for a sec. Please don't break anything." He left the room and it was me and Lola again. Alone. We both sat on the sofa.

"Woman, I've wanted to hear you say that for five years. And you come here raising all this hell. You screw a dude just hours after you screw me and the whole time, you don't tell me about the house. How could you do that? How am I supposed to believe you? And now you say all this now? I can't go back there, Lola. I swear I can't."

"Are you saying we can't try again?"

"Try again? Bitch, you lost my house!"

"I knew you'd be like this!" she said turning angry. "That's why I went to Chicago."

"You never said why you went to Chicago, Lola."

The doorbell rang.

"Aren't you going to get that?" Lola asked.

"Gent can get it. Answer the question. Why'd you go to Chicago?"

The doorbell rang again.

"You sure you want to know?"

"Damnit, that's why I'm asking, Lola!"

"I went to Chicago because—"

Then the doorbell rang a third time. But I heard Lola's response over it and it rocked me to the core. My knees buckled and I collapsed onto the sofa. Gent walked down the stairs, looked over to the living room area and saw my reaction. Not knowing what was going on, but sensing it was some heavy shit, he opened the door and mumbled something to the visitor, walked outside and closed the door behind him.

"So," I was nearly too choked up to talk. "You *were* pregnant. Past tense?"

"Yes," she said taking a deep breath. She nudged closer to me on the sofa and clutched my hand. "When I first found out I was pregnant, I sorta thought it would be another chance for us. But then I knew you'd find out about the house and wouldn't want another child with me. So I went to a clinic and did it."

"Jesus, Lola."

I was speechless. I couldn't be furious, although somewhere in her confession, I was pissed. I didn't even know if the child was mine but I wasn't happy she did it. It would've been awful to have another child with her. But even now, I can't call any of what I felt as joy. There was no joy. Only grief and heartache. And the more I thought about the fact she made that choice all alone, the more I felt sorry for Lola. I squeezed her hand back.

"Can you forgive me, Carlos? I don't know what's wrong with me. I'm never happy. I don't know what I'm doing anymore. I just know that I feel terrible. I'm always irritable and moody. And I just never thought it'd be like this."

"I know you didn't, Lola. I know that now."

We sat quietly until Jordan ran down the stairs in her costume.

"Jo Jo, come back. Ya folks still talking!"

"It's okay, Miss Mattie!" I yelled as Jordan ran toward us.

"You thoo sthill futhing?" Jordan asked as she propped her arms on my knees.

"Girl, what you say?"

"She's missing teeth, Lola, so it comes out that way," I said before addressing Jordan. "We're not fussing, baby. You're ready to go get candy?"

"Yes sir."

"Good. Tell your mama, 'bye' okay, Sweetie?"

"Yes sir. Gooth to see you, Mommy. Don't be a sthr-tranger."

Jordan gave Lola a hug, but I could tell Lola was shocked by the way Jordan handled it. And looking back now, I think Lola really wanted something good to come out of her visit. But you never know. I could see her using the situation somehow, angling for something. You can't overestimate Lola's ability to use a good tragedy to her advantage.

Then the front door opened and these two twin kids emerged: a butterscotch-colored girl in Raggedy Ann outfit and her twin brother dressed like Andy. Entering behind them was Gent and their aunt Vanessa. It was hardly a secret that Lola and Vanessa didn't like each other. But feeling totally out of place, it seemed like Lola waved the white flag. Lola gave Jordan another hug and a kiss and then got up to leave for good this time.

"Mommy has to go," she said to Jordan as she walked toward the doorway where Vanessa stood. I prayed those two behaved. I couldn't afford a child psychologist.

"When will I see you again?" Jordan asked.

Lola looked around and saw Gent, Miss Mattie, Vanessa and me there with a smiling Jordan and two other kids. I guess Lola added up that she wasn't part of the equation.

"That's up to your daddy, baby. It is all up to him. Bye Jordan."

And a deep sigh of relief later, that's how Lola left.

Once the Lola drama passed we took the kids trick-or-treating and Jordan had a blast. It was her first real Halloween, and Lola wasn't there to be a part of it. I stopped being angry and felt sad for Lola. But looking back, all she did was use me for financial security. I didn't mind giving to her. But I did mind her entitled attitude. And every time we butted heads, it amped me up to do more BBR stuff.

But with so much going on with the fellas, I couldn't depend on them to be my lieutenants in the revolution: Oscar couldn't get involved because of his new gig; Daniel worked extra shifts since he had a baby on the way; Gent was out of work and tended to his mom's recovery. With the exception of Rothman and LeVander, I was the last man standing for the BBR. So that left me to plan a massive BBR sit-in operation on my own, which was tough because real life threatened the revolution. After all, I had more pressing matters to tend to. Notably, I had to save my house.

When Monday, November 3 came around I only had two more days to save the house. The total due, which included the next month's mortgage and fees was $6,758, and I was strapped. I'd emptied the 401k to get the house in the first place and I just didn't have the money. That morning, as I got ready for work and Jordan gathered her things for school, I gathered all the phone numbers to the banks, lawyers and whomever to see what I could do about the house and stuffed all those notes into my work bag.

When I lifted the last set of papers, there it was staring at me. The ring. I paid a good lick of money for it. At least for me it was a good lick of money: $8,000. I'd read where pawn shops and jewelry stores had been bombarded since the market crashed, which hurt any chance I'd get anywhere near what I paid for it. But I had, about $1,300 in the bank and I needed that just-in-case money for groceries or any possible car trouble or whatever. If I could find $4,000—hell, I'd take even $3,000 for it—then I was certain I could talk the bank into a stay of execution.

"Fuck this," I said to myself. I grabbed it and tucked it in my bag.

After I dropped Jordan off at school, I walked into the office and Daniel was at the lobby security desk with a strange look on his face.

"Hey, man, what's going on? Everything alright?"

"You ain't got my messages? I left you a text."

"Sometimes I don't get a signal in that house. What you send me?" Then my phone went off, signaling the receipt of delayed messages. I looked at Daniel. He nodded me to check it. When I did, what I read floored me. I couldn't believe it.

"Layoffs? Oh my God, D. Have you been up there? How bad is it?"

"It's really bad, Los," he said with no humor. I'd never seen him so serious. "It's pretty sad up there, man. A lot of crying and shit going on."

My stomach got in knots. I couldn't lose my job. The thought of doing so scared the shit out of me. Too much was at stake. So I put off learning my fate a little while longer.

"I may as well kick it down here with you for a second. So you ready to be a daddy?"

"Nope, but I will be when the baby comes. That's a promise."

"Good. You seem happy, D."

"I am. I been waiting for something good, and that's Gina. I been stackin' cheese, too. I'm trying to make it so I can do some other shit than this ya know?"

"What, you thinkin' about going back to school?"

"That or start a business. Or maybe even do hair."

"Doing hair?" I looked at his dreads. "Seriously?"

"Nigga, I don't know. I just know I gotta do something. But I won't get into it until after the baby comes and she gets done with school. We'll figure the shit out one way or another. You got Gina's emails about the house?"

"Yeah, and I'm gonna call the bank today. I still don't have enough money though. Maybe she can go over it with me tomorrow night."

"What's tomorrow night?"

"Election night? At Gent's house?"

"Oh right! We'll be there. Say, what you gonna do with the ring?"

"What?"

"I was talking with Vanessa about rings and she said you still got the ring you were gonna give Lola."

"Why's V telling you—nevermind." I pulled out the ring. "You know where I can sell it and not get gypped? At least get a good price for it?"

"Hell yeah. Nigga, you can sell it to me." Daniel coolly pulled his dreads from his face and pulled them back over his shoulders. He leaned back in his chair and smiled.

"Really?" I asked.

I got a hold of myself and decided it wasn't time for pessimism. It was quite obvious what was up: Daniel was in love. I don't know when the hell that happened. But I will say this: when you get a woman pregnant, it'll make you a man or a mouse. Gina seemed supportive of him getting his act together so why wouldn't he give her a shot? But what if he didn't get his act together? What if he fell short of the glory of Almighty Gina?

I had to stop it. I was projecting my own chick issues on Daniel.

"You sure you want to spend your newly saved money on a ring? You do see how this economy is going, right? What if you need the money?"

"Los," he said as he stood up and placed his giant mitt on my shoulder. "I just have to step out on faith, man." Faith? I ain't had any of that in a while.

"I guess you're right, Daniel." I said just to end the back and forth. "So let's talk turkey. What you trying to give me for it, because I can probably get—"

"I'll give you 4Gs now. Another G in installments. So I'll give you $5,000 total."

"With 4Gs, hell yeah we got a deal. How soon can you get the cash?"

"Tomorrow." I looked at my watch. I needed to go upstairs.

"Deal. Let me get up here and see what the hell is going on." I took a long look at the ring. "I'm finally going to get rid of this bitch." I got on the elevator and took the dreaded ride to the newsroom floor. I feared the worst there and when the elevator doors open, it was what I expected.

Some sports columnists were huddled in a corner, seemingly to console our home and garden writer. A couple of editors were at the coffee station shaking their heads. It was like someone died in there. But my mind trained on one person. And when I found her, sadly, she was cleaning out her desk.

"No, V! Not you, too! What the hell is going on around here?"

"The other shoe is dropping, that's what's going on, Los. The world has gone to shit. Check your email. They sent out a company-wide memo."

"How many?"

"Thirty percent."

"Jesus."

"No. I'm pretty sure Jesus still has a job, but you never know who God had to cut from the payroll," she said trying to muster a laugh. She stopped packing and looked at me. "Why haven't you been to your desk yet?"

"Daniel warned me downstairs so I stalled by hanging with him for a little bit."

"Did he tell you that he's in the market for a ring?" she asked.

"Yeah, about that: you can't just go telling people stuff like that, V"

"Why not? You need the money, right? So sell it."

We got quiet again. Thirty percent? That was the 'A' in the *AJC*.

"You know they pinched Williams, too?"

"What? They fired the golden boy?" I whispered in shock. "How are they doing it?"

"Marty and Sam are calling folks in their offices. Sam told me."

"And Marty would tell me," I said as I turned my head and looked across the newsroom. Marty's office door was closed.

"This whole thing is just—" Vanessa stopped and sat in her chair and put her face in her hands. I pulled up a chair beside her and placed my hand on her shoulder. "You should go to your desk and wait for news."

"Okay. But I'll be back to check on you as soon as I find out what they're gonna do with me." I got up to go to my desk.

"Hey, Los?" she called as she waved me back over.

"I've been thinking about your situation. You may not want to hear this but maybe you should give up on your house."

"What? But you told me that—"

"I know what I've told you, but listen to me. The way things are now, you need to have some cash on hand. Sell the ring but don't put the money in the house."

"But I put the last five years into that house!"

"So? The house is a lost cause. Your mortgage will be under-water in a year. You still have a car note and student loans, so if you manage those, your credit will be fine. But you need cash for a rainy day. And we're in an economic shitstorm."

"Yeah," I said quietly as I walked to my desk. "You look like you're gonna be packing for a bit. I'll be back. Let me check my email."

I got a donut and newspaper from the break room and sat at my desk. I finally checked my email and saw the memo. Thirty percent. Wow. I looked across the office and saw people talking in hushed tones, packing moving boxes and in tears.

And then my phone rang. It was Marty.

"Hi, Carlos," he said. "Could you come into my office for a sec?"

"Okay."

Well, this sucked. I got up and took the short walk to Marty's office. When I got there, Marty looked like he was really having a bad day.

"Hi, Carlos," he said expressionlessly. "Shut the door. Have a seat."

I did both. And when I sat down, the first sentence out his mouth was a relief.

"You're not getting fired." The words felt like a stay of execution. I was so relieved.

"Well that's good news," I tried to say coolly as if I didn't sweat the situation.

"Don't thank me just yet," Marty said as he took off his glasses and rubbed his eyes. "Part two of this talk is for me to tell you that we have to pull the plug on the BBR."

I was confused. Thanks to *The Atlanta Journal Constitution's* financing, the BBR was a break-even to profitable venture. We sold thousands of T-shirts and were even able to sell a few ads on the website. Why shut that down?

"I don't understand, Marty."

"It's like this: the revolution has to end," Marty said. "It gets no plainer than that."

"But this makes no sense. We are doing alright on T-shirts, we're trending on twitter and the website visibility is up. What gives? You promised your full backing, Marty."

"Yes, I did. But everything has changed. We can't go on supporting something called The Broke Brothers' Revolution when the Dow seems to lose triple-digits points daily."

"Well, is it a financial issue? If so, I can probably run the website on my own and—"

"The website has to go away, Carlos. And you are prohibited from discussing the BBR in future columns."

"Wait? You're taking away the website *and* I can't write any BBR columns? You are going to kill what little momentum we've got! Right now, I have a brilliant sit-in/march planned and once John Rothman's case goes to court—"

"This isn't coming from me, Carlos," Marty said putting back on his glasses. His lean, triangular face showed how bad of a day he was having. If I'd known better, I'd say he had been up late drinking the night before.

"So who is it coming from? I mean, we've done some cool stuff the past eight months and I'm close to a major breakthrough. C'mon, Marty! I'm talking *Oprah*!"

"Are you shitting me, Carlos?" Marty said as he straightened up in his chair. The stock market has crashed. The values of 401(k)s have dropped 40 percent in one month's time. People are losing their

jobs left and right and all you can do is wonder why we're pulling the
plug on your crusade to not buy a woman a drink?"

I got Marty was pissed, and that was something he hardly did.

"Actually, the BBR is about more than—"

"Save it, Carlos!" he got up and pointed out toward the newsroom. "You see what's happening out there? Those are your friends—
my friends! And they're gone! The BBR gave us good copy. It gave the
paper a few more eyeballs. But *The Atlanta Journal-Constitution* is not
going to lose tens of thousands of readers who may be offended by
BBR coverage during these trying times when damn near everyone
is broke. I don't care how many T-shirts you've sold. We're pulling
the plug! The website shuts down tonight. The billboard gets taken
down later this week. And you are not to mention them in any of
your columns. Do you understand me?"

I got quiet. I couldn't argue his logic. The world had gone bust
and there was even talk of a second Great Depression. But I wanted
to talk about bar tabs.

"And if I refuse to shut down the BBR?" I asked.

"Then you're fired."

Chapter 20: The Broke Brothers' March on Washington

(Brother Carlos)

"Genthaniel. I know this your house, son, but I ain't in no mood for a whole bunch of niggas running around here. Especially if he lose."

"He ain't gonna lose, Ma," Gent said.

"This is America," Miss Mattie said. Now that Obama is a good man with a nice wife and some smart chillum. He should win. But I don't trust these crackas."

She walked back outside to get something. While she was outside, I turned to Gent, who finished dusting his flatscreen T.V. The doorbell rang and he went to answer.

"She can't be right, Gent," I said. "Obama's got to win. We need this one."

"Yeah, we do." He answered the door and it was Daniel and Gina.

"Heyyyyyy!" Gina and Daniel greeted as they entered the house. I hadn't seen Gina since Jordan's Chuck E. Cheese party, but she was glowing. She wore a big smile and her once-short hair seemed like it was growing out. I looked down at that belly and boy, was she showing. But when she rubbed her belly I noticed something else. She wore the ring.

"What's that on your finger?" Gent asked.

Gina smiled and before she could answer, Miss Mattie walked in and gave them both a hug. "There that ol' nappy headed boy is!" she teased while hugging Daniel.

"Hey, Miss Hawkins. How you feeling?"

"Oh, I feel good. Not as good as your girlfriend with that rock! Girl, you sure you can carry a baby and that rock on your hand?" Gina blushed.

"Oh, Ms. Hawkins, it's not *that* big."

"That's what she said," I snickered to Gent as we started laughing.

"So Miss Gina, does this mean you and this boy getting married?"

"Well that's just it," Gina said as she looked at Daniel. We—"

"Mista Daniel and Mith Gina!" Jordan yelled as she ran down the steps.

"Hi, Jordan!" Daniel said. "And call Ms. Gina by her new name: Mrs. Abercrombie."

"Okay, Missus Aba-com-bee." Jordan said as instructed. As for Miss Mattie, Gent and me, we had to digest what Daniel just said fed us.

"Hold on, D," Gent asked. "You mean to say y'all...y'all eloped?"

"We went to the courthouse this afternoon," Gina said, beaming.

The room got quiet.

"Were there shotguns involved?" Gent asked.

"Kwongrat-two-lat-shuns!" Jordan cheered.

"Jordan," I said. "Go in in the kitchen and get you a Capri-Sun."

"Yaaaaaaayyyyyyyy!" she yelled as she sprinted to the kitchen.

"She yells like that all the time?" Gina asked rubbing her baby bump with concern.

"Yeah, and she gotta cut that shit out," Miss Mattie said.

"So you just up and got married?" Gent asked. "Just like that?"

"Just like that. Daniel said he didn't want our kid out of wedlock. No offense, Los."

"None taken." I was happy for Daniel, but I wondered if he got himself involved with a nicer version of Lola: what Gina wants Gina gets. But Gina was a woman on a professional track who got knocked up by a deadbeat, ex-jock security guard.

And she was *happy* about it. Go figure, right?

"Well, God bless both of y'all, then!" Miss Mattie said. "Girl, sit yourself down! Man, fix your wife a plate or something!" Everybody got moving after that.

Folks started to show up as the night progressed. But per Miss Mattie's concerns, "not too many niggas" came through. Probably a comfortable 20 or so. I didn't know any of them though. Some were Gent's old coworkers, and Miss Mattie's doctor, Dr. Avery and her family came, which was cool, because she had two kids close to Jordan's age, so they could occupy each other. Dr. Avery's husband, though, was a drip. Gent and I sized him up. He was an alright-looking cat, I suppose. But he was a Poindexter. I mean, yeah, dude, goody for you and your Greek letters and your affiliation to this college and all that, but big deal. Dude had the social skills of an armadillo with Parkinson's. He did bring some food and booze, so Gent didn't diss him too much. Besides, Gent didn't peep Dr. Avery or her family too much because Landy was there.

It was fun to see Gent and Landy together, but they acted like they weren't together since Jordan was in the same room. You know my daughter has her reporter-father's nose and she was good at observing stuff. What made it trickier was that Landy asked Gent if he'd substitute teach for a while since he was out of work. Well, you know Gent. He thought about the pros and cons—he and Landy in such proximity at his goddaughter's school—and told her no. He figured if any of the parents knew that she was getting down with a teacher, it could be bad for Landy. I wasn't so sure it'd be a scandal.

"Is that Gent's new girl?" Daniel whispered to me as we watched from the hallway.

"Yep. That's her."

"Damn. She's sexy as hell! I'd tap the hell out that ass."

"Yeah, you're gonna have a fun marriage."

"Whatever, nigga. Is Vanessa coming?"

"I dunno. She may not want to hang since she lost her job. I feel so bad."

"Just be glad they let you keep your job. You got a mouth to feed."

"Yeah but it sucks that I had to give up the BBR to keep that job," I said. "And when I broke the news to Rothman, he was so disappointed. At least we raised enough money for his lawsuit. But now that the newspaper has silenced me and pulled the plug, the BBR is dead now. No more rallies. No more petitions. No more columns to pub rallies and petitions to draw attention. No attention means no *Oprah*."

"But getting on *Oprah* was a longshot anyway, wasn't it?"

"Yeah, but maybe that could've led to a book or something. I wish I didn't need my job. Then I'd take a chance and keep the BBR going on my own."

"Yeah, but nigga you had a billboard," Daniel said. "It's all good, right?" Then he pat me on the shoulder and grabbed a seat next to Gina on the sofa. The two kissed and started talking. It was a nice picture. I never saw Daniel so happy. So...*legitimate.*

I looked around and noticed that people in the party had broken up into cliques and I wasn't in any of them. And I didn't want to interrupt Gent, Landy and Miss Mattie's conversation in the kitchen. That was Landy's first real time meeting Miss Mattie. So I grabbed a beer and went outside and sat on the front steps. It was a nice, quiet moment I had to myself. And then a car pulled up and parked on the street.

It was Vanessa.

"Hi," she said. "I thought I should just drop in for a second.

"V," I said, smiling. "Stay a while. Even the Abercrombies are here."

"The Aber-whos?"

"Daniel and Gina. The Abercrombies? They got married."

"Already? Damn, was the ring burning a hole in his pocket?" I shrugged my shoulders. "Oh! What's going on with your house? Tomorrow's the fifth."

"I don't want talk about that, V. Let's just enjoy the night, okay?" When I twisted the knob to get back in the house, she put her hand on my back. "What's wrong?"

"You know, I saw that ridiculous Broke Brothers' billboard when I turned off of Memorial Dr., and that made me think of you."

"That I got a big ass head? That's what I think when I see it on the way to work."

"That billboard is nowhere near on your way to work."

"Yeah, but I still drive by it. Continue."

"Oh. Well...about you and Lola. Do you think she will always be in the way...of you being with anyone. I don't know. I was just wondering." I looked in her eyes.

"After the stunts Lola's pulled these last few months, she won't do shit with Jordan without my say so. Even if I have to file for sole custody, Lola no longer runs this. She'll only be in my life because of Jordan. And that's it."

"I see," Vanessa said as we found ourselves a little closer toward each other.

"Vanessa?"

"Yes, Carlos?" Her voice got as soft as a whisper.

"You're a good woman and a great friend."

"I feel a 'but' coming on." She sensed retreat. And she was right.

"I...I don't think, um...I don't think I can be out there for a while."

"Out where?"

"Dating. I don't think I can do this, right now. I feel something has happened between us lately and I really like it. It excites me, honestly, but I don't know if I can go the next step." She looked at me, shook her head and pulled away.

"I feel like a fool."

"You shouldn't."

"No, Los. I don't know what I thought was going to happen here."

"V, listen. I got so much going on right now. It'd be one thing if it was just me getting over the five-year thing with Lola, but you throw in an aborted kid, a housing crisis and a little girl to take care of. It's too much. I'm just glad to keep my job. The ground's been shifting under me this year and I need to sort stuff out. I'm no good to anybody right now. I want to trust this, but I can't. Lola's left me a little raw and I need to be still for a second. Does that make sense?"

"It does," she said as she dropped her head. "You make perfect sense, Carlos." She moved her fern-like crinkly hair from her face to be certain that I saw her eyes. "My line sister is a producer at CNN and has found a job for me."

"That's great, V! I knew you wouldn't be down long!" I hugged her but she didn't seem enthused about it. "What's wrong? That's good, right?"

"The job's not in Atlanta. I'd be covering Wall Street. I'd have to live in New York."

"Oh." The weight of the news made me sit on the steps. "When would you start?"

"Next week." Damn. The news felt like a body blow. She sat beside me.

"My God, that's soon."

"Yeah. I know."

"Are you gonna take it?"

"I guess I have to, don't you think?" I look back on this now and wonder if me responding to the possibly of an "us" earlier would've affected her decision to leave.

"V, you need the job—you can't turn that down." I grabbed her hand again. Funny how you feel so much for some people the moment you realize you can't have them. And when I think about all that time I wasted with Lola, it just makes me sick.

"Can we stay out here for bit longer, Carlos. Please?"

The Broke Brothers' Revolution   253

I put my arm around her and she put her head on my shoulder. Damn. With a bad economy, I couldn't take chances like I did with Lola. I couldn't tell her to not take the job. It wasn't my place to do so. I had to let her go. I had to consider what was best for Jordan and put my family first. That's what men do. And if that meant I'd be solo for a while then so be it. And I was okay with that decision. We sat on the porch steps for another good ten minutes, and we hardly spoke. We sat close and looked at the stars.

"Vanessa?" I said as I turned my face to her. Then she drew closer and we dove in for a kiss. She was ready for it. She wrapped her arms around me and squeezed.

"Wow," she said. "You have such soft lips."

"So do you. V. I didn't mean to—"

"You don't have to explain anything to me. You're a good guy, Los."

"And I'm gonna miss you at the office, V."

"Just at the office?"

We kissed again. But mid-kiss, I heard a creak of the front door. We turned and saw Jordan there, hands firmly on hips.

"Daddy-O, whattaya doin kis-thin Mith Banessa? Oh, hi Mith, Banessa!"

"Hey, sweetie. Um…I was just saying bye to your Daddy."

I looked at V when she said that. It splashed water on our moment.

"Bye? But you just godt here! Barack Obama is about to win!"

"How can say you Obama's name well but not some other words?"

"Because he's cute, Daddy."

"Oh wow," Vanessa laughed. "You're gonna have your hands full, Los."

Jordan kept looking at Vanessa. "Are you Daddy's new fwy-end?"

Shit. I had to be careful around Jordan. I didn't want her to get the wrong ideas.

"Well, baby, Vanessa's my friend, but—but—"

"Like I said, I only came to say bye to your daddy, Jordan. I'm moving away."

Jordan looked at Vanessa, and then looked at me. And for the first time since we moved out of the house—more than half a year earlier—Jordan cried. She turned around, stormed back into the house and ran upstairs. It confused the hell out of me.

"Carlos, I didn't know that would—"

"It's okay. Look, hang out here for a second while I go talk to her."

"I think I should go."

"I got to see about Jordan. Just be here when I get back, please."

When I got upstairs to Jordan's room the door was closed. I knocked.

She opened that door. "Yes, Daddy?"

"Have a seat on the bed. Talk to me. What's wrong?"

"Why is Mith Banessa going away?"

"She has to, baby. She has a new job."

"But I thought she was your fwyiend?"

"She is, baby."

"But so was Mommy and now both of dem are lea-bing!"

"Daddy will have friends, baby, but they all won't be able to stay."

"But I like Mith Banessa!"

"I do too. But she has to go away. I can't make her stay."

Jordan laughed. "You rhymed, Daddy."

"I swear, I can't have a serious conversation with you for two minutes." Jordan smiled. "Baby, listen. You got me, and I'm not going anywhere, okay?"

"Okay. I love you, Daddy."

"I love you too, Jordan." Meltdown averted. She gave me a hug. But mid-hug, a loud roar erupted from downstairs.

"What's dat, Daddy?"

"That's the sound of Barack Obama becoming president! Let's go watch history."

We walked down the stairs and everyone was screaming and hugging with big, happy faces. Jordan got carried from person to person, with each one taking the opportunity to explain to her the historical significance of the night. First it was Daniel and Gina. Then Miss Mattie. Then Gent and Landy. And even Dr. Avery and her lame husband.

I looked over by the doorway and saw Vanessa. In the celebratory chaos, things happened around us like it was New Year's Eve. Vanessa and I turned a bit from view of the crowd and hugged and kissed, too. But our affection had nothing to do with Obama.

"Is Jordan okay?" Vanessa asked in my ear amid the crowd noise.

"She'll be fine. She's just tired of the people in her world leaving her."

"Well as long as she's got you, she's gonna be fine."

"You are too, Vanessa. You're going to do well in New York."

It was a crazy scene. Everyone around us was so full of joy and enthusiasm. But we looked at each other with sad eyes. To break up our sadness, Vanessa walked over to everyone at the party to say her goodbyes: one last pat of Gina's belly here, a rub of Miss Mattie's newly-grown hair there. A wink at Gent and Landy and a kiss to Jordan.

I walked Vanessa out as the crowd settled into cellphone/text/call/everybody-in-the-world mode about Obama. When I got to her car I knew that was it. We stood there as we struggled to say goodbye.

"Call me when you're settled in. Facebook. Text, whatever. Just stay in touch, okay?"

"Absolutely," she said as she sweetly rubbed my face. "I don't care what Marty does or says. You're the leader of a major revolution, Carlos. After all, it can't be coincidence that we now have a black man in the White House." She winked at me.

And then we kissed again. And again. And again. And a one-minute sendoff turned into 10 minutes until we finally pushed each other away. It was long time for her to go.

"I gotta go, Carlos," she said. She gave me one more kiss and whispered in my ear: "We aren't all like Lola, Carlos, okay? Do you believe that?"

I nodded my head to agree her. We shared a final kiss. Then she got her body halfway in the car, paused for a second, and then looked to me.

"Question: was the BBR really just about paying for stuff?"

"No," I said. "It was about way more than that. A whole lot more."

She looked at me and smiled when I said that.

"That's what I figured," she said with a twinkle in her eye. "I'll remember that."

I didn't pick on it then, but I would later get why she asked me that. Good ol' V.

And like that, Ms. What Could Have Been was gone, and her departure nagged me for the longest time. Was I being too cautious? Did I really have to close that door? What if she was The One? I didn't know and I couldn't be sure.

The crowd finally dissolved and it was just Miss Mattie, Gent and a knocked out Jordan on the sofa. I carried Jordan up the stairs for bed. When I got to her bedroom, I remembered how happy she was when Gent said she could makeover her room. The warm pink colors, the toys she had accumulated. Even the little glitter and glue sign that read "Jordan's Room" on it all made me smile.

The one thing that Jordan's crying earlier brought to my attention was that she got attached to the people I brought around her. That comfort and stability was what I always wanted for her. I couldn't get it with her Mom. But I found it with Gent and Miss Mattie, and to a bigger extent, with Oscar, Daniel and even with Vanessa. Crazy, right?

So after tucking Jordan in, I walked down the stairs where Gent and Miss Mattie waited for me in the living room drinking scotch. The T.V. was in split screen to watch the post-election coverage on two different networks. Gent poured me a scotch as I took a seat on the sofa.

"Jo Jo in the bed?" Miss Mattie asked.

"Yes ma'am. She's tired. It's been a long day."

"Yeah," Gent said. "Why was she crying earlier?"

"She found out V was leaving." I said. I decided to leave out the mushy stuff. I wanted to keep those tender moments to myself.

"Poor Jo Jo," Miss Mattie said. "She got attached to 'Nessa, huh?"

"Yeah. Honestly, I think she's grown attached to you Hawkins, too. So, Gent, if you're still offering, I'd like to stay a little longer. Maybe sign a six or 12-month lease."

Miss Mattie and Gent smiled and looked at each other.

"Of course, brother. Y'all can stay as long as you like. And you don't need a lease, you know that. But what about the house?"

"I think I'm gonna try a shortsell, take the credit hit and hold on to my cash. Cash on hand is better than struggling to hold on to something that's losing value anyway. I...I...um..."

I trailed off. I was out of words. I think it was the accumulation of all the disappointment, the struggles, the bullshit—everything that got to me. I didn't want to cry. And I didn't cry. But I felt like a broken man. I sipped my drink and shook my head.

"I'm thinking about everything that has happened since—" I cut myself off again as I felt the water in my eyes. But I gritted my teeth to feign off the tears. That's when Miss Mattie slid over to my place on the sofa, sat down beside me and put her hand on my back, while Gent watched.

"It's okay, son," she said.

"Y'all know what my lunch plans are tomorrow? I'm goin' to the Walmart on Memorial Drive, and eat a sandwich in the parking lot while I watch them take down my billboard. And then the site will go dark and I'm gonna act like I ain't heard of no damn broke-ass revolution, because I was more focused on it than I was keeping a roof over my daughter's head. So I'm gonna sit there tomorrow and watch them tear it down, piece by piece. And then I'll go back to work and try to not get my black ass fired."

"What time you're going," Gent said as he started texting on his phone. "I can take a break from looking for a job and have a bite with you. Mama, you wanna come?"

"I can probably cook the lunch," Miss Mattie smiled.

"Yeah, I'll text D and he can come out, too," Gent said.

"Ya'll don't have to do that," I said.

"Yeah we do," Gent said. "Los, that's not someone else's room your daughter is sleeping in. That's *her* room. This isn't my house now. It's our house. Yeah, a whole lot has happened. But whatever happens next to you, Jordan, Mama, Vanessa, the fellas—whomever—just know that we're family and we got your back."

I nodded my head to show my understanding, and Gent took that as a cue to turn up the T.V. And the three of us watched as the networks repeated footage of Obama with Michelle and the girls walking out to meet the huge crowd at Chicago's Grant Park.

"I'm so blessed to see this," Miss Mattie said with tears in her eyes.

"Amen!" Gent said. "To Obama!" he said as we raised our glasses and sipped.

"Obama!"

Then my phone received a text message. It was sent a few hours earlier but I had just received the signal. I read it then showed it to Gent.

"Road trip?" Gent asked.

"Road trip," I confirmed.

＊ ＊ ＊

"God, it's cold!" Daniel said as we all loaded onto the Metro.

"Yeah, it's funny," Oscar said. "The folks up here said that it usually don't get this cold in D.C. I guess they were wrong."

"Yeah, they were wrong as hell," I said. It was the night before the Inauguration and Daniel, Gent and I took the 12-hour drive to hang with Oscar for Inauguration weekend. We braved the wintry weather up and down that highway to hang with our boy and take in some history. It was a bare bones trip for sure. We took my truck, split gas money and crashed at Oscar's apartment. Back home, Gina stayed with Miss Mattie and Jordan at Gent's place, although it was a bit of a gamble since Gina was like, seven months pregnant. But Landy said she'd drop in on them while we were away.

There were too many people in D.C that weekend for us to do any driving through the city. Besides, they blocked off streets everywhere. Thankfully, Oscar lived about a twenty minute-walk from The Mall. The night we arrived it was eight degrees. *Eight.* One syllable. Thankfully, we didn't have too far to go to get to this sports bar where apparently everyone knew Oscar's name like it was *Cheers* or something.

"Hey, man, I've made a few friends," Oscar said as we grabbed a booth. Our waitress was a showstopper. She had a deep, copper complexion, big dark eyes, pretty smile and a head full of crinkly reddish brown hair. And she smelled wonderful.

"Hi, Oscar! I see you brought some friends! I'm Nedra," she said as her titties were damn near about to bust out that black V-neck sweater. And she had a sexy accent. We all said "hi," placed our orders and she took off.

"Okay, so what the hell is she?" Gent asked. "She ain't just black."

"Ethiopian. And the town's full of 'em. Even the big ones are sexy."

"You hit that, didn't you?" I asked. Gent and Daniel waited for the answer. Oscar smirked as he turned to look at the flatscreen.

"Yep," Oscar said. "Just like that."

"Just like that? These women get horny like we do! She's like 26 and all she wants to do is text. And she only really texts when she wants some."

"Booty calls but no dating?" Gent asked. "Texts and no talk? Brilliant!"

"Not a dime spent," Oscar said. "And a lot of women are like that here. They'd rather text you instead of have a phone call so they can manage a whole bunch of people at the same time. I mean, some of them want me to move faster. I mean, they're giving it away. I don't even want all that. But when they meet guys like me: no kids and a job with benefits. They go crazy."

"Apparently, the exact opposite requirements for Gina," I cracked.

We laughed as Daniel flipped me the bird. Then Nedra returned with beers and our food and we got quiet as we checked her out up and down.

"So are you guys here for Obama?" she asked Gent. He was caught staring at her breasts. Didn't help that they were eye-level, either.

"What? Oh yeah. We came up from Atlanta. Ever been?"

"No, but I hear it's very nice. Oscar tells me about it. Are you guys from Senegal, too?" Too? We all gave Oscar a WTF look.

"No, that's just me," he said quickly.

"Oh well. Welcome to D.C., guys. I'll check on you later, okay?"

"Okay." She walked away and all of us scoped her ass. Nice.

"Senegal?" Daniel asked. "Nigga, why you lie and tell her that shit?"

"Well, I only told her that my Dad was Senegalese," Oscar said. "Besides, Ethiopian chicks don't mess with blacks. At least not here. Ya gotta be African. Or white."

"Nigga, you lying for booty?" Daniel said. I'm proud of you."

Oscar smiled. There was something different about him. He had developed a confidence I hadn't seen in him before. But I could tell he was in a bit of a tug-o-war with himself. Sure, he was doing what a lot of 30-year-old, red-blooded men do: sow wild oats. But he *was* frustrated. Would he get caught up in the cycle of empty sex and fast, fun living? I didn't know. Oscar didn't either.

We laughed and hung out a bit before we headed back to Oscar's. The plan was to have one last drink and smoke a cigar on his building's stoop before turning in for the big Inauguration. But when we got there, a FedEx package awaited him inside the gate.

Oscar opened it up and inside were four purple tickets to the Inauguration. Everyone had been seeking tickets so they wouldn't be like the other two million losers out on The Mall watching from far away. We were destined to be among those losers. Until then.

"Well, looks like we got four Congressional Issue tickets to the most sought after event in decades," Oscar said he skimmed over the letter.

"Hot damn! You must have put in for them or something."

"Naw, Los," Oscar said, smiling before he started to read:

"Oscar, I have not forgotten you. I am so proud to see that you are doing well in your new job. Here are 4 tickets for you and your Broke Brother friends, courtesy of Congressman Jack Ridenour. Enjoy. Angie."

"Wow!" I said. "This was all Angie. Jack Ridenour's so conservative, he'd support legislation to give the ghosts of aborted babies who grew up in the spirit world and become criminals to get the death penalty."

"What?" Gent asked. "How much you been drinking?"

"Not enough. You?"

"Ditto."

"Dude, you should have hit that Angie chick," Daniel said.

"No, I shouldn't," Oscar said. "She's married and y'all going to hell at a young age."

"How we going to hell?" I asked. "You're the one lying to them gypsies about being from Senegal. Don't they use voodoo?"

"She's not a gypsy. She's Ethiopian and she's Catholic. And y'all drunk asses need to keep it down. I got neighbors. Now shut up and get in the crib!"

The next day, we got up early and used the hell out of those tickets, and although we had to walk for-seemingly-ever we made it. Thank God we made it.

The Inauguration was better than the Million Man March, or any Greek Fest, or Promise Keepers or anything like that. All the pain, anguish and bullshit the four of us had endured up to that point was forgotten the moment we saw Obama sworn in. About an hour later while we were still on The Mall, I got a text. It was from John Rothman:

"Breaking news from Manhattan Superior Court. The ruling from my suit came in today. Guess what? I WON! Thanks for keeping me in the fight. BROKE POWER!"

That text really got me stoked, so I passed around the phone to let the fellas see it. And like I expected, it put a really big smile on all of their faces. While we all got swept up in the Inauguration party that was happening on The Mall we had our own private celebration when we got the Rothman news.

"Broke Power!" Gent started.

"Broke Power!" we all chanted. We did it for a while until some important looking people in our Inauguration section seemed kinda confused and pissed at us, so we piped down after that. But no matter. We were really happy for Rothman. To get that news that day was just icing on the cake.

After all, Barack Obama was our honorary Broke Brother. But John Rothman *was* our Broke Brother. Both victories were something four once-broken men needed: hope.

Broke Power, indeed.

The Broke Brothers' Epilogue

(Brother Carlos)

The next month, Landy got the perfect storm she needed. One of her teachers had to have back surgery and was likely to be out for the rest of the school year. Although Gent had already turned down her earlier advances to get him to substitute teach, he felt compelled to help his lady in a time of need. That, plus he could use the money.

But Landy had hopes that the experience would make Gent consider teaching full time since she was convinced he'd be good at it. But Gent wasn't so convinced. He tried to find new ways to fill up time so he could collect a check and dip. So he asked us to come to his classroom for show and tell with pics from the Inauguration for the entire day. He also scheduled it around Super Bowl weekend so we could all hang out at his house for his annual Super Bowl party. The timing was perfect for all of us, especially Oscar, who had some comp time from working the elections and was in town since he wanted to visit his folks.

It was a big weekend because Miss Mattie's birthday was later that week and although we all couldn't be there on the actual birthday, we went to church with her on Super Bowl Sunday (funny, the Catholic Miss Mattie wanted to check out the Baptist church Gent had been going to) and all of us, including Gina, Landy and Jordan went with her. It was the first time I'd gone to church since Jordan was born. (I know, it's bad.) But I had to start somewhere.

So the Monday after the Super Bowl, The BBR went back to school. Landy's school, which was Jordan's school, which was Gent's school.

"How many more of these we got to do, Gent?" Oscar asked as he grabbed a chocolate milk and placed it on his lunch tray. Ah, school cafeteria food.

"My planning period is sixth period, so you only got two more classes."

"Hey, I don't know much about teaching and shi–" Daniel caught himself as the lunch lady and another teacher in line looked at him. "*Stuff.* I don't know too much about this teaching *stuff.* But how you get a planning period when you sub teaching? I mean, what you got to plan?"

"My escape from here," Gent mumbled under his breath as he ponied up to pay $11 worth of school cafeteria food for the four of us. Each of us got one notecard-sized rectangle of pizza, a small Styrofoam cupful of corn and either a piece of fruit or applesauce. We sat at a table with some second graders and while we sat, Jordan's kindergarten class was leaving. When Jordan saw me, she waved. And since she's my daughter, she spoke to me. Loudly.

"Hi, Daddy! How's school?!" she yelled from across the cafeteria. She was talking much better since her teeth had grown back in. I put my index finger to my lips to give the "be quiet" motion. She smiled and walked off with her class, all the while pointing to me and telling her classmates that I was her daddy.

"I hope my girl turns out as cool as your kid," Daniel said.

"When is Gina due anyways, Daniel?" Oscar asked.

"April or May."

"You got a name for her yet?"

"I want Danielle. She wants something crazy and ethnic."

"What, like Tameka or something like that?" Gent asked.

"Naw, something like India."

"That's not ethnic," Oscar said. "India's a pretty name."

"Only if you're Indian."

"What?" Gent asked. "And you were doing so well too, D."

A little boy seated beside Daniel and across from me poked him on the shoulder.

"My aunt's name is India. She's a cool lady, so it could work."

"See, D?" Oscar said smiling. "There you go."

"Hello, sirs," Yolandra said as she approached our table. She's all business at the school, so we didn't dare call her 'Landy.'

"Hi, Ms. Arceneaux," we all said in unison, like freakin' children.

"How have your guests been, Mr. Hawkins?" she asked Gent.

"They've been great!" We all cheesed when Gent said that.

"Good. Could I have a quick word before your fifth period starts?"

"Yes, Ms. Arceneaux," Gent said as he raised an eyebrow and smiled slightly. "Should I follow you to your office now?"

"Sure. "It'll only be but a minute," she said.

Gent placed a napkin over his lunch tray and looked at us.

"Be right back, sirs," he said as they left the cafeteria.

"Now, I wonder if they ever—you know—at the school," Oscar said to me.

"Dude, she's looking out for me on Jordan's tuition. So I hope he's putting it to her."

"But Gent wouldn't do it at the school, would he?" Daniel asked.

"Y'all jokers got some short memories about Gent," I said.

"True," Oscar said. "I like her though. How old is she?"

"Dude, it don't matter," Daniel said. "She's smoking."

"Stop talking about this at the school." Gent said as he reappeared out of nowhere.

"How you get back so fast?" Daniel yelled. "We thought you were getting some."

"Not now. That's what the planning period is for," Gent said and he nonchalantly started eating again. Shaking off that stunning little statement, we started eating again and I noticed the boy with the Aunt India had a sad look on his face.

"What's your name, son?" I asked him.

"Quincy," he said slowly.

"Ah, Quincy! You like music?"

"Yes sir."

"Cool!" Oscar said. "Just like Quincy Jones!"

"That's my last name."

"Wait," Daniel asked. "Your folks named you Quincy Jones?"

"Yes sir."

"Is your name your Aunt India's doing?" Daniel asked.

"No."

"Did y'all haze this boy while I stepped away?" Gent asked.

"No sir," Quincy said. "But they asked how old Miss Arcee is." Then Quincy turned to Daniel to answer. "She's 35. I heard her tell some teachers after school one day."

"Thirty five?" Gent asked. "I can swing that. Thanks, Quincy."

"Gent, you may need to cover your behind a little more," Oscar said. "This kid's got some sharp ears. You heard everything we said here didn't you, Quincy?"

"Yep. But I could forget it all for a chocolate milk and an ice cream sandwich."

"A chocolate milk *and* an ice cream sandwich?" Gent asked, taken aback. "How old are you, you little extortionist?"

"I don't know what that is," Quincy said.

"An extortionist?" Oscar started. "Don't worry about that. Just know that it's you. Now how old are you?"

"Twelve."

"Well, Mr. Blackmailer, I will get your milk and your ice cream sandwich if it will buy your silence," Gent said as stood up to meet the ransom. "But know this: you're gonna have the shits with those dietary choices."

Gent got up to buy the items as Quincy and the fellas laughed.

"Why don't you have a milk, Quincy?"

"You see that girl at that table?" He pointed to a little red girl two tables away. I glanced at her, but when my phone vibrated, I checked it and missed his ID-ing of the girl in question.

"Hang on, Quincy," I said. "Let me check this." I looked and I had three texts. My phone sucks. Apparently, the only place I got good reception at the school was in the cafeteria, so I got all my missed texts at once. One from LeVander, who had been quiet since we had to pull the plug on the BBR, one from Vanessa, who had settled in at her CNN gig in New York, and one from Rothman.

"Are you listening, Mister?" Quincy asked.

"Just a second, Quincy," I said, scrolling through the texts. The first one was from Rothman: "Your friend Vanessa Howard told me to keep it a secret, but she used me for a story. It's on CNN.com today. I mentioned the BBR paid my legal bills. Broke power!"

That made me immediately scroll to Vanessa's text: "I did you a favor on CNN.com today. Check the site and search for your boy Rothman. And yes, you're welcome."

"Well that's funny," I said aloud.

"What?" Gent asked. Is everything alright?

"Hold on," I said. When I got to LeVander's text, it was a doozy: "I emailed the link to the Rothman story to my Oprah contact," he texted. "Don't want to get your hopes up, but you might want to clear your schedule next week. O's producer wants to talk with you." And then he texted me a smiley face. I should've been turned off because it was a dude using a smiley face in a text. But hell, the news did bring a smile to my face!

Holy shit. It looked like I was gonna be on *Oprah*. Now that's broke power!

"Sir?"

"Just a second, Quincy Jones!" I said as I passed Gent the phone. "Read that last text, Gent." When he read it, his eyes grew large and his mouth flew wide open.

"Are you serious?" he asked me.

"What?" Oscar and Daniel asked at the same time. I nodded to Gent to hand them the phone. They started reading. And it was fun to see their face change from confusion to joy as they read. No one said anything. We just sat there and smiled.

"Sir?" Quincy asked as he nudged my arm. I was so excited, I forgot about his ass."

"What, Little Boy?"

"The girl I was telling you about? She's over there. See?" He pointed to a cute, longhaired reddish-brown girl who weirdly looked like Lola if she were a kid.

"I gave her my milk money so she can get an ice cream."

"Do you give her your milk money a lot, Quincy?"

"Yeah."

"So you buy her milk but she still sits with those boys right there?"

"Sometimes with different boys. I try to stop giving her money, but then she talks to me more, and that makes me want to help her."

I looked at the guys, and they looked at me. They knew where this was headed. Oscar laughed and shook his head, Gent pumped his fist and Daniel nudged me with his elbow to keep me talking to the boy. I looked around to see if anyone else was looking. I checked, LeVander's text message one more time to make sure it actually said what I thought it said. And yes, it still did.

Then I leaned forward and the rest of the fellas leaned in too as I asked Quincy perhaps the most critical question of his young life:

"Quincy, have you ever heard of Broke Power?"